ENTHRALLED

'Mistress, please allow me to kiss your pretty foot.'

'What's it worth?' She nudged my chin with her big toe. The sensation shot all the way down to my cock. I opened my mouth but no words came out. She'd taken the power of speech from me.

'Would you die to taste it?'

I nodded and felt a sharp, silver toenail scratch my bottom lip. By now my cock was a throbbing bulge in the black pouch.

'Is that little prick of yours aching?'

'Yes, Mistress.'

'I could make you come just by touching your face with my big toe.' She shook her head in pitying disbelief. 'You can't help yourself can you?'

'No, Mistress.'

'Go on, get down and lick it then.' She pushed my head down onto the carpet with her foot and, holding the sole above my face, continued to munch her breakfast cereal.

ENTHRALLED

Lance Porter

The LAST
WORD *in*
FETISH

nexus

enthusiast

This book is a work of fiction.
In real life, make sure you practise safe, sane and
consensual sex.

First published in 2007 by
Nexus Enthusiast
Nexus
Thames Wharf Studios
Rainville Rd
London W6 9HA

www.nexus-books.com

Typeset by TW Typesetting, Plymouth, Devon
Printed and bound by Clays Ltd, St Ives PLC

ISBN 978 0 352 34108 2

One

*'But you'll never fuck me.
Do you understand that? Never.'*

I like to look at pretty women – I really can't help myself. In the summertime, when they put on their short skirts and cross their legs so carelessly, you would find me in the local park, on my belly on the grass, praying for a glimpse of heaven. Or if not there, I would be wandering around the shopping malls, lusting after the giggling young fashion queens. When a real stunner passed me on the high street, I was compelled to turn and follow her. I'd creep along in the wake of her swaying buttocks, trembling with a secret ecstasy. My only intention was to look, mind you, nothing more, but I'd risk getting flattened by a double-decker bus to keep a tempting female ass in view.

There's much more I could tell you and I will in due course. But first you must understand this: I became a voyeur out of necessity, not choice. I tried everything imaginable to make the acquaintance of beautiful and glamorous women, but I failed miserably. Rich, handsome, talented – I was none of these, and like most ineligible bachelors I led a life of quiet sexual frustration. My one solace was masturbation and hardly a day went by that I didn't open a magazine or put on a video and pay tribute to some maddening bitch – and I return to that much-maligned word in all of its primitive glory.

I had no reason to suspect I would be singled out from among my kind and that my desperate prayers would be answered. But this is what happened, for better or for worse.

She visited Giorgio's for a purpose that evening and the moment I stepped through the door she knew I was her man.

She was sitting alone at the bar, perched upon a tall chrome stool in classic style, one long, tanned leg crossed over the other. Raising a glass of wine to her lips, she sipped it indifferently, and then eased back against the bar rail and slowly re-crossed her legs, pointing her extended foot towards me. Her toes flexed proudly beneath the thin sandal straps and the red nails glistened darkly in the low light. I watched entranced as she drained the last of her drink and idly surveyed her surroundings. The way she bobbed her foot up and down told me she was bored.

I managed to keep my legs steady as I walked towards her but I could feel the prickle of perspiration on my face. I stuttered an introduction, telling her truthfully she was the most beautiful woman I had ever seen. She looked me over appraisingly before she replied, 'I'm Jasmine.' (The name evoked the exotic – waves rolling over white sands; a fragrant tropical breeze stirring palm leaves; naked feet and swaying hips – and it suited her absolutely.) 'Who did you say you were again?' I repeated my name and watched her face light up.

'Well, Matt,' she said with a grin, 'haven't you noticed that my glass is empty?'

I estimated she was ten or fifteen years younger than me, but even so I felt intimidated by her astonishing beauty and confident manner. I didn't even consider pulling up a stool and remained standing awkwardly at her side. Her eyes wandered while I spoke and she continued to bob her foot to the music. I was desperate to make an impression and talked rapidly about anything that came into my head. She calmly sipped her wine, looking more gorgeous from one moment to the next.

I felt I meant nothing to her and, more profoundly still, that I could never mean anything to such a woman. The realisation depressed me, yet her show of indifference only inflamed my desire. She was vengefully sexy, I remember thinking even then, her body too much of an asset for one woman to possess. Her breasts were thrust forwards like two indecent trophies, and again and again my gaze was drawn into her gaping cleavage and down to her magnificent hips and thighs, which stretched the short black dress taut across her lap. Even her fingers aroused me, the long manicured nails painted a bold red to match her toenails. I had an irresistible craving to see her naked.

An inner voice demanded I tell this woman I'd fallen in love with her. I knew I did not stand a chance and I was prepared for the rejection and the humiliation – ready to walk out of Giorgio's and die in the street. One look into her maddeningly beautiful eyes and I forgot myself completely. My inhibitions vanished and all sense of reason melted away.

But I was not to get the opportunity to make a fool of myself so easily. Before I had a chance to speak, she uncrossed her legs and climbed lightly off the stool. Once on her feet she straightened her dress and, with a degree of concentration that was heart-breaking to watch, smoothed it over the tops of her thighs and adjusted the thin shoulder straps. She was leaving – just like that. Disappearing forever. The idea was intolerable. I watched in disbelief as she picked up her handbag from the bar.

'Where are you going?'

'To meet a friend.' She started on her way, heels clicking on the floor tiles. I looked on helplessly as she carried that dream of a body further and further away from me. Her ass, which I now saw in its full glory, swayed proudly and seemed to taunt me with each step she took.

'Stay here,' she called back without turning her head.

I waited. I did not even consider going into the town centre to meet up with my drinking pals as I'd intended. I sat on the vacated stool, which was still warm and where the air smelt faintly of her, picked up her glass, which had wine left inside, and examined the bold red imprint of her lips on the rim. I wished she'd spat into the drink, left behind more scraps of herself. I grew miserable, imagining she'd abandoned me to meet another man, one of those sculptured hunks, blessed by fortune, who always get to fuck the Jasmines of this world. I ordered beers and tortured myself with the idea that she was lying in his arms and kissing him with abandon, while I awaited her return like a faithful old Labrador.

Time passed slowly. Customers came and went, friends greeted each other and nearby several couples started to dance. I soon retreated to the back of the bar. Standing alone, I became conscious that a handful of regulars who'd observed me talking to Jasmine earlier kept glancing across, as if they'd placed bets on how long I'd stay. A man I knew vaguely, who was sitting at a table close by, shrugged his shoulders in a gesture of condolence. I resented all this attention and refused to accept its meaning. I held a bottle in my hand, drank steadily and focused on the doorway, silently cursing every fool who walked in.

Towards the end of the night when everything looked hazy and hopeless, she stepped through the door and lit up the whole of Giorgio's. She was even more stunning than I remembered. Her hair was darker and silkier, her lips fuller and a more intense shade of red. She seemed taller, too, her shapely legs impossibly long. Walking at her side was a fabulous blonde, dressed like Jasmine but all in white, down to her high-heeled sandals. Black and white, night and day, the contrast was utterly arresting. This spectacular pair should have been strutting along catwalks in Paris or Milan, triggering flashlights with each step. They approached like two magnificent predators – beautiful and deadly.

'What do you think?' Jasmine asked her companion. The blonde looked me over even more coldly than Jasmine had done earlier; then she turned away and folded her arms. Quite drunk by now, I felt bold enough to take the initiative and introduced myself to her. She responded by rolling her blue eyes and whispering something into Jasmine's ear. She went to a stool further along the bar, crossed her legs tightly and paid me no further attention.

'Your friend is a little precious,' I said to Jasmine, trying to make light of the snub. Jasmine grinned mischievously and glanced over at the blonde.

'Maybe you'll get a chance to tell her yourself one day.' Then in a changed tone she asked: 'Why did you wait here for me?'

I told her that I'd fallen in love with her.

'I know you have,' she laughed, taking a step closer to me. She dragged a fingernail down the length of my tie and stared darkly into my eyes. 'I know how much I turn you on and the best thing is I haven't even tried yet.' She ran her tongue across her lips leaving them moist and glistening. 'I bet right now your little cock is stiff, isn't it?' She tucked her finger down the front of my pants and pulled my crotch tight against her own. I could feel the swell of her cunt beneath the thin dress and was embarrassed by the obviousness of my arousal. She pushed her thigh between my legs and brought her mouth close to my face. Her breath was hot and smelt strongly of whisky.

'I could make you come right now. Would you like me to make you come in front of all these people?'

I begged her not to. My voice was weak, no more than a gasp. She increased the pressure of her thigh against my bloated and helpless cock.

'I say when and where you come, is that clear?'

I nodded, drowning in the closeness of her.

'Did you wait here because you thought you'd take me home tonight?'

I shook my head.

'Tell the truth. You wanted to fuck me.'

I said nothing.

'Well, don't you want to fuck me?' Her thigh was rubbing against my balls. I could feel them begin to spasm. 'It's your last chance to answer.'

'Yes,' I said fighting the urge to come. 'I do.'

'But you'll never fuck me. Do you understand that? Never.'

I nodded mutely, too overwhelmed by the feel and scent of her to offer any dissent.

'That's good,' she said, her lips curled in satisfaction. 'Now I'll give you what you deserve.' She grabbed my tie like a leash and led me away from the bar to a corner where couples were slow-dancing. People gaped as we passed and I heard a woman snigger.

Once in the corner, she pushed my back against the wall and pressed her mouth hard against mine. The suddenness of her attack stunned me and I felt her tongue slide between my lips as I struggled to catch my breath. Gasping, I reached around to squeeze her ass cheeks, but when my hands found their prize she knocked them away.

'You don't have permission,' she hissed, releasing my mouth for a second.

I stood against the wall with my hands at my sides and her tongue resumed its assault. She wedged her leg between mine and began to stimulate my cock with lewd, knowing movements. My enforced passivity made her even harder to resist than before and in a few moments she had me at the brink of orgasm. It took all my willpower to keep the cum inside my balls.

'Think you can resist me?' she laughed. 'I'm going to make you wet your pants right here in front of all these people and there is nothing you can do to stop me.'

I didn't doubt her for a single moment.

She gave me one last penetrating kiss, pushing her long tongue to the back of my mouth, then turned around and pinned me against the wall with her firm young ass. My cock strained madly inside my trousers and she wriggled it into position between her jutting cheeks. Placing my hands on her hips, she began a sluttish dance, throwing her long, scented hair back into my face and grinding against my imprisoned cock.

'Now it's time for you to come,' she said. She used my hands to tease up her dress, while continuing to roll her ass. One side of the hem nudged up higher than the other and I was given a peek at a perfect ass cheek. She looked at me over her shoulder and spoke through tousled hair: 'I just want you to know that I didn't put on any knickers this evening.'

That was all it took, a few smutty words and a filthy smile. The thought of her hot cunt wriggling naked beneath the dress and practically spread over my cock was more than I could bear. I shut my eyes and surrendered to her erotic tyranny. I came violently and fell back against the wall.

When I opened my eyes she was standing before me, a picture of elegance and composure, not a hair out of place. She held an open lipstick in her hand and was smiling triumphantly. I watched, paralysed, as she dragged my tie to one side and used this stick of red grease to scrawl large numbers across the front of my shirt. She stepped back and admired her handiwork.

'Call me,' she said and then walked over to the blonde who was waiting to leave. Arm in arm they headed for the door, glowing and vibrant, the night spread out before them.

I felt suddenly isolated and utterly ashamed of myself. The whole bar seemed aware of my disgrace, every face twisted and scornful. Stiff-legged, cock still dribbling, I pushed my way to the exit, vowing never to set foot in Giorgio's again.

Once outside I walked away quickly but stopped beneath a street lamp before I'd gone very far. I looked down at my shirt and was seized by panic. The lipstick numbers were horribly smudged and I could barely distinguish one red blur from another.

Two

*'Don't hold back,' she said. 'Give in to it.
You all do in the end.'*

The following evening I sat hunched over the phone
frantically trying different numbers. I must have
disturbed half the city before a male voice confirmed
I'd reached Jasmine Del Ray's residence. My spirits
plunged for a moment but it quickly became apparent
that I was not speaking to a boyfriend. Something in
the man's manner, a certain stuffiness I suppose, led
me to imagine he was an older relative, or – and this
impression was fairly vivid – a butler. He informed
me politely that Jasmine was unavailable and
couldn't say when she'd return. I left my number with
him and waited restlessly, watching the minute hand
creep around the clock.

I called three more times and spoke to this same
individual who never revealed his name or indicated
his relationship to Jasmine. And though he main-
tained a detached and respectful tone during each
short exchange, I sensed he was jealous of me. During
the last call a suppressed hostility developed between
us, a childish rivalry that took me entirely by surprise.
Disconcerted, I put down the phone and went to bed.

I lay awake, as I had the night before, reliving the
events at Giorgio's. Her scent was still whirling in my

nostrils, and I could feel her tongue flicking the back of my mouth, her ass grinding my cock into submission. I jerked off savagely and fell into a short, fitful sleep.

When I woke up her image was still burning in my mind. I saw her perched on the stool, swinging her foot. I watched her smile victoriously and walk from the bar, her cunt barely hidden by the wisp of a dress. She was in my balls all night long.

I was glad when morning came. I took a long, cool shower and set off for work. I was at that time a manager in the personnel department of a large insurance company – need I say more? The annual ritual of recruiting new staff was underway and I was looking forward to losing myself in the pages of statistics and forecasts that were waiting on my desk. But Jasmine dominated my thoughts the whole day and I was constantly reaching down to adjust my cock. I simply couldn't concentrate and made some stupid errors as I prepared my report on the computer. Fortunately, my assistant, Kim, bless her soul, spotted them in time.

'You look worn out,' she said, coming across to my side of the office. 'Were you out on the town last night as well?'

I checked her over as she leant forwards and inputted the data. Her attention was absorbed by the scattered papers and her fingers moved expertly over the keyboard. She had joined the company from university almost two years ago. I'd interviewed her myself and chosen her over a more experienced candidate because she was the better looking. That went against all the rules, of course, and common sense as well, but Kim turned out to be a first-class assistant – intelligent, enthusiastic and always cheerful. At the rate she was learning, I reckoned she would soon be able to do my job. Now and then that thought used to worry me.

Kim was averagely pretty, with short, light brown hair, a slim figure and a clear, fresh complexion. Her best feature was her wide green eyes which gave her a calm and gentle appearance. She was a welcome sight on a dreary winter morning, I can tell you, and I took fewer days off sick after she joined me in the office. We had an excellent working relationship, which extended to taking lunch together and drinking at the company bar on Friday evenings. I had a feeling that something serious might develop between us, despite the age difference, and I'd been waiting for the right moment to ask her out on a date.

But now, as I looked at her stooped form, I couldn't help comparing her to Jasmine. I felt terribly cruel as I did this, sadistic even. Kim was cute, as I said (though the knee-length grey skirt and frumpy yellow blouse did her no favours). I know she could turn heads. Many a guy would have been proud to sport her. But Jasmine eclipsed her with one shake of her magical ass.

'There,' she said, stepping back from the computer. 'Lucky at least one of us is awake this morning.'

I merely nodded.

I tried calling Jasmine whenever Kim left the office. The same male voice answered each time and told me politely, but with an undercurrent of hostility, that she had not returned. A game developed between us: I did all I could to extract new information from him and he repeated the same well-rehearsed lines over and over again. He was like one of the operators in the firm's call centre and stuck rigidly to his limited script. In total, I spoke to him for maybe an hour, but at the end of it all I still had no idea who he was or where Jasmine might be. I didn't know whether to

11

expect her back that evening, the following afternoon, at the weekend or sometime after the next
lunar eclipse. She was unreachable and everything
about her remained a tantalising mystery. Each time
I called he was careful to remind me that he'd taken
my name and number, that we'd double – triple –
checked it was correct, and that all I could do was
wait. Wait. Another half hour would pass; I'd send
Kim off on an errand and pick up the phone.

I returned to my flat that evening to see the light
on the answering machine flashing excitedly. Leaving
my case standing by the front door, I ran over and
hit the play button. There was a long, suspenseful
silence followed by a mysterious buzzing sound; a
female voice was just discernible beneath it. The
message finished with the rattle of somebody clumsily
hanging up. I played it repeatedly, straining to hear
the few distant words, listening for anything that
would reveal the identity of Jasmine. I turned the
volume to maximum, put my ear against the speaker,
but heard only a half-human language drowned
beneath a deafening mechanical groan. In a flash of
inspiration, I snatched up the receiver and dialled
1471. Somebody had called just five minutes before
I'd put the key in the front door but withheld the
number. I cursed myself for not leaving the office
sooner.

Once again I spent the evening beside the phone. A
friend called wanting to know why I didn't show up
in town on Monday night and, right after him, a
vague acquaintance from work who started to give
me another depressing account of his wife's illness. I
was equally abrupt with both of them.

Around nine o'clock I realised that I hadn't eaten
anything all day except a sandwich at lunch and
phoned for a pizza. I finished half of it before I lost

my appetite and threw the box on the floor in disgust. I called Jasmine three more times but hung up as soon as I heard the unctuous male voice. He was beginning to put violent ideas into my head and, besides, it was just too painful to be told that Jasmine was not available. I called it a day and went to bed.

But I couldn't sleep. I propped myself up on the pillow and browsed through some back issues of *Playboy*. The world's most gorgeous women smiled invitingly at me from the glossy pages. They posed naked or in glamorous lingerie, tastefully revealing their carefully groomed cunts in richly furnished bedrooms, beside the crystal blue waters of swimming pools and on sun-drenched beaches.

Since my early teens I'd dreamt constantly of being involved with women like these. The women I dated invariably disappointed me. They were generally warm, affectionate and eager to please me – I mean no disrespect to them – but they never satisfied my deep craving for the luxurious female body. When they undressed I felt cheated, as if yet again I was accepting a dismal parody of all that I longed for. Some of the women I brought home were even unwilling to remove their clothes unless the light was switched off. It hurt me deeply to witness such crippled self-esteem, but I never tried to talk them out of their decision.

Whenever a hot body at a nightclub really got into my balls or some leggy babe passed me on the street it was inevitably the prelude to bitter frustration. I pulled out my hair trying to figure out what I had to do to become acquainted with these women. They stayed at the very edge of my life, as if obeying some secret injunction. There was simply never an opportunity to establish contact with them. They carried themselves with an enviable self-assurance and seemed not to need any man, least of all me. They thrived on life and basked in the excitement they generated. I spent my days wondering where they lived, where they worked, how they managed to remain so elusive. At the sight of a gorgeous woman dangling on another guy's arm, I'd be consumed by envy. It was beyond my comprehension. What did it take to possess one of these magnificent creatures? I wasn't ugly. I had a job. I couldn't work it out.

I could stare at pictures of beautiful women all day long, my cock and I united in longing. I subscribed to *Playboy* and *Penthouse* and bought *Club*, *Mayfair*, *Model Directory* and other magazines whenever the girl on the cover caught my eye. But on the whole, self-proclaimed pornography failed to meet my requirements and I was much more likely to pick up a copy of *Elle* or *Cosmopolitan* than waste my money on a hall of horrors like *Fiesta*, *Forty Plus* or a hard-core sex mag. My favourite videos were all purchased over the counter at HMV and Virgin Megastore, not from the shifty porn mongers in the back streets of Soho. Many of them, like my collection of celebrity workout tapes, didn't even carry an 18 certificate. Nakedness is not a prerequisite for getting me off, depictions of sex largely unnecessary – a firm ass in a tight leotard has done it for me many a time. And the things you can see in music videos these days if you look closely enough and have a good pause button on your remote control.

Still, my blood boiled whenever I heard anybody whining about the evils of top-shelf magazines and calling for them to be banned. I was ready to take to the streets in defence of all filth. I had the vague suspicion that there was a conspiracy against guys like me. I discerned a mean-faced alliance, made up of *certain* feminists, househusbands, born again

Christians, Sunday policemen, reformed cons, the NUS, the Mothers' Union, aging beauty queens, and other neurotics, brazen hypocrites and sycophants, that was intent on denying me the chance of even *looking* at beautiful female bodies; meanwhile, the same lucky bastards as always had full permission to go on shagging the world's top bitches.

I did make love to a beautiful woman once, but I had to travel all the way to Las Vegas for the privilege. A few friends who are insatiable gamblers suggested the trip and while they threw away their money in the hotel casino, I took myself off on tours of the strip clubs and peepshows. I was amazed by some of the women I saw in these places, shameless creatures with maddening bodies. In the larger clubs I was thoroughly spoilt. Up on the main stage there would be naked dancers sliding down poles, legs akimbo or crawling around the perimeter and allowing grateful men to stare into their cunts. Others would be writhing on customers' tables, garters stuffed with dollar bills. I didn't know where to look; the world's choicest tits and asses beckoned from every direction. I wanted to stay in Vegas forever – I swear there is no better city on earth. And when the week was over and we boarded the plane to fly home, I cursed God for making me an Englishman who needs to work for a living. But at least I had the memory of that fuck.

It had never been my intention to pay for sex – I simply requested a table dance. I sat very still as a spectacular woman with flowing blonde hair stepped up to do me the honour. I felt slightly uneasy at first, concerned that other customers would see the lust that was burning in my eyes. Smiling down at me from massive platform sandals, she began to gyrate her pelvis and at the same time used her thumbs to stretch the sides of a black thong high over her broad hips. Her oiled skin glistened in the spotlight and I could see the ripples of muscle in her toned thighs and stomach. She let go of the thong straps to slide her hands up to her big, naked breasts, cupping them lovingly and jiggling them for me. Then she showed me her ass. She turned around, bent forwards and shook it right in my face. She had pulled the thong tight between her cheeks and the crotch was moulded around her pouting cunt. My eyes fixed on the outline of the lips and the few wisps of light, pubic hair.

When she turned around again and saw the lump in my pants, she climbed down from the table and silently led me to a small private room beyond the stage. She told me the price and then the rules. I was to sit in a leather armchair. I was to keep my hands on the armrests and on no account attempt to touch her.

I obeyed and she stood between my open legs and dangled her plump breasts in my face. She rubbed those beauties together, pushing the nipples close to my eyes. The moist heat of them, the blend of scented oil and woman-sweat, made my head spin. She pulled them away and started to play with them selfishly, pinching and twisting the nipples and making the sweet sounds a man wants to hear. Lifting one breast to her mouth, and without taking her eyes off me, she began to flick the nipple with her long, curling tongue, teasing it and teasing me. She did the same to the other nipple and finished by sucking on it. She made it look so delicious I began to drool.

She spun around and sat herself heavily on my cock, catching me by surprise. I gasped at the sudden pressure and the heat of her naked ass. Her whole purpose now was to make me come and she wasted no time. Her movements were strong and insistent.

She wriggled her ass almost vindictively and moaned in contrived ecstasy. There was no subtlety. She was dry-fucking me like the expert she was. I tried to resist. I didn't want to come so quickly and especially not in my pants. The idea appalled me and it still does. But save pushing her away there was nothing I could do to stop her milking me with her skilful ass.

'Don't hold back,' she said. 'Give in to it. You all do in the end.'

She focused her movement into a tight circle and I closed my eyes and bit my bottom lip as she stirred my imprisoned cock towards ecstasy. After maybe a minute of this exquisite torture she changed technique and began to bounce on my lap. She had me now and she knew it. Straight backed and aloof, like a rider in a saddle, she hammered me to a gasping climax. She continued to roll her ass while I came. She spread her hot crack over the length of my spasming cock and coaxed every last drop of cum into my trousers.

Fortunately, there was a bathroom where I could clean myself up. It had just the right facilities, including a dispenser of paper underpants. The presence of this machine reassured me; I was not such a deviant after all. When I came out she was bending over adjusting her sandal straps and the sight of her gaudy nakedness made my cock hard all over again. I paid her, tipped her handsomely, and asked if there was any way I could fuck her properly. I offered her a small fortune for the chance. She was suspicious at first and told me that going out on dates was against the rules of the club. But after I increased my initial offer she agreed to meet me in a hotel lounge the next evening.

She turned up fit for the Oscars wearing a diaphanous white dress, jewellery and delicate silver sandals. She looked like a character from a pornographic fairy tale, a Cinderella turned whore. I paid for a room, ordered champagne and she gave me her body for an hour.

I wasted no time. I unzipped the dress and it fell to the floor, revealing her awesome nakedness that seemed virgin all over again. Kissing on the lips or the face was forbidden, but I licked every inch of the rest of her body. I even took off her shoes and kissed her feet, the heels, the soles and each of the toes. I spent an eternity with my tongue buried inside her tangy cunt while she lay on the bed and absently stroked my hair. Eventually she lifted my head and reminded me that she had to leave soon. I rolled on a condom and fucked her in a frenzy. I wanted all of her, her whole magnificent body at one time. I lay on top of her, sucking her nipples and spreading her ass cheeks with my hands. I stared at the perfect face I was not allowed to kiss, marvelling at her lips, her tiny nose, the long lashes of her closed eyes. I was in love with her ears, her slender neck, her golden hair. I came in tribute to her effortless beauty.

I wanked myself to sleep for the third night running. My dreams were dense and overwrought with images of Jasmine. The next day at work was as long and unbearable as the previous one. The deadline for my report was approaching and I sat through an interminable meeting with the other managers, nodding, smiling but hearing nothing. I didn't have the opportunity to call Jasmine all day.

I arrived home shattered but still restless. The answering machine was flashing again and my heart raced, but none of the messages was from Jasmine. I called her and the same male voice answered. I was on the verge of swearing at him and just managed to slam down the receiver in time. I looked around the room; the pizza was still there in the box on the floor. I grew nauseous looking at it. I couldn't bear to stay in my flat a moment longer.

I got in my car and drove around aimlessly. Then I had an idea. I returned, parked the car and walked quickly around the corner to Giorgio's. I had not forgotten my humiliating exit or my vow, but now I was borne along by a surging conviction that overrode every other consideration – Jasmine would be there.

I sat at a table and gazed at the stool she'd used, at the upholstered seat her ass had rested on. I was tense, worried that the bar staff were whispering about me, sure that the regulars were pointing fingers and having a quiet laugh. Yet I stayed put, because here, in the place she had once been, I felt that she was not entirely lost to me. I drank two bottles of wine, constantly checking the door, willing her to appear.

I slept soundly when I returned home and fell into bed. But I woke up with a devil of a hangover and a cock that gave me no peace.

The next day was Friday and when we finished in the office Kim invited me to the company bar. I trailed along reluctantly and insisted we take a table hidden away in the corner. I drank a coke and spoke in monosyllables.

'Matt,' she said, after a long silence, 'I know it's really none of my business and I'm probably out of line asking, but is something wrong?'

'What makes you think that?' I found it hard to hide the irritation in my voice.

'Since Tuesday you've looked like a judge has passed the death sentence on you. I'm not the only one who's noticed.'

'It's just a virus. I'll be right as rain next week.' I tried to sound flippant and picked up my coke; but I could tell she wasn't convinced.

'That's some virus. I hope I never catch it.'

I was fit to drop when I got home, but nervous energy kept me going. I snatched up the phone and hit the buttons hard in sheer frustration. The male voice answered and, sounding like a worn-out record of myself, I demanded to speak to Jasmine. I was ready to hang up rather than deal with his grating apology; but suddenly I realised he was telling me a whole new story. Jasmine, he said, was flying back from New York at the weekend. She was expected home on Monday. I thanked him for the information. I actually thanked him.

Never did a day pass more slowly than the following Monday at work and several times I almost broke and called her from the office. I was tense when I arrived back at the flat and worried that she would not want to speak to me. I forced myself to sit it out until nine o'clock – for some reason it seemed the right time to call, long enough past dinner and not too late to seem intrusive. I poured myself a glass of vodka to give me courage. I gulped it down, waited, but my hand was still trembling as I dialled. I counted seven rings before someone finally lifted the receiver. I held my breath for a long second . . . then a warm, seductive voice filled my ear.

'Jasmine,' I said – all the music returned to that name – 'it's me, Matt.'

'Who?'

'Matt from Giorgio's. Last Monday night? Remember?'

There was a heavy pause before she answered.

'Oh.'

'I've been trying to call you for a whole week.'

'What do you want?'

'How was New York?'

'I said, "What do you want?"'

'You said to call.'

'And?'

'Can I meet you for a drink?'

'I don't think so.' She intoned these words like an often-used refrain.

'Just one drink. Any place you like.' I became aware of my hand clutching the arm of the chair.

'I'm busy all week.'

'How about the weekend? . . . Please.'

She let that final word hang limply before she spoke.

'Say that again.'

'Please.'

'Again.'

'Please.'

'And one more time.'

'Please.'

A burst of irreverent laughter followed.

'I might be at Apollo on Saturday night. Don't call me again, do you hear?'

I sat listening to the silence she left behind.

Three

*'What kind of relationship do you plan to have
with a woman you can never fuck?'*

On Saturday night I paced up and down the long
queue outside Apollo, searching for my beloved
Jasmine. For days I'd had a gnawing anxiety that she
would not show up. Now I began to fear she'd sent
me here as a cruel prank – it was not difficult to
imagine her laughing at me with a boyfriend in a
fancy restaurant across town. I took my place at the
back of the line, determined to go through with the
night even if I had to spend it drinking alone. I
couldn't go home while there remained even the
slightest chance of seeing her. There was no turning
away from that ass of hers.

I had made a little progress towards the entrance
when my eyes were drawn across the street. There, in
the relative darkness, I saw a white Mercedes pull up.
It seemed to have appeared from nowhere and
glowed phantom-like in the night. I watched the
driver climb out, straighten his peaked cap and take
two stiff steps to the rear door, which he opened
rather cautiously. He stood back with his head
lowered, giving the impression he was weighed down
by an immense sadness. A moment later a pair of

shiny black boots swung into view and the spiked heels were lowered to the ground. Joy exploded inside me as Jasmine revealed herself.

She was wrapped in a black leather jacket that narrowed at her waist and flared stiffly above the top of the boots, from which her proud, bare thighs emerged. Without addressing a word to the driver, she stepped coolly across the street and past the waiting horde. Her name burst from my lips as she came by and she turned her hypnotic brown eyes towards me.

'Do you think I'm going to wait in a queue?' she snapped and continued on her way. 'Follow me.' Her legs moved with daunting elegance in the high boots and I was keenly aware of my own clumsiness as I trotted after her.

The bouncers greeted her with oily grins. These tall, impressively built men behaved like puppies in her presence. The most senior of them escorted her to a door a little way on from the main entrance and opened it for her. She rewarded him with a cover-girl smile and went inside. He blocked my way as I tried to follow, puffed out his chest and asked to see my gold membership card.

'I'm with her,' I said.

He didn't budge until Jasmine confirmed it.

'It's okay. He's one of mine,' I heard her say.

He gave me the once-over and stepped aside, slowly.

She was standing at the cloakroom counter. She unfastened and removed her jacket and I watched in wonder as she exposed a white crop-top that struggled to contain her strong, restless breasts. Then I saw the rest of her. God save me! Shiny black hot pants that were so tight I could clearly make out the mound of her cunt. The silver zipper tread, which

23

gaped open inches below her bellybutton, plunged down into this triangle of tight creases. It was a roller coaster ride for the eyes.

'Hang this up.' She shoved her jacket at me. It was warm from her body and the smell of it turned my world red. 'And don't lose the receipt.' She proceeded to the VIP lounge, leaving me free to gaze at her departing form. Her ass cheeks flexed greedily with each high-heeled step and chewed the yielding latex in the crack between them. I passed her jacket to the attendant, breathing in its scent, and then gave him my own. I paid him, slid the tickets into my wallet and rushed to join her.

The atmosphere in the VIP lounge was easy and relaxed. Many of the faces I saw were at least a generation older than those waiting in the queue outside. The men were, frankly, smug, every last one of them; the women, who were noticeably younger and prettily dressed, circulated like hollow angels. At the near end was a well-polished bar with an abundance of gleaming brass. Narrow panels divided the floor space into cosy alcoves in which cushioned chairs and couches were arranged around low tables. Signed photographs of celebrities, professional athletes and sports teams were displayed on the walls in heavy frames. Installed above the bar was a bank of flashing video screens which showed the main club arena below from a variety of prime positions. From the comfort of your chair you could observe the crushed masses heaving on the dance floor, spy into dark corners, study the drunken expressions on unsuspecting young faces. The lounge also had a discreet dance floor, a subtle invitation to greater intimacy. It was located before the door that led down to the inferno below, and this sequential arrangement suggested inevitability, the way of all flesh.

I found Jasmine in conversation with a silver-haired man with an orange tan whose audacity amazed me. He had one of his paws on her arm and was squeezing her like a lecherous uncle. I stood awkwardly at her side, unsure how to react. I made a show of looking into a mirror on the wall and adjusting my tie. The old-timer gestured to the bar and asked her what she was drinking. She sweetly declined his offer but kept him hanging around with her suggestive smile. I listened to them and it dawned on me that she was flirting with the owner of the club.

'Get me a Long Island Tea,' she said to me.

I was glad to go to the bar, as it gave me something to do. I ordered the cocktail and got myself a Budweiser. She was still chatting with the owner when I returned. I stood at her side again, holding a drink in each hand.

'Why don't you find a place to sit?' she said.

She shook her head as I walked away and the owner whispered something too faint for me to hear. I found an unoccupied table and put down the drinks. I sat and waited, sipping the Budweiser from the bottle. My eyes returned to her constantly. I marvelled at her complacency as well as her rare beauty. She stood in full view of all the tables, igniting the flames of unspeakable desires with her barely clothed body and those outrageous boots that had no other purpose than to be stared at, admired and – yes – feared. I could feel the heat rising all around me, see male faces darkening with lust. She shook with sudden laughter and sent delicious ripples running up and down her longed-for flesh.

When she came across to the table all trace of flirtatious humour had gone. She settled down on a couch, put her arm on the rest and crossed her legs. The hot pants rode up obscenely, exposing the swell of her ass in profile. While she sipped her drink, she swung her extended leg, lightly kicking the edge of the table with her boot.

'I wish you'd use a glass for that,' were the first words she said to me.

I apologised. I went straight over to the bar and fetched a glass. 'You look wonderful,' I told her as I poured my beer into it.

'Really.'

'I don't know what else I can say. You know how I feel.'

She turned her gorgeous eyes towards me at last. 'What do you want from me?'

'A relationship.'

She laughed at that. She genuinely thought it was funny. 'Didn't I tell you that you'd never fuck me? What kind of relationship do you plan to have with a woman you can never fuck?'

'They happen . . .'

A sarcastic smile on a beautiful woman's lips cuts to the heart of you. I felt my gaze drop as I struggled to convince her that I could renounce all my sexual ambitions, if that is what it took.

'Look at you,' she interrupted. 'Your tongue has been hanging out since I took off my jacket. You're positively drooling over my tits and ass right now.' She swung her leg towards me and prodded my shin with her boot heel. 'I bet you felt that in your stiff little cock, didn't you?'

My cock was throbbing insanely.

'Go and get me another drink. A whisky this time, with ice.'

Steadily the lounge began to fill. Acquaintances of Jasmine came across to share news and gossip and gasp over her outfit. They wouldn't leave us alone and I ran back and forth to the bar buying one round of drinks after another. I was soon out of cash and had to leave my credit card with the barman. I was learning one thing about Jasmine: she loved to drink; and with each glass she became more generous with her body. She behaved like a heaven-sent slut. She let men hug her waist, plant wet kisses on her arms and shoulders ... and that smile. For a short time a girlfriend perched on her knee and the pair of them made a crude pretence of being lovers, licking each other's tongues to wild applause. I had not forgotten the strong taste of whisky when she'd kissed me at Giorgio's. I prayed I'd get lucky again – a long, dirty snog, a sly squeeze of that shiny ass, those magnificent tits rubbing up against me. Galloping thoughts.

I made small talk with those sitting close to me and began to enjoy myself. I had attractive young women all around me, spicily perfumed and play-acting the way they do. It was a rare treat; I was in an oasis. But I never forgot Jasmine and watched her longingly. I didn't get so much as a glance in return, not even when I placed her whiskies down in front of her.

There were pools of condensation and spilt beer on the tabletop and a girl next to me grew irritated at having to wipe the bottom of her dripping glass.

'Where are the beer mats in this place?' she complained. Jasmine suddenly stopped talking and turned herself towards me.

'There's one right beside you,' she said to her friend.

The girl looked at me puzzled and I attempted a smile. I had an awful sense of foreboding.

'Isn't that right?' Jasmine continued, taking a sip of whisky and staring at me.

I was too incredulous to reply and felt my cheeks burning.

'What-is-your-name?' she said very slowly in the manner of someone talking to an imbecile. This made her friends laugh and now they were all looking at me expectantly.

'. . . Matt,' I was finally compelled to say.

'Good boy.' She swallowed the last mouthful of whisky and placed the empty glass on the table. I felt the gust of her exuberance. 'We all seem to have finished our drinks,' she said with a devilish smirk. 'I think it's time you fetched some more *beer*, *Matt*.' There was a roar of laughter and I forced myself to join in. For the next hour it was a running joke. Every time I went to the bar there were shouts of 'Mine's a beer, Matt.'

Later on somebody tapped my shoulder as I was balancing a tray of drinks.

'Is she your woman?' he asked.

'Yes,' I replied.

'I'd slap her.'

Such bravado! If I hadn't been holding the tray, I'd have swung for him.

It was sometime after midnight when the local basketball team strode into the lounge like lords of mankind. These enormous men – two of them black, the others white, all wearing fancy blazers – made a profound impression. Every head turned in their direction, including Jasmine's. They gathered around the bar and one by one reached down to shake hands with the owner, who looked like a sunburned gnome in their midst. The bottles of Budweiser they picked up from the bar were lost in their gigantic palms and they put on a fine performance, moving their bodies boisterously and giving each other high-fives at every opportunity. The women at the table couldn't keep still. They loved the American accents, the loud, complacent drawling. The athletes had noticed them in return but could afford to play it cool. They grabbed their Buds and filed across the lounge, headed for the excitement below. One of the black guys, who had a shaved head, made firm eye contact with Jasmine as he passed.

I was only at the bar for a minute but returned to find that Jasmine and her girlfriends had disappeared. I felt ridiculous as I set down a full tray of drinks in the middle of a deserted table. I was in no mood to talk to the few guys who were left behind and sat in silence, struggling to suppress tormenting thoughts. It was hopeless though, and I moved to a chair where I had a clear view of the video screens.

It didn't take long to locate Jasmine and her huge black partner among the press of bodies. They had taken up position in the centre of the dance floor and appeared on two screens. I watched with a mixture of revulsion and fascination as they came together for a pulsating dance number. They were like two fine animals in rut, supreme specimens of the species performing a burlesque drama of cock and cunt. She turned her back to him and he responded to the provocation of her shaking ass with stiff jerks of his pelvis. Their simulated fucking was more obscene than the real thing. It was all tease and temptation. Jasmine was dancing for me and a thousand other pairs of hungry eyes, as well as for her enamoured stud. One camera caught the rush of sexual excitement on her face – the public display of her lust for a single man. My stomach twisted into a tight knot, a sensation that the word jealousy hardly begins to describe. The image of her flushed face multiplied, filling screen after screen, as if some demon had seized control of the system and wanted to crush me with the weight of my obsession. I went back to my seat and forced myself to make conversation.

Hours seemed to pass before a glowing Jasmine returned with her prize stud. They sat on the couch and he encircled her with a long arm. He kept his thighs wide open, oblivious to the enormous space he was consuming and people crowded around to shake his hand and slap his palms. Jasmine was captivated by his every word and swooned at the sound of his deep rumbling voice. She stroked his thigh as he spoke and never took her eyes from his face.

Pleading for a pause in the flow of questions, he reached for one of the Budweisers on the tray; but his fingers recoiled when they made contact with the bottle. He was quick to take advantage of his discovery.

'Where I come from we like our women hot . . . but we drink our beer ice cold.'

I felt the roar of laughter he got in response was hugely exaggerated.

Jasmine threw a quick glance at me and I was trotting over to the bar almost before I realised it.

I returned bearing more drinks to find her reclining with her back against the armrest and her legs draped across her stud's thighs. They were playing a childish game. He would walk his fingers up the length of her boots and along her bare thighs, seeing how far he could advance before she pushed his hand away. After several attempts he managed to reach the soft flesh of her inner thigh and snatched at the zipper of her hot pants. She slapped his hand playfully as he tired to tug her fly open. After this victory he sat back and took a long swig from a chilled Bud. She watched him adoringly.

I, too, drank from the bottle. It felt good. I was defying Jasmine and laying down a challenge that only she and I could understand. I loosened my collar and tie and tried to make eye contact with her. The stud noticed me staring but showed no hostility. He raised his bottle to me.

'You haven't introduced us,' he said to Jasmine. 'Who's your friend?'

'I don't know.' She gave me a filthy look. 'Who are you?'

'The name's Matt,' I said and held out my hand. 'How do you do?'

'No, your real name,' she snapped. Even the stud was shocked by the venom in her voice but not for long. The smile returned to his face and now it revealed a salacious curiosity.

'Tell him your real name,' she repeated, looking gorgeous and vixen-sly. I quickly put down the bottle, hoping it would be enough to pacify her. Without taking her eyes off me, she picked up a sopping beer mat. She dangled it casually between the tips of her long fingers, letting it drip onto the table. 'I won't ask again,' she said in a bored tone of voice.

Still I did not speak. I smiled apologetically. I pleaded with my eyes, my whole subdued being, but I already sensed it was hopeless. It was my misfortune to worship the flesh of a woman who held me in utter contempt. I watched helplessly as she casually flicked her slender wrist and sent the beer mat spinning towards me, spitting juice on the way. It struck my chest and slid down my shirt to land on the top of my trousers, leaving a sticky wet trail behind.

'This,' she said decisively, 'is beer mat.'

I stood up and walked away, letting the beer mat drop to the floor. She had humiliated me so badly this time I could not conceivably stay at the table. I went down to the main club. I was relieved to be anonymous among so many people but Jasmine's terrible laughter was still ringing in my ears. I stood at the edge of the dance floor with a crowd of weary guys. Silently we watched the women dancing. How powerfully their young hips moved.

I then remembered I had the cloakroom tickets in my wallet and the idea of stealing Jasmine's jacket came to me. It would have been a fitting act of revenge, but I have to admit I was also aroused by the thought of possessing something she'd worn – I'd not forgotten the smell of the leather mixed with her wild perfume.

I returned to the lounge with the intention of walking straight past Jasmine to the cloakroom. But when I saw that voluptuous body lying tame in the stud's arms I lost all desire to go through with my plan. I didn't want to creep away only to be remembered as a thief. Instead I would make it appear to everyone present that I was rejecting Jasmine, despite her enslaving beauty.

I stopped at the table and put down the cloakroom ticket in a pool of spilt beer. I'd planned to say something cutting, but in the event I simply walked away without uttering a word. I was halfway to the door when I heard her call my name; her tone was calm, almost friendly. I turned around slowly, trembling in anticipation of the sight of her.

'Be a dear and fetch my jacket before you go.'

My mouth fell open. I simply could not believe what I was hearing. The audacity of this bitch seemed to have no limits. She stretched lazily against her stud and ran her fingers over his smooth head. Her pouting lips sought his flesh and she kissed him tenderly under the chin. She turned her attention to me again.

'Don't you have a little job to do? Run along now.' Her stud was watching me as if I were an oddity, a pitiful product of a fallen nation.

'You must be joking,' I said.

'No, Matt, I never joke. Not with you. This is your last chance.' There was unmistakable menace in her voice now.

I came back to the table, determined to appear strong.

She rose slowly to her feet and I marvelled at the spectacle of her body in the revealing outfit which now appeared barbaric. (I was not the only man looking down at her boots.) She took her beaming stud by the hand and led him towards the dance floor. She let me inhale the raw scent of her and feel the shocking heat of her body as she brushed past.

'Bitch,' I hissed sharply, loud enough for everyone around to hear.

That single word stopped her. Dropping her stud's hand she took a step towards me. She was formidable beyond words. The heels lifted her to an unnatural height and she placed a hand on either hip as if preparing for a piece of violent melodrama. Her eyes were smouldering with outrage, daring me to defy her just one more time.

'What did you say?'

I remained silent, blinking stupidly. I could feel my will crumbling in the face of her rising fury. At that moment she looked more beautiful than any woman I could ever imagine.

She spoke again: 'Get my jacket.'

I did as I was told. While she stood watching, I carefully peeled the ticket from the tabletop and hurried through the door to the cloakroom. I believed I could redeem myself and win another chance to see her. I had to believe it.

She was slow-dancing with her stud when I returned. I laid the jacket carefully on the couch and, ignoring all the dreadful names shouted at me, took a last look at the woman who'd dominated my thoughts night and day for two weeks. She was moving herself sensually against the muscular body of her partner and his massive hands gripped her waist as if it were a slender stem. With a nod of her head she signalled for me to approach and I walked over quickly, hoping for a word of encouragement. Her stud loomed behind her as she spoke.

'You did it in the end but you took too long.'

I apologised.

'Even worse, you really pissed me off.' She reached out and slapped my face hard. It was enough to stun me. 'Now get out of here and don't ever bother me again.' She returned to the arms of her dark lover and he led her to the back of the dance floor.

The bouncers held the doors open for me and I walked like a zombie through the lounge and out into the street, forgetting my own jacket. The cold air outside numbed the stinging in my cheek but far worse than the pain or the humiliation was the finality of her last words. I climbed into a waiting taxi and mumbled directions to the driver.

As we pulled away I noticed the white Mercedes was still parked in the same position across the street. The driver sat motionless in the front seat, as if he hadn't moved the whole night long.

Four

*'Don't get too excited.
Your next lesson is to learn how to wait.'*

Nothing could take my mind off Jasmine. I turned to the models in my magazines but the pages of flat, unmoving bodies were no substitute for what I'd lost. I sat beside the phone fighting the temptation to pick it up. I carried on imaginary dialogues with her. I begged her pitifully and even in my fantasies she mocked me without mercy. Late on Sunday evening I gave in and called her only to hear the male voice tell me she was not at home. I had visions of her on a luxurious bed fucking her athletic lover. Her legs were wrapped possessively around his waist and she was moaning gratefully as he plunged his bolt-hard cock in and out of her yielding cunt.

The week that followed returns to me only in disjointed fragments. I remember the distant, despairing look on Kim's face and the mountain of paperwork on my desk, which grew and grew. I remember I failed to attend an important meeting and that some women overheard me in the firm's cafeteria as I swore down the phone. I remember I tried to enter the VIP lounge at Apollo but was blocked by the heavy body of a bouncer. Most vividly of all I recall my lucid, alcohol-fuelled dreams in which I was tormented by Jasmine. In one she wore the shiny black boots and hot pants; her legs were long enough to make me dizzy, her ass impossibly voluptuous. Hands on hips, she strutted down a line of baying admirers and, unable to stand on two legs, I crawled after her frantically but could not keep up. I would wake up drenched in sweat.

After many days of trying, I finally reached her on the phone. I expected her to be angry when she heard my voice; instead, she merely sounded impatient, as if I were interrupting something. In the background I could hear excited female voices.

'Give it up,' she said. 'You blew it big time.'

'Let me have another chance. I'll do anything.'

'Why should I bother with you?'

'Because I utterly adore you.'

'And what makes you any different from all the others who say that?'

'I'll show you. I'll do whatever you want. Anything.'

'No, I don't think so.'

'Please, just one more chance.'

'Are you begging me again?'

'Yes. Yes, I'm begging you.'

'That's too bad because you haven't earned that privilege yet.'

'Please.'

'Goodbye, Matt.' She hung up the phone and cast me into darkness. But she had pronounced my name, recognised me in some small way, and that gave me reason to hope.

I held out for a whole week and called her again. She did not sound surprised to hear from me and let me speak. I began in the way I'd carefully rehearsed but my voice still faltered.

'I would like the privilege of begging your forgiveness.'

'All right, go ahead,' she sighed.

'I beg you to give me one more chance to show you how much I adore you.'

'Are you down on your knees?'

'Yes,' I said and quickly knelt down on the carpet.

'Good, because that's where you need to be whenever you ask me anything. Now hurry up and say what you have to say. I'm getting bored.'

'Let me take you out one night. Anywhere you want to go.'

'Is that all?' I sensed she was ready to put down the phone.

'I'll do whatever you want me to.'

'What's your name?'

' . . . Beer mat.'

'Say it louder. Say you're a soggy beer mat.'

'I'm a soggy beer mat.'

She laughed, laughed like a beautiful and healthy young woman. 'Go to the wine bar on Saturday night and if I'm not there go to Apollo; and if I'm not at Apollo try all the other clubs in town. But don't call me. Whatever happens don't you dare call me. You won't get another chance to go down on your knees and beg if you do.'

I went out on Saturday night knowing I would not see her. I made my way diligently from one location to the next performing a ritual for her. Obeying her instructions made me feel connected to her and I had the sense I'd taken my first secure step into her world. I felt proud, superior to the crowds of drunken clubbers I brushed shoulders with.

I resisted the urge to call her during the days that followed. It was easier than before, now that I believed I would hear from her. I was less agitated

and in my dreams she became less ferocious, sometimes stroking my head and even letting me lick her
hands and thighs. I now rejoiced in the lust that kept
me bound to her and refrained from wanking as
much as I possibly could so that my desire intensified.
My cock, when it was swollen with her spirit, was the
only companion I needed.

I was able to function at work again and went for
lunch with Kim several times. We chatted about small
everyday things. The smile returned to her face and
she even made a joke about my virus. She was cute
but when I looked into her naïve green eyes I saw
only Jasmine.

Eventually I received the long-awaited phone call.
She said simply to meet her in town the following
afternoon and designated a bench at the top of the
pedestrianised high street. I went to work in the
morning and around midday told Kim I felt a cold
coming on and took the afternoon off. When I got to
the meeting place Jasmine was already sitting on the
bench in the pose I adored, one leg crossed over the
other. She wore a dark business suit with sheer
stockings and a skirt that left a distracting amount of
thigh exposed. On her feet she wore tight black
stilettos, cut low around the toes. Her hair was
gathered above the nape of her neck in an abundant
French pleat and her glorious features were enhanced
with a touch of mascara, a hint of blue eye shadow
and a subtle gloss on her lips. She was a perfect icon
of the modern professional woman, a tailored display
of sexuality, sophistication and power.

She remained seated, swinging her leg enchanting-
ly, while I stood before her hardly knowing what I
should say. It was the first time I'd seen her in
daylight and she dazzled me. Men who walked by
expressed their crude interest without any inhibition,

twisting their heads around to take a second and third look at her. I was thrilled to be associated with a woman who without even trying sent waves of excitement rippling up and down the high street.

'I hope you brought your credit cards,' she said.

I tapped my trouser pocket just to reassure myself and nodded. She uncrossed her legs, treating me to a flash of stocking top, and rose to her feet. I watched her set off in the direction of the shopping mall, lost in admiration for her legs and the brisk, decisive strides she took.

'Come on, I don't have time to waste on you,' she called back. I quickly caught up and tried to start a conversation but her sarcastic remarks soon discouraged me. I walked in silence at her side listening to the relentless click of her heels against the pavement.

Once inside the shopping mall she made straight for the escalators and took me up to the designer boutiques. It was less busy here than on the floors below, the atmosphere soft and light, and I became aware that I was walking among a finer class of consumer. Charmed women drifted past clutching fancy carrier bags emblazoned with names and logos. Jasmine strolled at a leisurely pace, as much on show herself, it seemed to me, as anything displayed in the windows. She glanced at some of the displays but did not pause until we came to Gucci where her eyes fell on a collection of priceless shoes. We stood gazing into the window each with our own thoughts.

There were maybe a dozen shoes, displayed like fine works of art on slim white pedestals of differing heights. Each shoe was illuminated by its own small spotlight, which cast it in dramatic relief and gave it an unearthly quality. My eyes were drawn to a mule with a thick wooden sole and a chunky wedge heel that tapered outwards towards the base. A single band of black suede, which left the toe area exposed, was the only means a woman had of keeping this object attached to her foot. It stood over six inches tall at the heel, daunting as a sentry, an unsettling parody of a shoe.

'Do women actually walk around in things like that?' I asked.

'What do you think we do with them?' She turned away and went over to the shop opposite. The skirt she wore was not excessively tight but fitted close enough for the twitching outline of her ass to reveal itself as she walked. There was no hiding those divine globes of flesh; they demanded attention at all times. I caught up to her, my cock stiffening, and followed her into the shop.

The lighting inside was warmly hued and enticing, and a sweet, spicy, supremely feminine fragrance invaded my nostrils as soon as I stepped across the threshold. I became light-headed and my heavy cock lurched like a drunk, forcing me to alter my stride. I had entered a shrine devoted to expensive lingerie and found myself limping after Jasmine through an exhibition of wildly erotic garments in satin, silk, cotton and lace.

The merchandise was displayed on circular steel rails, which resembled space-age totems, and the rows of panties and bras presented a feast of colour and texture that made my mouth water. They dangled seductively from their tiny hangers, inviting thrusting breasts and firm female asses to fill them, stretch them, give them shape and purpose. I stopped and turned full circle, marvelling at the bold display of such intimate items. It was as if I were peeping up the skirt of every woman in the land.

Two slate-coloured mannequins stood in the centre of the floor, raised on a platform. One was naked except for a metallic-blue satin basque trimmed with silver lace. Her sister was dressed in a half-cup bra, sharply cut red panties, suspenders and dark stockings. Their eyes were heavily made-up and they gazed blindly into the distance like ships' figureheads. Hanging on the walls were arty black-and-white posters of models posing in underwear against classical backdrops of temple ruins and amphitheatres. Behind a counter two pretty assistants chatted while they threaded panties onto hangers with practised efficiency.

The customers – all female – were engrossed in the task of selecting garments to adorn the secret parts of their bodies. They wandered slowly from rail to rail, occasionally removing a bra or pair of panties to inspect more closely. They would hold the delicate piece of merchandise out before them, appraising it critically, and seemed to enjoy running it between their fingertips and stretching the elastic. Their behaviour was so intimate that I was afraid to be caught staring. I felt like an intruder and became profoundly conscious that I had no place in a shop like this. I moved closer to Jasmine trying to justify my presence to curious eyes.

Jasmine was a highly discriminating customer and slid garments quickly around the rails until something caught her attention. I watched her lift up a bra-and-panty set in black wet-look satin. She considered it briefly and held it towards me.

'Here,' she said, already resuming her search.

I regarded the sexy articles with uncertainty and she glanced at me crossly.

'Hold.'

I quickly took the hanger from her fingers and held the feminine items against my leg. Self-consciously, I checked the location of the other customers and looked over at the assistants. Jasmine passed me two more hangers suspending the same bra-and-panty sets, one in red and the other in white. I took these without hesitating but wondered how I could keep my growing burden concealed.

She walked to another rail that displayed a selection of more traditional panties. She picked out several pairs of silky camiknickers in rapid succession and literally dumped them into my arms. I set about distributing the merchandise between my two hands, anxious that I did not resemble some kind of living clotheshorse. Showing not the slightest regard for my predicament – though I think she did smile darkly for an instant – she waltzed across to the other side of the shop and began selecting packets of stockings. She shoved a bundle into my hand as soon as I caught up and, as an afterthought, piled several more packets on top. I swayed to keep them balanced but could not prevent one from tumbling to the floor and attracting the attention of a woman at the next rail. Jasmine made a loud tut-tut sound and pursed her shiny lips.

As I crouched down to retrieve the packet I'd dropped, the others spilled from my hand making a frightful noise. One of them struck the tip of Jasmine's shoe and lay motionless on the floor before her. Mumbling an apology, I stretched my hand towards it but she kicked it out of my reach and I was left to watch her clicking heels disappear behind the base of the mannequins. With bitter determination, I gathered the packets together and hung them from my fingers. When I stood up again, the woman at the next rail was still watching me with an unreadable expression on her face.

Jasmine was waiting impatiently to pass me a negligee. It was metallic-blue and silver like the basque on the mannequin. I went over to her, gesturing that my hands were already full, but she simply draped it over my shoulder. I felt ridiculous and, struggling to sound polite, I made a suggestion:

'Wouldn't it be easier if I laid these on the counter?'

'If you don't like the way I shop, you're free to leave.' She selected another negligee, red with a black lace trim and longer than the first, and draped this one over my other shoulder, not caring that part of it caught on my ear. She looked around deciding what else to buy. She was commanding and beautiful in her dark business suit. The tied-back hair enhanced the strength of her features, which in an instant could become severe and intimidating.

She led me across the shop, past a middle-aged woman who was staring at us with a hand over her mouth, back to the panties. We stopped at a rail of sexily cut garments and she pulled out a tiny black thong, the kind which surely only models must wear and has no other purpose than to add emphasis to the enticing cleft between an already magnificent pair of ass cheeks. My cock was squirming as she unhooked the frivolous thing from its hanger and let it dangle from her fingertips.

Despite my predicament I found the sight irresistible. I would have given anything for her to wear that Y-shaped string beneath her smart business suit. I was already picturing it working itself into her intimate creases as she walked down the high street. I imagined the meetings she would attend, the contracts she would sign while this piece of pricey cotton secretly gnawed away at her.

'Take it.' She held the thong out to me, oblivious to the chain of filthy, enslaving fantasies it was stimulating. I was eager to snatch it from her fingers

43

but my hands were full. All the other customers were gaping at us now.

'I won't ask you again,' she said sharply. Carefully, I raised the hand in which I was clutching the colourful selection of camiknickers. She shook her head meanly.

'I don't want you to carry it in your hand.'

'What?'

'Open your mouth.' She waved the thong in front of my unblinking eyes.

'No,' I pleaded in a dry whisper.

'Have you already forgotten what you promised on the phone? I'll tell you one more time. Open your mouth.' There was not a trace of pity on her adorable face. She was fully intent on stuffing the thong into my mouth. I knew that if I resisted no amount of begging would win me another chance with her.

I opened my mouth for her. I stood in the middle of the shop like a hungry fish tempted with a piece of dangling bait. I was aware of heads shaking and faces illuminated by sudden insight. Jasmine revelled in her easy triumph; she would feed me at her leisure. My frozen eyes watched her hand. It came slowly towards my wide-open mouth, lowering the thong almost to my lips. Suddenly it dropped out of view. I felt her tuck the thong into my shirt pocket.

She walked across to the counter and waited, tapping her red-varnished nails impatiently. I was quickly at her side and laid down the merchandise before the assistants. The young rascals didn't lift a finger to help and merely looked on with open amusement. When my hands were finally free, I pulled the thong from my shirt pocket and tucked it away among the packets of stockings. A snigger burst from one of the assistants and she immediately picked up the wisp of material and unfurled it before all our eyes. As if this was not torture enough, she held it by the waistband like an exhibit, letting the plunging crotch section dangle obscenely above the counter. The three women exchanged knowing looks and I was convinced they all shared a dark secret and could see the workings of my sorry soul. Still smirking, the girl laid the thong on a bed of tissue paper and proceeded to fold it, ever so slowly, ever so deliberately. The fuss she made was truly absurd and I had a burning urge to tell her that there was simply nothing there to fold. She clearly enjoyed the sight of me squirming.

I turned my head towards the doorway and the brightness outside. I longed to leave the shop; the heavy feminine odour hanging in the air oppressed me terribly now. But the assistant operating the till worked at a tormentingly slow pace. She picked up one item at a time, entered the price by hand and then passed it to her colleague whose job it was to pack the dainty carrier bags. The process was unbearably protracted and it seemed to take forever before the total cost flashed up in green lights. Suddenly I was staring at an astronomical figure, more than I earned in two weeks. It seemed criminal to demand so much money for a few items of lingerie.

The assistant addressed Jasmine: 'How would you like to pay, Madam?'

'With his credit card.'

I dug into my wallet, rooted out my card and placed it on the assistant's petite upturned palm. I felt sick.

'Thank you, sir.' The sweetness in her voice was brittle. She swiped the card through the machine and laid the bill on the counter for me to sign. I took a pen and felt the women watching in satisfaction as I stooped to sign my name. I was conscious that I was handing over two weeks of my labour in order that the woman standing beside me could adorn her glorious body with luxurious lingerie. I consoled myself with the thought that one day I'd see her wearing some of it. I passed the signed bill to the assistant.

'Get the bags,' Jasmine ordered and walked over to the doorway. I winked at the assistants as I did her bidding. I wanted to show them that I was just a generous guy indulging his temperamental girlfriend.

'She's had a bad morning at the office,' I said in a low voice as I gathered up the half dozen little packages. But they knew better. The frozen smiles on their pretty faces told me they'd seen this drama before.

The bags displayed the shop's name and distinctive logo and left no doubt about what they contained. I walked along at Jasmine's side advertising the fact that I was carrying her precious underwear for her. I'd long dreamt of strolling through a mall in the company of a gorgeous woman, glowing with pride as other guys looked on enviously, but this was a nightmare. It was clear to everyone we passed that we were not lovers or even friends. She alone was the focus of men's attention. I was her besotted drudge, her lingerie caddie, nothing more. My only purpose was to save her unnecessary exertion during her afternoon shopping trip.

She made her sullen porter follow her into other shops with evocative foreign names. She wandered slowly through the aisles, though mercifully she did not purchase anything else. I was in constant anxiety of what she would do should my credit card be rejected. When she'd seen enough she rode the escalators to the ground floor. Here Jasmine and the bags made an even starker impression and I wished she'd let me walk at her side instead of insisting I trail three paces behind.

We left the mall and I followed her the length of the high street, listening to the relentless click of her heels and watching her ass – crying for her ass. We passed a group of vigorous young men who stared at her, then at me, then at the bags. The sight of their grinning mugs made me sick with loathing.

She finally stopped at a taxi rank.

'Good,' she said, 'you're slowly starting to learn.' For the first time that afternoon her tone was not harsh and I felt encouraged. Anticipating a reward my cock jumped in my pants.

'Don't get too excited. Your next lesson is to learn how to wait.'

She opened a taxi door and told me to put the bags on the back seat; when I'd done this she climbed inside. She sat sexily, crossing her wonderful legs, uncaring that the top of her stocking shot into view.

'How long do I need to wait?' I asked.

'Until I call.'

'When will that be?'

'I don't know,' she said dismissively. 'Maybe never.'

She pulled the door closed and gave directions to the driver. I watched her relax in the seat and grin at something he said. Her face glowed brightly, free of all concern. She had already forgotten that I existed.

Five

'I could make you do anything, couldn't I?'

I checked my answering machine from work at every
opportunity and sat by the phone each evening
willing Jasmine to call. My friends did manage to
drag me out for a few drinks occasionally, but while
they were laughing and slapping each other's backs,
I'd suddenly fall silent, convinced Jasmine had called
and left a message. I'd slope off to a nearby phone
box full of hope only to return a little while later
tormented by images of her dancing with the basketball player. Picking up my pint, I'd picture his long
fingers peeling off the fancy underwear I'd bought for
her.

More than two months after the shopping trip I
was walking through town, facing another frustrating
evening at the pub. It was a typical weekday evening;
the clubs offered reduced admission and cheap beer
and the high street was crawling with students. In no
hurry to get to my destination, I followed a pair of
cuties down a busy side road where I was delighted
to discover the light from the bars and restaurants
picked out the subtle lines of their underwear. Even
from three car-lengths away I could distinguish a pair
of high-cut panties through a white satiny dress. But

48

I was not able to savour my discovery. The women came to a sudden halt outside a Greek restaurant, exchanged a few words, and against my silent protest took their smooth legs through the door.

I sighed to myself, as I always did when this kind of thing happened, and glanced around, hungry for more bare flesh and panty lines. That's when I caught sight of the white Mercedes parked across the street. I approached it slowly without breathing, afraid it was a mirage that would evaporate if I moved too quickly or let out a breath. It was parked in front of a cocktail bar and my eyes scanned the customers sitting at the tables in the bright window. A silent cry of joy escaped me. Jasmine was among them.

She was wearing a red sheath dress and leaning forwards with her elbows resting on the table. Her back made a graceful curve and her ass protruded over the back of the stool as if offering itself to an imaginary cock. Facing her was the icy blonde from Giorgio's. Her lips were less generous than Jasmine's and painted candyfloss pink, giving her a girlishly petulant expression.

Jasmine's chauffeur was at the table too, facing the window. He was in uniform but had removed his cap, which he held on his knees. I saw now that he was older than me, perhaps in his late forties, and had a rather distinguished appearance. His beard, greying at the edges, was carefully groomed and he had a prominent and wrinkled forehead. Were it not for the chauffeur's uniform, I'd have taken him for a university lecturer, a doctor or a scientist – a man used to commanding respect. Yet there he sat between two vivacious young women, shoulders hunched and eyes lowered, unmistakably their subordinate. Jasmine suddenly snapped her fingers while continuing to chat with her friend, and without a moment's hesitation he

49

sprang to his feet and scurried away from the table. I walked on past the window to the end of the street.

I was jealous, insanely jealous. It was more painful to see Jasmine with this man than it had been to watch her dance with the basketball player. The chauffeur – the voice on the phone, I was certain – and not her handsome stud was my true rival. I'd begun to accept that I'd never fuck her and my ambition now was merely to spend time in her intoxicating presence, carrying her lingerie through shopping malls if that was what she demanded. But as long as she had another stooge to drive her car and jump to her commands, her world was closed to me.

I went back to the window for another look at Jasmine, peering from the shadow of a doorway this time in case she glanced out into the street. I watched the chauffeur return bearing two extravagant cocktails which he placed one in front of each woman. They observed him disdainfully, like two spoiled daughters who'd bent their father absolutely to their will, and there was something in the steady gaze of the blonde that sent a shiver through me. Only when he was sure the women were satisfied did he resume his place at the edge of the table. He had no drink for himself and once more sat with his head bowed and shoulders hunched. Jasmine and her friend paid him no further attention. They sipped their bright drinks through long transparent straws, nibbled pieces of fruit and licked their sweet lips.

I walked to the end of the street again and around the block. On the way back I stopped beside the Mercedes and looked down at the back seat, trying to judge where on the leather cushion Jasmine had rested her latex-clad ass. How long had she sat there? I wondered. Five minutes? An hour? I was lost in contemplation and when I turned to face the window again I saw Jasmine and her friend preparing to leave. My rival, as I now thought of him, put on his cap and, standing behind each woman in turn as she climbed to her feet, slid the stool away from her pretty ass.

I crossed to the other side of the street and waited for them to come out. My rival was first to emerge. He trotted to the car and held the kerbside door open while the blonde lowered herself onto the seat. Jasmine walked around to the other side of the car where I had a clear view of her. The red dress was stretched to its limit by her long-legged and curvy loveliness, and the pinched outline of her waist, so narrow and graspable, made my knees go weak. My rival scooted around to open the door for her and she patted him affectionately on the cheek. She settled into her seat and he closed the door, hiding her from view as she raised the hem of her dress to cross her legs. I walked into the road as he drove away, hating him with a violence that made me tremble.

That night changed everything. I knew I would grow old and die waiting for Jasmine to call. With little thought as to where I was going, I drifted towards the pub and stood gloomily among a crowd of friends. After a few sips of beer I slipped away again, carrying myself with the nervous determination of a junky. I went straight back to the cocktail bar hoping against all reason to see Jasmine in the window, then wandered around town searching for the white Mercedes. I plunged through a dizzying succession of streets, drawn on by the hopelessness of my quest and the empty promise of every corner. Eventually, I came out by the river. I was out of breath and my feet were aching. I leant on the embankment rails and gazed down at the moon's reflection scattered across the rippling surface of the black water. A nagging drizzle had begun to fall and I had never felt lower in spirits or more capable of abandoning myself to desperate actions. I contemplated tracking down my rival and killing him. A plan started to take shape but the clatter of a passing truck broke my concentration. I was left quaking at the brutal thoughts I'd entertained. Jasmine was turning me into a monster. I took a deep breath, closed my eyes and made a resolution to forget about her forever. I would force myself to try other women. I needed sex. I'd starved myself for months. The face of Kim suddenly appeared to me. Yes! Kim. Dear Kim. Generous, understanding, gentle Kim.

It was not an easy task persuading Kim to come out on a date. Things had changed between us and she was cooler towards me than before. I had to spend days pestering her before she agreed to join me for dinner at a restaurant. The evening got off to a bad start. She showed up late wearing an unsightly floral skirt, a shapeless duffel jacket and barely any make-up. I knew better than to compare her to Jasmine; even so, whenever I looked at her I felt a twinge of disappointment.

We ate quickly and talked a little about work. Her body language cried out to me and the other customers that we were dining as friends and not as potential lovers. She refused to drink more than half a glass of wine and I finished most of the bottle myself along with my own beers. I felt quite drunk when it was time to pay the bill and I vowed I was going to fuck my pretty little assistant that night one way or another. We left the restaurant and I started walking quickly towards the centre of town.

'Where are you going?' she asked, dawdling yards behind me.

'I fancy a club,' I said, without slowing down.

'I'm not dressed for a club. And anyway, clubs aren't my scene.'

'Just a drink, Kim, and then we'll leave.'

I led her straight to Apollo. There was no queue and we were soon sitting at a table beside the dance floor, a Bud in front of me, a glass of wine in front of Kim. I tapped my foot to the techno beat and watched the handful of girls who were up dancing. Slowly the place began to fill.

'What are we doing here?' she shouted over the music.

'You're not enjoying yourself?'

'Don't you feel embarrassingly out of place?'

'Why should I?'

'Those girls out there dancing are young enough to be your daughters.'

We began to argue. Kim, usually so polite and diplomatic, accused me of being pathologically immature.

'If this is where you and your friends come for a night out, I feel sorry for you.'

'You think I should stay at home with my slippers on, don't you?'

'I'm just wondering what grown men see in girls barely half their age.'

'Why don't you ask Michael Douglas or Rod Stewart that question?'

'It's pathetic.'

'I really don't see the problem.'

'Maybe you're going through a mid-life crisis? That would explain your weird behaviour lately.' She sat back in her chair and turned her head away from me.

Inwardly fuming, I went to fetch more drinks. The night I'd so carefully planned was turning into a disaster. I'd lost my touch and forgotten how to woo a woman. Kim should have been a walkover. She was my assistant for Christ's sake!

I decided to change my approach. When I returned from the bar I confessed that I was restless and discontent with bachelor life. I hinted strongly that it was time I thought about settling down. She mellowed somewhat and showed a little sympathy but there remained a glimmer of suspicion in her eyes. With continual coaxing she finished her second glass of wine and the alcohol came to my aid. She unfolded her arms and relaxed in the chair. The outlines of her pretty breasts were just discernible beneath her sweater. I reminded her of the good times we'd had working together and we both began to reminisce.

She still refused to dance but I managed to steer her to an empty couch in a dark corner of the club. We sat down amid snogging couples, hidden behind a wall of bodies. I put my hand around her shoulder. She was warm and smelt attractively sweet. I felt genuine desire for her. Her skin was fresh, her lips familiar and inviting. I leant across to kiss her.

She responded by pushing my face away and sliding to the corner of the couch where she sat, knees pressed together, thoroughly distraught.

'What the hell are you trying to do?' she moaned.

'I thought you felt the same way I did?' She had made me look a fool and I was having trouble remaining calm.

'You really don't get it, do you?'

'Get what?'

She glared at me for a long moment with eyes I'd never seen before. 'Oh, never mind.' She gave a sigh of exasperation and folded her arms. I was livid and said something that I immediately regretted.

'Don't forget, little Miss Prim Pants, I'm your boss.'

She turned her face towards me. It was red with the wine. Her eyes were moist and her lips were quivering. 'You're sadder than I thought, Matthew Crawley.' She stood up.

'Wait,' I said. 'I'm sorry. I didn't mean it like that.' She shook her head wearily and walked away. I looked at her body. Man, oh man! She really had something, even in that shapeless Oxfam skirt. There was a cute little ass wiggling beneath it all. I watched despairingly as she threaded her way through the crowd. I kicked myself for screwing up my one best chance.

In the office the next day she was the perfect assistant. She made no reference to the night before and neither did I. But we never took lunch together again and on Friday evening she made a point of going to the bar with her own friends. Jasmine reasserted herself in my thoughts. She returned with a vengeance. She taunted me for thinking that having once laid eyes on her I could ever be satisfied with a mouse like Kim.

I held out for three more days, then called her. She answered the phone herself and I fell instantly under her spell. Her voice was a rich, throaty purr and my cock began to stiffen at the first sound of it. I longed for her, for the tiniest morsel of her. She could have talked me to an orgasm without even trying. She had only to breathe her name in my ear and I was ready to erupt.

'Jasmine,' I said cautiously, 'it's me, Matt.'

'You.'

'I couldn't wait any longer.'

'I'd forgotten all about you.'

'I need to see you.'

'Didn't I tell you not to call me?'

'It's been months.'

'Are you trying to make excuses?'

'No, I just thought . . .'

'You disobeyed me. You've blown your very last chance.'

'What?'

'Goodbye, Matt.'

'Don't go.' I pressed the phone tight against my face. 'I'll take you shopping. You can choose whatever you want.'

'Do you have any idea how desperate you sound?'

'I don't care.'

'I could make you do anything, couldn't I?'

There was no need for me to answer.

'If you were here I'd tell you to get down on your hands and knees. I'd make you crawl to me. I'd make you grovel at my feet, just for fun.' Her voice was triumphant and cruel, yet also playful and teasing. She was toying with me, revelling in the power she exerted over me. As she spoke, I pictured myself begging like a dog and gazing up imploringly into her mischievous brown eyes. Yes, I was prepared to do this, to entertain her in any way she demanded. I would pit my desperation against her indifference.

'Give me one more chance,' I pleaded.

'Doggy.'

'Please.'

'Why should I?'

'A chance.'

There was a long pause before she spoke. 'You'll need to be punished for disobeying me.'

'Anything.'

'But I just can't be bothered to think of the punishment.'

'Please, you have to.'

'No, I don't think so.' She sang those words, her voice rising and falling like a teasing skirt caught in a summer breeze.

'Punish me, please.'

'Say that again.'

'Punish me, please.'

'Oh, all right then, if you insist. But you've got to think of the punishment yourself. And it had better be a good one. If I don't like it no amount of grovelling will help you. Call me at the end of the week.'

I was frantic. I lay awake each night dreaming up punishments for myself. Was I supposed to suggest something painful? Something that would risk my reputation and position? Her mind was a mystery to me; she was as capricious as she was beautiful. I racked my brains for the whole week and it was all for her, a young woman who scarcely gave me a second thought but who could deny me everything I hungered for with a single sentence, a few musical words: 'No, I don't think so.'

All day Friday I turned ideas over in my head, rejecting each one. Reduced to an anxious wreck, I left work early and drove home. What could I offer this beautiful tyrant who ruled my mind, body and soul? The congested streets gave me no answers. My adoration, my dedication, my money meant nothing to her. She wanted me to suffer, that was all; and I feared I'd fail to satisfy her even in this capacity. Waiting at a set of traffic lights, I began to tremble. 'Jasmine,' I heard myself saying, 'I deserve the harshest punishment you can inflict. You should refuse to see me ever again.' It sounded extraordinarily clever. It would appeal to her, I was sure. But what if she called my bluff and actually made that my punishment? Surely she would not miss the chance to be so delightfully wicked? For the rest of the journey I tried to get the idea out of my head but it was no good. In some deep, self-preserving part of me, it seemed, I wanted to put an end to my insane relationship with Jasmine. Or was it just that I wanted to suffer, horribly?

I got home and went straight to the phone, feeling a reckless urge to plunge into the abyss that I knew was waiting for me. I picked up the receiver and began to dial, but at the very last moment another idea came to me. Inspiration from the devil. I hung up and sat on the couch. Speaking out loud, I rehearsed my lines carefully – I had to strike just the right tone to make it work. When I felt ready I called her.

'I've thought constantly about the punishment I deserve,' I said solemnly. 'But the truth is you could never punish me.'

'Don't be so sure,' she said rising swiftly to the challenge.

'You could never punish me because anything that was your will would be a pleasure to endure.'

She laughed. She was moderately impressed. 'Very clever, Matt. Maybe I underestimated you. You're not as dumb as you look. You do amuse me ... slightly.'

'Then I can see you?'

She thought for a moment. 'Yes, I'll give you one more chance. But remember that if I did choose to punish you your little life wouldn't be worth living. You know that, don't you?'

'Yes.'

'I'll meet you in the Park Hotel on Monday at two o'clock. If you're late ...'

Late! She had to be joking.

When Monday arrived I called in sick and took the whole day off work. I tried to eat but the smell of toast turned my stomach and all I could do was stare

58

at breakfast TV and count the minutes. Towards midday I drove into town, parked the car and paced up and down the high street, constantly glancing at my watch. By one o'clock I was making my way to the hotel. I sat stiffly on a couch in the lobby, eyes fixed on the entrance. Slightly dizzy with hunger, I began to dream she would take me up to one of the rooms and let me fuck her. Squeezing my cock into that precious cunt of hers was the only thing on my mind. I was prepared to suffer any humiliation to get between her legs.

The Jasmine who came through the sliding glass doors a long time after two o'clock resembled one of those smiling mannequins rich men show off at horse races and garden parties. Her hips swayed sedately beneath a tight Marilyn Monroe skirt, and the broad shoulders of her matching red jacket moved with a stiff elegance. A wide-brimmed hat cast a gentle shadow over her face and self-contented smile. I watched her clip across to the reception desk on brilliant-red stiletto heels, trying to connect this marvel of poise and tailoring to the woman who'd got drunk on whisky, talked like a slut and dry-fucked me in the corner of a cheap wine bar. Key in hand, she came over to me and I stood up expectantly. She ignored my greeting and lowered herself into an armchair.

'You look wonderful,' I said taking my seat again.

'How original,' she replied, smoothly crossing her stockinged legs. I struggled to think of a worthy compliment as I watched her fingers, which were encased in beige kidskin gloves, playing with the key. 'You don't have long so start talking. Tell me why you keep pestering me on the phone.'

She listened to what I had to say with a disarming smirk and began to tap the key stiffly against her thigh. My thoughts drifted to the room upstairs, the waiting bed . . . her tanned ass cheeks slowly parting . . .

'You're transparent,' she interrupted. 'From the moment you first looked at me it was obvious what you wanted. Why not just come out and say it?' Her dark eyes challenged me while her body worked its magic on my cock. She grinned in satisfaction as I pulled the front of my jacket over the growing bulge in my pants. 'Didn't I say you'd never fuck me? Do you think I'll change my mind?'

'No,' I said quickly.

'What a pathetic lie! You think about fucking me all the time. Well, don't you?'

'Yes.' There was little point pretending otherwise. My straining erection was making me squirm in my seat.

'Do you feel uncomfortable discussing sex with me?' she teased, swinging her leg and twirling her foot. It was all a game to her. We sat facing one another – I contending with the pain of my desire for her and she openly entertained by the spectacle. It was as if she wanted everybody passing through the lobby to observe the fundamental relationship between us. The staff behind the reception desk made no secret of their interest.

'Shall I tell you two facts?' She pursed her lips in a mildly lascivious manner. My trapped cock was at her mercy and her words, when they came, carried a smooth, feminine authority.

'Fact one: If you fucked me it would be better than you ever imagined, even in your dirtiest daydreams.' She paused to let me consider that cock-engorging prospect. 'Fact two: You'll just have to take my word for it because you'll never get the chance to find out.' She was gloating as she said this, enjoying the sight of my impotence and frustration, yet I adored her more than ever. I gazed at her worshipfully. I was tantalised by the idea that beneath her elegant society clothes was a fabulous cunt, an animal cunt that could relieve the ache in my restricted cock, a prize cunt that was hers to give or withhold as she saw fit. Slowly she re-crossed her legs, forcing my gaze to travel from her glistening stiletto heel, up her exquisite calf and thigh to where that most superior of cunts was hidden. I was staring at pure temptation. I was ready to sell my soul for the chance to fuck her.

'It's obvious why you sniff after me,' she continued in the same sneering tone. 'The real question is: Why do I bother with a man like you?'

'I don't know,' I said.

'Shall I tell you?'

I nodded.

'I might have a use for you one day.'

'When?'

She laughed at my eagerness. 'I haven't even told you what I *might* want to use you for yet.'

I can only guess how this conversation might have developed because at that moment Jasmine suddenly stopped talking and stood up, her body shivering with excitement. I saw him a moment later and all my hopes for her slightest indulgence (the chance, maybe, to demonstrate my dog-like devotion in one of the rooms) were dashed. He was a hulking blond with a deep tan and jutting jaw. He crossed the lobby in a few powerful strides, seized Jasmine in his thick arms and pressed his mouth firmly against hers. She arched herself against his rigid frame, crotch straining up towards his, and tilted back her head under the pressure of his kiss. He engulfed her in his embrace and she clung to his broad shoulders. His arms crushed her jacket and his hands rested masterfully on her ass.

When he released her lips, Jasmine's face was flushed and her hat sat at a crooked angle. He loosened his embrace but continued to hold her admiringly in his arms. He glanced down at me but asked no questions and his eyes returned to feast on the body he would soon enjoy. They kissed again and after exchanging a few sickening words he let her go. She pressed the key into his meaty paw and after patting her ass he headed over to the elevators.

'Your time's up, Matt,' she said, her eyes following the man she would soon have. Her jacket was crumpled around the shoulders, her hat still askew.

'When can I see you again?' I asked, despairing at the prospect of waiting months for another chance.

She looked down at me and for the first time ever I thought I saw an expression of pity on her face. She glanced over at the reception desk, at the guests who were dotted around the lobby, and lowered her gorgeous ass into the chair. This time she did not cross her legs and kept her heels on the carpet, her knees dangerously wide apart. Then, without a hint of apprehension, she wriggled the tight skirt up her thighs until she had exposed the tops of her stockings. She resumed her lewd, open-kneed pose, willing me to stare. The challenge was more than I could face. The woman I adored was all but flashing me her crotch in a hotel lobby. My cock was foaming and I had to look away. Through the corner of my eyes I watched her raise her ass from the chair and reach a gloved hand between her legs. Nonchalantly, she pulled a pair of red panties from under the skirt, tugged them over the top of her thighs and rolled them down the length of her nylon-clad legs. She leant forwards in the chair and without hurrying guided the delicate garment over each of her high heels. Rising to her feet, she quickly straightened the skirt and then swung the panties in front of my nose.

'Here,' she said flatly, 'I won't need these.'

I reached out to grab them but she lifted them away teasingly.

'Promise not to call.'

'I promise.'

'You won't get another chance.'

My hand was outstretched, my gaze fixed on the tiny red prize that she dangled from her gloved fingertips just beyond my reach. I was aware that we had an audience. The sight of a grown man frozen in his desire for a young woman's panties was simply irresistible and sent a stir through the lobby. But the embarrassment I felt at being the object of such scrutiny did not free me from my craving. On the contrary, as I sank in humiliation Jasmine grew in cruel magnificence and the panties she'd worn – *those panties that had been between her legs* – were the greatest prize on earth. She tossed them onto my lap and walked away.

'Have fun,' she said. 'And don't forget to exhale occasionally.'

I picked them up with clumsy, trembling fingers and felt they were still warm and alive with her flesh. I stuffed them into the front pocket of my jacket and watched her stroll pantyless to the elevator.

You can be sure that I made a great occasion of sniffing Jasmine's pretty panties. I resisted the urge to bury my nose in them immediately I was outside the hotel and away from contemptuous faces. For most of my adult life I've sought the opportunity to savour the intimate aroma of beautiful women's panties, but with a depressing lack of success. (Take my word for it, beautiful women know the value of their used panties and guard them jealously from hungry guys

63

like me.) My gratitude to Jasmine was boundless and I treated her panties as a rare and precious gift.

I returned home and placed them carefully on my pillow. They ignited my bachelor bedroom. The waistband and tapering crotch piece when spread flat offered an impression of Jasmine's hips and cunt that was both vulgar and sublime. I threw off my clothes, releasing a huge, lumbering cock, then lay down on the bed, as if beside a lover. I inched my lips towards the panties, kissed them reverently, and took them fondly in my hand. Then I turned on my back, closed my eyes and slowly lowered them over my face. The cool lace and silk rested lightly across my nose, my cheeks, my lips, my chin. Now my face knew the secret pleasure of Jasmine's ass wrapped in its luxurious lingerie.

I breathed in expectantly, about to realise a dream. But I could detect only the fresh scent of the fabric. I inhaled more deeply but still I failed to discover the womanly odour I craved. I slid the panties over my face, sniffing for Jasmine's essence as if my whole life depended on it. My nose was soon rooting in the tiny crotch piece and I sniffed hungrily at the thin wad of cotton until my lungs ached. Slowly, very slowly, it began to yield the aroma it had absorbed, but it was a mere whisper of her cunt scent. The odour was so impossibly subtle I had to believe Jasmine changed her panties three or four times each day, never allowing one pair to collect the full extent of her sexual musk. It was the meanest trick ever played; she'd given me a starvation ration of her cunt to sniff.

I pushed the cotton gusset up into my nostrils and savoured the tiny bit of her I had. I wanted more. I needed more. The tease of cunt odour left me gasping and desperate and vividly aware of the thing I was being denied. While I snorted and beat my meat, I was tormented by an image of Jasmine in the room at the Park Hotel. She was crouched on a king-size bed, her ass arched high in the air, a supreme and grinning bitch. Eager to take the cock of her golden stud, she held her cunt wide open with her fingers and the sight of that glistening wet candy had the cum shooting from my balls until late into the night.

Six

'What should I make him do next?'
she asked playfully.

I recognised him immediately, though he wore a brown jacket and pants instead of the chauffeur's uniform and his once luxurious beard had been shaved away to a stub of a goatee. He emerged from a crowded aisle and even gave a polite nod as he steered his shopping trolley past mine. I stood blinking for a moment, then swung my trolley around and walked after him. Weeks had gone by since the meeting in the hotel lobby; Jasmine had still not called and her panties had been sniffed clean.

I followed my rival through the supermarket torn by conflicting emotions. He was shopping for Jasmine – it never entered my head he was here for any other reason – and that knowledge was hard to bear. Yet it also gave me an incredible thrill to watch him fill the trolley with her needs and desires. I noted each product he selected, the size, the brand, as if it revealed something essential about the woman I adored. That afternoon at Sainsbury's I learnt, among other things, that Jasmine had a taste for Italian food and French wine, ate Alpen for breakfast and drank freshly squeezed orange juice, had her toilet cleaned with Domestos and wiped her gorgeous ass on reams of yellow Andrex Velvet.

My rival seemed to have grown since the night he'd sat between Jasmine and the blonde. I caught up to him and walked along at his side for a stretch comparing our builds. In my violent daydreams I knocked him about as if he were a stuffed toy; but as I glanced across at his fleshy hands and broad shoulders I knew that a real confrontation would be very different. He slowed to scan the shelves of groceries and I stared hard at his face. I focused on the strange goatee and moustache, wondering what had possessed him to adopt this unflattering style – if indeed it had been his choice at all. It looked like the work of a cruel barber, a punishment or reminder of some crime. The thick mass of hair beneath his nose and around his mouth had been shaped to resemble a blunt, bulldog-like snout. There was no mistaking this. What is more, two heavy jowls were now exposed and these, too, had something disturbingly canine about them. He nodded at me for a second time and walked on towards the checkout tills, still without an inkling who I was or what I had just seen in his face.

I abandoned my trolley and waited near the doors while he paid for the groceries. There's Jasmine's faithful hound, I thought to myself. He'll lie obediently at her feet and jump at her every command. But he'll fight to the death with anyone who tries to take his mistress away from him.

When he came out I followed him to the white Mercedes. The car reminded me of Jasmine in her high boots and teasing black shorts, and waves of jealousy surged through my body as he opened the boot. I sat behind the wheel of my Volkswagen and watched him loading the carrier bags one by one. I turned the ignition key and revved the engine, trying to provoke him. He glanced over his shoulder once but otherwise did not react. He continued to fuss around with the bags, rearranging them several times before he closed the boot; then he pushed the rattling trolley all the way back to the supermarket entrance. I drummed my fingers hard on the dashboard; this big man's mincing ways were beginning to exasperate me.

My fingertips were sore when I finally slid into first and followed the Mercedes from the car park and onto the bypass. We soon left the city behind us and a few miles out he turned off the main road. He led me through tree-lined avenues and down narrow winding lanes, driving carefully as if the exacting Jasmine herself were in the back of the car, demanding the smoothest of rides. There were moments when I thought he was playing a game with me, taking me on a fruitless tour of the city's most desirable suburbs – I'd come to expect only frustration and disappointment in my pursuit of Jasmine's ass. I stayed with him, though, and my patience was eventually rewarded. At the end of a picturesque lane, bordered on either side by trees and sandstone walls, he slowed almost to a halt and then turned smoothly through a pair of heavy wooden gates. They were closing behind him as I drove past but I caught a fleeting glimpse up a driveway to a magnificent white house.

The discovery of the house marked a turning point in my relationship with Jasmine. I drove home that afternoon noting each turn I made, my mind swarming with the possibilities that were suddenly available to me. I wasted no time. Once the sun had set, I put on a dark sweater and jeans, grabbed a flashlight and retraced my route. As a precaution, I parked the car in front of a nearby church and covered the rest of the distance on foot. The road was quiet, not a soul was about.

I located a part of the wall where some narrow gaps between the blocks of sandstone provided footholds. I gazed up at the dark barrier before me. The reality of what I was preparing to do struck me now and I felt afraid of what I was about to become. Until that evening my pursuit of attractive women had been legitimate and discreet. I did what all men do: I looked. So what if I intervened a little, improved my positioning, so to speak? After all it was no crime to turn around and follow a little tease along a busy street or even tail her into a department store or up an escalator. If I had the slightest suspicion I was becoming a nuisance, I would stop or walk away, even from the finest of asses. Intimidation really wasn't my scene. My dream since adolescence was to move through the city invisibly.

To climb over the wall would be to cross the line I'd drawn for my own sense of moral integrity. It would also make me a trespasser or even a stalker in the eyes of the law. Yet how could I resist the temptation, the challenge? From the day I followed my first ass, nervously, at a distance, imagining everybody knew my game, I understood the relationship between desire – true desire – and transgression.

I reached up and gripped the wall with stiff, frightened fingers. They had no strength in them and it was willpower alone that kept me fastened to the rock as I scrambled upwards, missing the foot holds and scraping my knees. Once on top I held a crouching position. Temples throbbing, I looked down into the garden and across at the bright, fairytale house in the distance. I felt giddy as I prepared to jump. I felt I was about to plunge into a lower and unexplored realm of myself.

I landed heavily on a patch of stony ground between clusters of shrubs. The crash was deafening, it seemed to me, and I lay there, cold with fear. I expected spotlights to flare up, dogs to start barking, the moon to shout out in alarm, but the night went on as silently as before. I was an intruder in Jasmine's garden and I was the only person on earth who knew about it.

I got to my feet, brushed myself down and explored nervously, keeping to the dark edges of the garden. I did not dare turn on the flashlight and stumbled over rocks and tree roots. I told myself repeatedly that I did not have to achieve anything on the first visit, that in a little while I could climb back over the wall and drive home. My heart was beating in my throat and it made me sick to think that my desire for a woman could drag me through such an ordeal, make a common criminal out of me.

The front of the house was brightly lit; but as I crept around the garden I discovered that the rear was much darker. The only illumination came from a large French window. The light seeped through closed blinds across a patio and reached as far as a swimming pool, where it reflected off the water. I saw my opportunity, though it took me a long time to gather enough courage to leave the cover of the bushes. On heavy and unwilling legs, I approached the window, freezing for a moment when an owl hooted. I drew level with the pool and wiped away the sweat that was stinging my face, then tiptoed the remaining distance taking short, strained breaths. It was the most terrifying walk of my life.

Let me tell you what I saw when I pressed my face against the glass and peered through a gap between the blinds. I will never forget it. It was my first glimpse into a forbidden world. Gathered in the room

70

was a company of astonishingly beautiful women. I am talking about the kind of angels who sunbathe nude on Caribbean beaches and light up the pages of glossy, perfumed magazines; the kind you see smiling for cameras as they're whisked from airports to hotels to fashion shows; the kind who glow in sequinned evening gowns and drape themselves over the arms of rich and famous men. They had kicked off their shoes and sandals and were curled up on comfortable couches, sipping drinks and nibbling snacks. If I listened hard enough I could just detect the low murmur of their conversation, punctuated by bursts of excited laughter. What words did these fabulous creatures exchange? What ideas managed to entertain them?

Jasmine presided over the occasion and looked more spectacular than any of her guests. She wore a flimsy black negligee and lay on a couch at the far end of the room, a study in sensuality and sloth. Her back was against the armrest and her feet dangled over the corner of the furthest cushion. She was feeding herself tapas and each time she laughed she wiggled her perfectly formed toes. I crouched at the window gazing at the long naked legs she displayed, my breath hot and anxious against the glass. I expected a heavy hand to come crashing down on my shoulder at any moment and put an end to me and my sinful pleasure.

What happened next gave me as much of a jolt. The door to the room opened suddenly and in crept a male creature who was now scarcely recognisable as the man I called my rival. He was naked – a mound of pasty, hairy flesh – except for a tight black leather pouch. This device encased the cock and balls he'd been cursed with, making of them a pitiful appendage beneath his overhanging belly.

Jasmine watched her drudge wheel a silver trolley around the room, collecting empty glasses from the pampered guests and offering them new drinks. The young women were clearly used to such slavish attendance and paid scant attention to him. He went about his work diligently, getting down on hands and knees to gather dishes and platters, and they accepted his service as they did their own beauty and good fortune. Their curvaceous bodies were made for indolence, his aging male muscles for low work and their pleasure.

As the drudge was about to leave the room a cherry fell from the glass of one of the women. Without any prompting he walked over from the door and retrieved it, much to the delight of Jasmine's guests. No sooner was he back at the trolley when another cherry dropped on the carpet, this time to the accompaniment of giggles. Once more, without the slightest hesitation or sign of annoyance, he walked across the room to pick it up. It lay close to the feet of a baby-faced blonde and she watched contentedly as he lowered his heavy frame before her.

The women began a game with him. They plucked the cherries from their cocktails and rolled them across the carpet for him to fetch. They sent him scurrying from one end of the room to the other and had him digging out cherries from among their discarded shoes and sandals. He soon gave up walking, sank in his debasement and chased after the cherries on all fours. If one landed within kicking distance of a woman's foot, he was required to wait while she flicked it away with her toes. This way they made him crawl from one pair of playful feet to another, like some hopeful, panting hound. When they had no more cherries left they used other fruit. They tossed pieces of melon and pineapple up into the air for him to catch in his mouth and made him chew on wedges of lemon. They dipped their fingers into their drinks and flicked the sugary liquid into his face. He knelt obediently before them and they awarded each other points for hitting him in the eyes.

When they finished their game the drudge was a disgrace, his body wet and sticky, his face smeared with fruit pulp. Yet this wretch of a man dared to lift his head and look appealingly towards Jasmine. My heart stopped for him. But the expression on her face, though aloof, was not harsh. She nodded once and, as if a thousand bells had rung, he bounded across the room and crouched before her. She made him wait there while she sipped her drink; then she casually pointed to her feet, which were now crossed at the ankles. At that sign he stretched his head forwards and began timidly to lick her delicately wrinkled soles, careful not to irritate them with his hairy snout. Jasmine reclined prettily, like some gracious goddess, and watched her pet male pay homage to her. But he was soon forgotten as she and her guests resumed their easy chatter. She crossed and re-crossed her legs without regard for him, and he followed her ever-moving feet with his long eager tongue.

This extended display of grovelling devotion and supreme indifference, and the orgy of humiliation which had preceded it, forced me to acknowledge Jasmine for what she was – a diabolical beauty. I should have been outraged by the scene I was witnessing, or at least sickened into sobriety. Yet I desired her more intensely than ever. I would have given my soul to exchange places with the debased creature in rapture at her feet. I will spare you the details of what I did with my cock outside the window but I hesitate to call it wanking. My hand was driven by a primitive energy and the orgasm, released after only a few tugs, ripped through my body like a revelation. I returned to the car feeling light and carefree and floated through the darkness all the way home.

It is surprising how quickly you accommodate yourself to a new moral order and eagerly do those things you once held taboo. I became a regular spectator at Jasmine's soirees and each time I climbed over the high wall I left another piece of my old, guilt-ridden self behind. I still had occasional attacks of conscience and days when I felt terrifyingly alone in my life as an outlaw; but the suffering these lapses caused me was insignificant when compared to the joy that was transgression's reward.

I grew bolder and, after a month of visits, I brought a sleeping bag with me and stayed in Jasmine's garden all night long. At dawn I concealed myself in the thick shrubbery behind the pool and waited patiently. The sun rose into a cloudless sky and in the early afternoon I had my reward when Jasmine and her friends came out to play beside the pool. They wore bright bikinis, skimpy thongs, and some strolled about topless. Their pert tits bounced joyously and their ass cheeks rolled with a more fundamental exuberance.

These were blissful days, marred only, as I have said, by the stubborn residue of a puritan upbringing and the lingering anxiety that I might be caught. I had reached a state of contentment for the first time in my adult life and desired only that things stayed as they were. I had come as close to Jasmine as I believed I ever could, closer than she had ever intended, and it gave me great satisfaction to know that I was stealing pleasure from her. She denied me her cunt but I could gaze at her almost naked body until I had my fill.

I became familiar with Jasmine's guests, especially the ones who visited frequently. I recognised some from Apollo and also the icy blonde who, I learnt, was called Jennifer. The others had names like Kelly, Chastity, Danni, Star and Raquel, and personalities to match. The drudge was always in attendance, his cock all trussed up in the tight pouch. He kept these beauties supplied with drinks and snacks, and when they were out beside the pool he carried around towels and got down on his knees to dry their feet. He found deep fulfilment in his menial work and, when Jasmine let him crawl over to where she was lounging and lick her soles clean, it seemed he longed for nothing more in this world.

The women did not always harass him but if one started a game, the others would soon join in. They toyed with him casually and thought up a hundred different ways to ridicule and humiliate him. They made him suck up crisps and nuts they'd trampled into the carpet beneath their shoes and used their lipsticks to write demeaning names and epithets on his naked flesh. I gasped at the cruelty of these young women, some of whom I had seen on the covers of magazines, fresh-faced and innocent, beaming at a beguiled public. When they sat around the pool I could hear the words they exchanged and their sadistic inventiveness never failed to astound me. They encouraged each other's wickedness and spat the foulest abuse at the impotent male who danced attendance on them. Their eyes sparkled with a cruel passion at such moments and they pressed their thighs together and wriggled excitedly on their sun loungers. They showed their victim no mercy.

A calm settled over the women whenever the drudge served as Jasmine's footstool or was allowed to worship her feet during the course of an evening. The cringing male embodied all that was vile and lamentable in the species, as the lipstick names scrawled over his body made clear. He crouched down low and Jasmine rested her pretty heels upon his broad back in accordance with a brutal law that privileged her absolutely. Her guests breathed contentedly, aware at some level that they, too, were supported by a grovelling ugliness which dared not resist. When I looked into the glazed eyes of the drudge as he bore the gentle yet irresistible pressure of the supreme creature above him, I saw a man who had truly found his place in this life.

I spent my days at the office and as many nights as I could outside the windows of the mansion. Even when Jasmine was not at home I would often lurk in the grounds enjoying the proximity to the house and recalling scenes from other visits. I became familiar with her routine. She would disappear for days, sometimes weeks, and hold a party for her friends when she got back. She always looked different on her return – her hair restyled, her skin glowing with a fresh tan. While she was away I sometimes called the house and had a little fun with the drudge. I no longer hated him now that I could see my beloved Jasmine at will, and even developed a certain admiration for my rival. He was more devoted to Jasmine than I could ever be, willing to suffer every type of humiliation to be in her presence. But it tickled me to hear his butler voice, the polished pronunciation, the clear intonation, when only a few nights before I'd seen him crouched like a dog, lapping champagne from the high-heeled shoe of a giggling teenage girl. I could hardly resist the temptation to call him by some of the names the pretty little brats liked to scribble on his body.

I should mention I purchased a video camera and shot hours of excellent footage of Jasmine and her friends, which I played whenever I had a spare minute or was prevented from driving out to the house. I planned eventually to edit, index and catalogue my tapes, but the material they contained made it impossible to achieve the concentration necessary for such work.

Over time I detected a change in the relationship between Jasmine and her drudge. She would observe him closely as he attended to her guests, though her dark eyes gave no indication of her thoughts. He worked all the harder to impress her and the young women had enormous fun with this beaten and confused creature. Their favourite game was to make him kneel at the side of the pool while they took turns to push him in with their feet. Then, with water dripping from his body, they forced him to crawl on his belly and lick up scraps they threw from their plates. One afternoon he slithered into the path of Jasmine by mistake. Raised on towering white heels she glared down at him as if he were an insect about to make a mess on the bottom of her shoe. He scurried away, terrified, and she stepped over the wet trail he'd left, shaking her head ominously.

I was there to see how it all ended for him. Jasmine had returned from a long absence, and came out to join her guests wearing a high-cut black bikini. She had been ripened by a tropical sun. Her skin, a gorgeous Brazilian bronze, glistened with oil, and as she strolled to the poolside the languorous sway of her hips evoked the rolling contentment of warm oceans. Nature was parading one of its masterpieces before my grateful eyes – a truly beautiful woman in her physical prime. She was divine that afternoon and knew it herself. Had she called my name – any name – I'd have bounded from my hiding place straight to her feet.

She stretched out on a sun lounger, took a drink from the kneeling drudge and watched her friends amuse themselves with him. They soon grew tired of their games, however, and for the rest of the afternoon the drudge was ignored. He crawled around the pool like a neglected dog, eager to provide entertainment for the guests and win favour with Jasmine. He stared hopefully at the food on their plates and sprang to four-legged attention each time a foot moved towards a shoe. When a pretty Australian kicked him in the ass he spun around eagerly. But she was in no mood to play; she merely wanted him to move out of her way.

All the while he cast anxious glances towards Jasmine, who was too busy chatting with Jennifer even to notice him. Not until the sun was beginning to set did her eyes fall on the man she had turned into her dog. The smile dropped from her lips and with a curt nod she gave him permission to approach. He crawled joyously to the foot of her sun lounger and waited on his hands and knees for the next command. She pointed to her feet and he set to work licking them for all he was worth. Resting on her elbows, she looked down at him with a bored expression, presenting her toes to his eager lips and pulling them away again. Jennifer smiled approvingly as Jasmine teased her drudge in this lazy manner. She even leant over and whispered a suggestion and both women sniggered. Finally Jasmine pushed away the drudge's face with her foot and ordered him to stop. He sat on his knees, gazing hungrily at her toes, while the two women decided his future.

Eventually Jennifer stood up and stepped into a pair of thong sandals which had low, spiked heels. Glancing forlornly at his mistress, the drudge shrank before the pale perfection of her friend. Jennifer was indeed a beautiful woman and only my predilection for sultry, exotic types stopped her competing for Jasmine's crown. She bent to kiss Jasmine's cheek and I wondered what bound these two women so closely. They were as different in character as they were in appearance. Jasmine was sensual to the core of her being; her ass swayed by instinct and enslaved by nature. Her colder northern sister was not half so generous; her ass was the device of a calculating mind. Jennifer walked towards the house, arms folded, sandals slapping against the soles of her feet. And the drudge crawled behind her, his frightened gaze focused on the springing silver heels. Jasmine smiled to herself as he went. Her skin glowed magically in the last amber rays of the sun. She yawned contentedly and closed her eyes.

Later that night when I was leaving and still wondering about the scene I'd witnessed by the pool, I noticed a blue light flashing in the treetops at the front of the garden. It was a chilling sight and when I peeped over the wall my worst fears were confirmed. Two police officers were inspecting my car in that sly way they have. (I'd become complacent by this stage and taken to parking a few houses away.) I felt the weight of the video camera hanging by its strap from my shoulder. No longer did it contain images of Jasmine and her girlfriends but hours of incriminating evidence. I did not even need to consider; my hands set to work of their own accord. I ejected the cassette and tore out the tape, yard after yard of it, ripping it with my fingers, chewing it between my teeth. Down at the local police station a team of uniformed men would grin viciously if they were ever allowed to peer through the eyes of Matthew Crawley.

I dug a hole among the shrubs and buried the mangled pieces of tape and the camera. I waited, crouched at the base of the wall. Soon I heard a car drive away and the blue light vanished. But I was still too afraid to leave the garden, worried they'd set a trap for me. I sat on the ground for another hour damning myself for being so careless before I found the courage to climb over the wall. I walked quickly to the car, glancing around in all directions. On the way home I invented a story to explain why I'd been parked in the road for so long. If they were waiting for me I'd tell them I often took a stroll in that neighbourhood after work and on weekends. There were some fine old houses there, you know, and the gardens were just beautiful. Then I'd confess, with a slightly embarrassed smile, that I'd walked further than usual this evening and lost my way. In fact, wasn't that a more likely explanation than the truth?

Nobody was waiting when I got back to the flat. I immediately set about destroying all the tapes I'd made and dumped them in the communal bin. I lay awake the whole night refining my story, but I never did hear from the police. To this day I still don't know what it all meant. Probably nothing. But all the same, I lost my tapes of Jasmine and I'd been frightened away from her house for good.

Work began to demand more of my time. I was behind schedule implementing a series of very complex directives and there was one problem after another with the new software we'd had installed on the computer network. I'd been opposed to its introduction from the very start but my low opinion of the Information Revolution was not widely shared.

80

The managers in the other departments were working late into the evenings and I'd run out of good excuses for leaving the office at five each day. Kim was a real asset to me during this period. She took my place on an IT course and pretty well ran the show. But I needed to be around to scribble my signature and type in my password.

I found myself watching her sometimes and wondering what in the world had led me to make a pass at her. She was undeniably pretty – especially if you caught her at a good angle – but how could she or any woman hold your attention after a weekend of watching Jasmine beside her pool? Frankly, I'd been so wanked out when I got to the office each morning I'd scarcely noticed Kim at all. Remarkably, my aloof attitude had made her warm towards me. She'd fled in tears the night I'd revealed my desperation; but she was attracted, or at least intrigued, by the reserved character I'd since become. Shortly before the incident with the police she'd even invited me to the company bar. I'd gone along reluctantly because I suspected that Jasmine would be holding a party that evening. Kim commented on my restlessness but refrained from asking too many questions. We talked mostly about work and she'd mentioned she was thinking of applying for promotion. I wished her good luck and promised I'd write her the glowing reference she deserved. I could see she wanted to discuss the subject further but I was really itching to leave by this time and made my excuses. The prospect of seeing Jasmine lying around in her underwear was making my cock hard and I felt surprisingly tipsy as I got to my feet. Kim was staring at me oddly and I wondered what she was thinking – but just for a moment. Getting to Jasmine's house was all that had mattered to me.

Over two weeks had passed since I'd watched the drudge being led away by Jennifer. It was late on a Tuesday afternoon and both Kim and I had skipped lunch to work on a project whose completion deadline had already come and gone. My desk was overflowing with correspondence, pages of statistics and reports waiting to be read and signed. I was also putting together a presentation that I was supposed to deliver to some new personnel at the end of the week. I remember looking up from the computer screen, despairing of ever writing a compelling introduction to my talk. I searched the ceiling and walls for inspiration and my eyes came to rest on the door, just as it swung open. Everything after that happened at the very edge of reality, as in the long, slow moments before a high-speed collision. Jasmine came into my office. She smiled at Kim and walked across the floor towards my desk. She was wearing a conservative blue trouser suit with a short jacket, but her feet were naked and displayed in silver, spiked-heeled mules and her toenails were painted metallic red. I felt disorientated. My gaze fastened on her as if she were the only recognisable object in the room. She knew nothing had changed. She knew that I was still hers. She stood commandingly before my desk and spoke to Kim.

'You don't mind if I talk to him for a few moments, do you?'

Kim was silent, rendered speechless like me; but I caught a disturbing glimmer in her eyes before Jasmine's magnificent body obscured my view. Without another word she cleared a space on my desk, sending papers sailing to the floor. She turned her back to me and sat down, crossing one leg over the other and leaving me to stare at her ass, which was crushing the corner of a file.

'It's your lucky day.' She was speaking to me but looking over at Kim. 'I'm going to give you the chance you've been begging for. The chance to make yourself useful to me.' I sensed she was preparing to humiliate me, here in my office, right in front of my assistant.

'Couldn't we talk about this somewhere else?' I suggested cautiously. I was red with embarrassment. She had left the door wide open and anybody passing could see her perched on my desk, her beautiful ass astride weeks of research and analysis.

'Where do you suggest we go?' she teased. 'A wine bar? A nightclub? A hotel lobby? Or would you prefer to talk about it in a lingerie store with my panties hanging from your mouth?'

I prayed Kim would excuse herself. She was usually so intuitive and I was baffled why she hadn't already made her exit and closed the door after her. Instead she sat firmly behind her desk and watched her boss surrender to his imperious female visitor.

Jasmine tossed her long hair over her shoulder, confident that I would not contradict her again or offer any resistance. I merely hoped that she would spare me further embarrassment and quickly arrange the time and place of the next meeting.

'I need you from tomorrow,' she said. Then, changing her tone, she addressed Kim: 'Of course, if that's all right with you?'

'That's really his choice,' Kim said coldly.

Jasmine surely smiled at that reply. She stood up from my desk and, keeping her back to me, straightened her trousers, pulling the smooth fabric tight against her flesh. I was mad with desire for her, even in this humiliating situation, and my eyes feasted on the firm swell of her ass. I searched in vain for her panty line and my cock almost burst through my fly

83

as I realised she was wearing nothing beneath the trousers, except, perhaps, the tiniest thong.

She reached across the desk, took a pen from my shirt pocket and scribbled an address on the first piece of paper she found.

'It's your choice,' she said and stuffed the pen back into my pocket. 'You've got one night to decide and the rest of your life to regret it.'

She walked away, seeming ready to leave the office at last. But she hadn't finished her sport with me yet. One of the sheets of paper she'd knocked from my desk had sailed into the middle of the room and now it caught her attention. She prodded it with her shoe.

'What a mess you've made in here.' She had a wicked grin on her face. 'Are you going to leave all this paper on the floor?'

'No,' I murmured with as much dignity as I could manage. I knew better than to argue. One word of dissent and she'd find a far more humiliating task for me to perform. I hoped she'd be satisfied with watching me pick up the scattered sheets of paper. I couldn't bring myself to look at the expression on Kim's face as I came from behind my desk and got down on my knees in my own office.

'Men are such pigs,' she said to Kim. 'How do you put up with him?' She kicked the stray sheet towards where I was crouched and stood over me as I shuffled the others into a pile. Her naked feet in the silver mules were inches from my face. Her toenails glistened obscenely. I wondered how long it had taken the drudge to paint them for her.

She went and sat in my chair. She swung her legs up onto the desk and stretched them carelessly, kicking more papers and files to the floor. I crawled around picking them up and she leant back and watched me, hands clasped behind her head.

'You're slow,' she complained. 'I'm beginning to have second thoughts.' I looked up at her imploringly, my eyes begged her not to torment me any longer. She sat there proudly, a queen bitch in slutty silver heels.

'Is he always this useless?' she asked Kim.

'That depends.'

'Does he leave you to do the tidying up?'

'Usually.'

'Matt,' she said, 'be a pet. Go over there and tidy her desk.'

'What!' The protest was involuntary, instinctive.

'*Beer* mat,' she repeated calmly, tapping one of her heels on the desk, '*crawl* over to her desk and tidy it for her.'

I did as I was ordered. As slowly and reluctantly as I dared I crawled across my own office carpet to where my assistant, Kim, was comfortably seated. I did not look up. I could not bear to acknowledge myself to her. My gaze fell below her desk where I could see her legs, crossed at the ankles. She was wearing her loose black slacks, which I hated, and a pair of flat loafers which I hated even more. It appalled me to be forced to serve a woman dressed in such sexless clothes. I was sure she put them on just to mock me.

Kim sat in her chair, arms folded and gazing straight ahead, while I fussed around her, my head bowed. I knew Jasmine was observing me and I feared she was considering other ways to humiliate me. Kim remained expressionless as I shuffled papers into neat piles, put pens back into their holders and did the best I could to arrange the hundred and one little objects that covered her desk. She let me do my work without comment, but occasionally she placed her hand on something indicating it was to be left alone.

85

'Send him back over here when you're done with him,' said Jasmine.

'That's enough,' Kim announced in a flat voice a few moments later.

I was about to walk back to Jasmine, but thought better of it and got down on my hands and knees again. I crawled over to her, hoping that now she would leave me in peace. I halted in front of my desk and looked up at the soles of the silver mules. Jasmine's victorious gaze sailed over me towards Kim.

'What should I make him do next?' she asked playfully.

'I don't know,' said Kim.

'Throw something and he'll fetch it for you.'

'I'd rather not.'

'Do you want him to bark for you?'

'No, thank you.'

'Would you like him to lick your feet?'

Never in my life had I felt so abject, so insignificant, as I did then, listening to these two young women talking, quite literally, over my head.

'Maybe you should go now,' said Kim, politely but firmly.

I thanked her with all my wounded heart.

Jasmine directed her gaze down at me. 'You're lucky. She's embarrassed for you and I'm getting bored.' She swung her legs off my desk and stood up. She walked around to where I sat on my knees and I cringed as she reached a hand down towards me. I expected a sharp slap across the face, a stinging reminder of her complete domination of me. Instead she patted my head with surprising tenderness and there was a hint of affection in her proud smile.

'You see?' she said to Kim. 'They're just like dogs.' She continued to pat my head and even stroked my cheek with her long, sexy fingers. The touch of her warm flesh against my face was electric. I felt the sensation shoot down to my balls and along my throbbing cock. I belonged to her. I was her dog, her slave or whatever else she chose to call me. She pressed a fingertip against my lips.

'Kiss,' she said.

I did so, hungrily.

'Stop,' she said.

I stopped at once.

'Now my feet.'

Without hesitation, I lowered my head towards her feet. I suddenly longed to abase myself before this glorious woman, here, in the middle of my own office. The idea was wildly stimulating and the blood in my veins turned to fire. All my desire was focused on those perfect feet, arched seductively on their profane silver altars. But she stepped away before my lips could reach their sparkling prize and I was left staring at the floor. I groaned in disappointment.

'Maybe one day I'll let you. If you're very, very good,' she said. She walked out of my office, pausing in the doorway and allowing me to savour her beauty a few moments longer. I'd seen her many times but still I thought: this woman is too wonderful to be true; she has been unfairly blessed by a cruel god. If she'd snapped her fingers I'd have crawled after her. I'd have followed her on my belly through every office in the building even if my only reward was to be kicked in the face once we got outside.

Seven

*'I make the rules and change the rules
whenever I feel like it.'*

It is a strange experience to visit a woman's house,
not as a guest or prospective buyer or even as a
builder, decorator or tradesman, but as a candidate
drudge. I hardly knew how to behave or what to say
as Jasmine led me from room to room, pointing out
my lowly duties in the casual and condescending
manner of a young woman used to total obedience.

We started in the kitchen. 'This is where you'll
spend most of your time,' she said, stepping about in
her high heels, vaguely curious herself about the
utensils hanging from the walls, the racks of spices,
the array of electronic devices. She stroked a gleaming work surface, feeling the cool marble beneath her
fingertips. 'And don't bother to tell me you can't
cook.' She indicated a row of books on a shelf. 'Just
follow the instructions.'

She set off again, hips swinging impatiently in
designer denim cut-offs and I followed her out into
the hallway. The area, roughly square in shape, was
illuminated by bright sunlight pouring in through two
tall windows set either side of the front door. Against
the far wall, a carpeted staircase swept to the upper

floor. From the hall I was shown the dining room, the lounge and the entertainment rooms. She allowed me a brief glimpse inside each before she pulled the door shut again. It was clear she resented having to spend time with me.

'Keep them spotless,' she said. 'No dust. Not anywhere. Understand?'

'Yes,' I replied, staring at her belly button which was in plain view beneath a tight peach tank top. I quickly dropped my gaze down to the floor. She was wearing tall, white sandals and her nails were painted a pale pink.

'Vacuum every day. But never when I'm around unless I tell you to. OK?'

'Yes.'

She pointed to a door she had not opened.

'The same goes for the bathroom. Spotless at all times. And polish this floor regularly.' She dragged the sole of her shoe over the mahogany tiles leaving a dull smudge behind. She pointed with her toe. 'I mean, I don't want to find this sort of thing.' She walked briskly towards the stairway. 'There are bathrooms up here as well, clean them all every day.'

I was close on her heels as she ascended. It was the treat of a lifetime, I can tell you. I wished the stairs would go on forever and that I could press my face between the rolling globes of flesh above me. I would happily have died in there.

'This carpet needs to be vacuumed like all the others,' she said without turning her head. 'And if you're going to stare at my ass, try to be discreet about it.' When we reached the landing my cock was crying out for relief and there was sweat around my collar.

'Come on,' she said. 'I want to show you my bedroom.'

Keep your art galleries, your cathedrals and your palaces – there is no place on this earth so fascinating, so mysterious, so stocked with treasures as the bedroom of a beautiful woman. Jasmine had made hers a shrine to herself. The curtains were still closed and a crystal chandelier hung from the ceiling, its sparkling light glancing off mirrors mounted on pink walls. The mirrors were as tall as I was and reminded me of patient suitors worn thin with waiting. When Jasmine entered the room, they seemed to spring to life and vie with one another to display her body. There were no pictures on the walls, no ornaments or graven images to compete with the multiple reflections of her form, which she briefly paused to contemplate.

In the weeks and months that followed I would spend many hours polishing these mirrors which, due to her insistence that I divert my gaze whenever she undressed, became windows onto scenes of forbidden loveliness. In fact, it was in her bedroom, not in the kitchen, that I did most of my work each day. The time required to keep this room in its immaculate condition staggers belief. The nooks and crannies where dust accumulates. The places you find hairs, stains and other things. The mess that a beautiful woman leaves behind.

I could describe Jasmine's bedroom in fabulous detail, talk about the theatrical dressing table, the Persian cushions, the candles that burnt in her honour, the vases of unacknowledged flowers – I cleaned every square inch of it by hand. But on that first occasion, my attention was absorbed by her magnificent four-poster bed. The gilt frame was adorned with lace and the bed itself was a soft plane of virginal whiteness. She led me towards this plat-form on which she'd fucked and would fuck again, but which now lay smooth and calm like a snow-covered field. It gave no hint of the scenes it had staged, or even that she'd slept there, except for a solitary lipstick mark on the pillow – a salacious red crescent.

'Change my sheets every day, unless I tell you otherwise,' she said. 'And don't forget about the carpet.'

She walked over to an en suite bathroom and stood in the doorway.

'If I've used the bath, clean it out. I like it to shine. And make sure there are always fresh towels here.' She looked at me hard. 'Don't forget the toilet. Scrub it thoroughly every day. And I mean that. I'm very particular about where I put my ass.'

Next she went across to a pair of sliding doors and pulled them open to reveal a deep walk-in closet that housed her vast collection of outfits.

'Everything in here is your responsibility.' She stepped aside to let me see the extent of my work. 'All my shoes must be ready to wear, so shine them regularly and never let them gather dust.'

I looked at her army of shoes. I'd never dreamt one woman could own so many pairs. They stood proudly on wall-mounted shelves along one side of the closet. On the upper shelves were her dress stilettos, all shining brightly and awaiting the appropriate occasion. Beneath these were the faithful sandals – her preferred footwear – slingbacks with dainty heels, formal sandals, strappy sandals, beach sandals, dancing sandals, a hundred and one variations on the theme of arching, wrapping and displaying the feet. On the lower shelves were 70s-style platforms, fashion clogs, the shoes she'd worn to my office and a pair of oil-black mules with leopard skin straps. At the bottom stood her avant garde creations, footwear made for the catwalk from moulded vinyl and Perspex. And, last of all, standing in a line on the floor, were her boots – ankle high, knee high, thigh high, some with square heels others with dagger heels. There were shoes in boxes, too, gifts waiting to be unpacked.

Jasmine drew my attention to a large wicker basket that stood just inside the door. She told me to open it.

'Do my laundry every day and always check the labels. Most of this is hand wash or dry clean only.' I counted at least three pairs of panties lying on top of the colourful pile – jewels simply discarded and forgotten about. She pushed the lid closed, her upper lip curling slightly. 'You'll have time for that later. Just don't ever let me catch you.'

I followed her back onto the landing, aroused by what she'd so casually implied. Her low estimation of my nature was becoming ever more seductive. She was creating me, breeding something monstrous from a germ deep inside. Out on the landing she gestured to the other rooms.

'My friends use these when they sleep over. You obey them just as you obey me.' She looked at me closely for the first time and I felt naked and dirty before her. 'It's a lot to do and I have my doubts you'll be up to scratch. I'd have a couple of you working here but one little pervert living under my roof is quite enough.'

We went down the stairs and back into the kitchen where she opened a door that I'd assumed led to a pantry. It was, in fact, the laundry room and when she flicked on the light, a bare fluorescent tube, I saw a sink, a washing machine and a drier. The floor was bare stone and there were no windows; the walls were whitewashed plaster. At the back of the room was a narrow bed.

'I almost forgot,' she said, 'this is your place. I call it the boys' room.'

Arranged around the bed were an old chest of drawers, a dining room chair, a Formica table and a battered bookcase. There were still signs of the previous occupant: a brown tweed jacket slung over the back of the chair, a pair of scuffed Oxfords next to the bed, writing paper on the table and, on the rickety shelves, a dozen or so books and a curious leather folder.

'You stay in here when I don't need you.'

I didn't notice the rod at first; or rather, I did not immediately realise what I was looking at. It rested across two steel brackets on the wall above the bed, like an artefact of some kind. Jasmine grinned as she witnessed my belated recognition.

'Go and fetch it,' she ordered.

I did as instructed. I went over, took down the rod from the wall and carried it back to her. It was much heavier than I'd expected. She took it from my hands and flexed it, testing its suppleness, showing her familiarity with the object. She looked ravishing as she reacquainted herself with her dark punishment stick.

'In future you'll be down on your knees when you present this to me.'

I obeyed the silent command of her eyes and sank to my knees. I gazed into her smooth navel and my cock rose towards this yawning orifice, which contracted minutely each time she inhaled. She walked around me lazily, her shoe soles rasping over the rough stone floor. I was aware of the warmth of her bare legs, the scent of her skin, the calm rhythm of her breathing. She stopped in front of me and, with the tip of the rod, delivered a light yet stinging blow to my cheek. I had never felt more vulnerable – or more alive.

93

'This is for when you really piss me off.' She placed the tip of the rod under my chin and raised my face until I was gazing up into her smouldering eyes. 'Or, then again, I might just beat you because I've had a bad day.' She smiled at me in that taunting way she had. I was an object for her, a thing to be whipped and beaten at will.

'Put it back,' she commanded.

I was relieved to do so. I returned the rod to its place on the wall and noticed several dark smudges on the chalky plaster. Some of them were obviously fingerprints and seemed to have been left by frantic hands. I wondered how many men had lifted this black stick from the wall. What thoughts had raced through their heads as they went to be beaten for the crime of their desire? I left the rod suspended above the bed, a slender yet menacing presence. It would be a perpetual reminder of Jasmine's tyranny and, more terrifying still, of the dismal potential that resided within my own self.

I followed Jasmine back into the hall, through the lounge and out into the garden. I felt more comfortable in the daylight and in surroundings that I was familiar with. She walked briskly towards the pool and sat down in one of the cushioned chairs. I remained standing while she talked.

'You take care of the garden and keep the pool clean. And you have to wash the windows too ...' She paused. 'But you don't know the half of it, do you, Matthew Crawley?' She was having serious doubts about my ability to satisfy her. 'There are ways I like things done and ways I like men like you to behave.'

I thought I had a good idea what she meant. Yet watching the drudge perform and even imagining myself in his place was scarcely preparation for the role I would assume. The spectator always keeps his deeper self intact, no matter how closely he identifies with his surrogate; but in becoming the drudge myself, I would undergo a transformation and turn into the object of my own fascination and horror.

'From now on you'll address me as Mistress at all times,' she said.

'Yes, Mistress.' The word rolled off my tongue with a naturalness that startled me.

'Also, unless you're working, you'll get down on your knees when you're in my presence. And you'll crawl like an animal whenever possible.'

'Yes, Mistress.' I dropped to my knees instantly.

'You really are desperate to please me,' she laughed. 'What do you hope to get out of all this?'

I lowered my gaze, afraid to reveal my desire for her.

'Don't hide it. I've told you – men like you are transparent to me. I know exactly what you want. I can see your excited little prick from here.' She crossed her legs tightly, creasing the thin, faded denim around her crotch. The impression of her cunt was unmistakable. 'Here's the deal. You can look all you like. Sometimes I quite enjoy having men like you drooling over me. And when your work's done, you can go to that little room and fiddle with yourself to your heart's content.'

I knew this would happen every day and so did she.

'I'm moody,' she continued. 'I make the rules and change the rules whenever I feel like it. Your job is to obey. Do you have a problem with that?'

'No, Mistress.'

'Some days I want you dressed in a G-string and pouch. On other days the sight of your naked body will disgust me. Sometimes I'll let you hang around me. At other times you'd better stay out of my sight or you'll suffer. You'll have to learn to read my mind if you want to avoid getting punished. And as I told you, I might come home one day and beat you just for the fun of it.'

She let me digest this and went on.

'But there is one thing you can be sure of. One hard fact you can cling to in your confusion.' Her voice became harsh. 'You'll never fuck me. Not ever. I want to hear you say that.'

'I'll never fuck you, Mistress,' I said. I felt I was castrating myself for her. She made me repeat the sentence over and over again, laughing dryly as I shed my manhood at her feet.

She closed her eyes and a contented smile spread across her face. For a while she forgot all about me kneeling on the ground. Everything revolved around her cunt and she had it there, securely between her legs.

'If you're good,' she said eventually, 'and if I'm in the mood, I might let you lick my feet clean. They're very pretty as you can see.' She lifted her shoe until the heel was only a tongue's length from my mouth. 'Would you like that?'

'Yes,' I said breathlessly.

'That should be, "Yes, *Mistress*."' She pursed her red lips and shook her head in pretend annoyance. 'You failed the test so you don't get your treat. You don't even get the chance to beg for it.' She twisted her foot playfully, letting me admire her fabulous white sandal from different angles.

Suddenly she uncrossed her legs and sat up straight in the chair. I moved back afraid. 'You're hanging around like a bad smell,' she shouted towards the house. I looked over my shoulder and was startled to see my old rival approaching on his hands and knees, wearing only his G-string and pouch. He was a pathetic sight and had made a dreadful mistake in deciding to present himself to Jasmine in his drudge's attire. Had she not already spurned him in all of his grovelling nakedness? The limp hairy flesh he displayed was an insult to her and her eyes burnt with a fury I had not seen before. As he reached the pool, she waved me to one side. Sitting on my knees, I watched him crawl to her feet.

'I told you to go,' she said and with revulsion crossed her legs again. He dropped flat on his belly beneath her raised foot, offering himself to her as a sacrifice. He was trembling all over, either with joy or fear, I could not tell. Her lack of reaction gave him courage and gingerly he craned his neck, stretched out his thick tongue and began timidly to lick the black underside of the shoe which dangled above his head. He cleaned it thoroughly and proceeded to plant servile kisses up the length of the heel that jutted threateningly towards him. Then he traced his busy lips over the sides of the sole and kissed the criss-crossing straps that bound her foot. He displayed great skill; his hairy mouth did not once make contact with her flesh.

Jasmine remained indifferent to the wretched creature silently appealing for mercy beneath her feet. She examined her perfect fingernails and absently surveyed her well-tended garden. The drudge's efforts were useless; she did not even glance down at him. I realised she was allowing this little drama to run its course for my benefit.

After five minutes had passed she snapped, 'Cut that out now,' and kicked him square in the face to make sure he understood. There was a dull cracking sound – the pain must have been excruciating – but he did not cry out. He rolled onto his back and lay there, motionless and prone. She made him wait a long while but when she got to her feet she was swift and brutal. She loomed over him and viciously ground her heel (the same one he had licked so hopefully) into his cheek. Still he did not cry out. She stamped on his face several times in quick succession, making him writhe in mute agony. Then she put her hands on her hips and crushed his nose and mouth with her sole, twisting her foot slowly but purposefully and with a contempt that came naturally to her. She reduced him to unprotesting dirt beneath her shoe.

'There, you got what you wanted.' She gave her heel a last vindictive twist and stepped away from him. Hands on hips, she walked forwards and stood with her ass towards both of us. 'Now clear out before I call the police.'

For a few moments I thought she was talking to me as well.

Jasmine's terms were very simple. She dictated them while reclining on a sun lounger. I knelt on the tiles at her feet; the sandals, which I had removed, stood side by side in the space between us. If I wanted to become her drudge, she explained, I'd have to give up my job at the insurance company and move into the room next to the kitchen. I shuddered at the prospect of surrendering so much to this woman. She would not even agree to a contract that would guarantee me certain minimum rights and a small degree of security. She laughed at the idea, calling it quaint and old-fashioned. She would employ me as her skivvy for just as long as it pleased her – that was that. And when she grew tired of me she'd simply throw me out.

'That might happen the day after you move in,' she joked, flexing her toes, enjoying the look of distress on my face. 'You know, I could suddenly change my mind about all of this and kick you out before you've even unpacked.'

I appealed to her. I said if I were allowed to keep my job I'd contribute all of my salary to her household. She listened to me, her face displaying an unnerving mixture of boredom and contempt – an expression beautiful women reserve for men who have nothing to offer them.

'I can make more money in one afternoon than you earn in a whole year,' she said.

I was in no doubt about that. The salary of a middle manager was pocket money in comparison to what she could command for modelling lingerie.

'Your only value to me is the work you do around the house.' Her tone was dry and businesslike. 'The only thing you can give me is your time. To make this arrangement worth my while I want you at my disposal twenty-four hours a day.'

I pleaded some more. I implored her to be generous and at least promise to keep me for a specified length of time.

'How long do you want?' she asked.

'A year, Mistress.' It was the first thing that came into my head.

'That's way too long. How about three months?'

'Six months at least, Mistress.' There I was, a grown man begging on my knees for the right to be a slave for six months.

'No, still too long,' she said after a brief reflection.

'Three months, then, Mistress. I'll accept three months.'

'Too late. I've withdrawn the offer.' She shook her head and smiled gorgeously. It was pointless trying to negotiate with her. She did not have to grant me a single concession.

She sat up and swung her long luscious legs towards me.

'Now that you've finished quibbling, you can make yourself useful and put my shoes back on.' She held out one splendidly arched foot and then the other and I carefully slipped on each of the sandals. As I fastened the tiny silver buckles around her ankles, she reminded me that there was an abundant supply of desperate men.

'It's a buyer's market. Your value is so low you almost don't have one. There's nothing you can offer me that I can't get for free.'

I felt ... I knew that I could stand up and walk away. I still had my job. It would take time but eventually I'd be able to look Kim in the eye again. Worse sins than mine are forgiven, if never quite forgotten. My reputation was tainted and the jokes would continue for a long time to come. But I could deal with that – life is messy. I was kneeling close to the spot where only a short while before a shell of a man had grovelled on his belly only to be viciously trampled on by the very shoes I was fastening to her feet. I feared that my own fate would be as awful as my predecessor's and that in a year, a month, or perhaps only a week's time I'd be dismissed in a similar manner. Maybe these same shoes would bring my own useless grovelling to a short and painful end? For a fleeting moment my office seemed a warm and welcoming haven and the plain, asexual Kim beckoned to me as the ideal female partner. But the sugary vision vanished quickly. I was deluding myself, distorting the reality and forgetting my nature. Even if I could drag myself away from Jasmine, the debilitating craving for beautiful women would come along with me.

When her sandals were securely fastened Jasmine stood up. She towered over me like an immense statue and I saw in her face and glorious figure the embodiment of all my desires. She had spoilt me, given me a taste of a pleasure I could ill afford. How could I ever find satisfaction in magazines and videos again? She was my destiny and she knew it; I could feel my cock growing stiff in my pants, struggling to climb towards her.

I wanted to fuck her, that was all. But she denied me her cunt even as she swung her tempting ass right in my face. Other guys fucked this exquisite bitch and she moaned for them. There on my knees on the hard ground, I wondered how Jasmine cried out when she got a good, stern fucking. Did she groan, whimper and squeal, reward her studs with musical panting? My nose was inches from her denim-wrapped cunt and I contemplated its plump triangular outline.

'You seem to like it down there on your knees,' she joked. 'Most guys do. It's obviously where you all belong.' She turned around slowly, brushing my face with one of her powerful hips, and presented me with a view of her buttocks. The shorts were cut high at the back and her tanned cheeks protruded rudely beneath the frayed and uneven hem.

'Do you like it?'

I nodded dumbly, too engrossed in the feast of soft ass-flesh to utter an intelligible word.

'I thought so.' She reached a hand behind her and gently patted the taut denim. 'An Arab Sheikh once offered me a million dollars if I'd let him kiss this cheek and two million if I'd sit on his ugly face. But you don't have that kind of money, do you?'

'No, Mistress.'

'That's a shame because you know what I call an "ass man" without money?'

'No, Mistress.'

'An "ass man" without money is just an asshole.'

'Yes, Mistress.'

'You're nothing but an asshole, Matthew Crawley.'

'Yes, Mistress.'

'Well, asshole, get out of here. You've got a day to tie up your miserable little life.'

I left the house in a hurry, wishing I'd been allowed to plant a worshipful kiss on that heavenly posterior.

I handed in my resignation the same afternoon and the next morning dropped by the office to collect a few personal items from my desk.

'You're a fool,' said Kim. 'Look at what you're doing to yourself.'

'It's really none of your business.'

'There must be something wrong with you.'

I glanced across at her. I saw a timid young woman in her dour working clothes. She'd make some gentle soul a perfect wife one day and together they'd raise a brood of well-adjusted kids. I felt a sharp contempt for her and the poisonous domestic life that she had to offer. If I was a failure by her standards, then so be it. The status of dutiful husband and proud father had eluded me, I understood now, because deep down it held no appeal. I'd pursued it half-heartedly, just as I'd once pursued Kim, kidded myself along when all I'd ever truly desired could be summed up in two magical words: Jasmine's ass.

I should have ignored Kim, our outlooks were as different as those of two warring nations, but I felt compelled to say my piece. I was a bag of swirling emotions and I knew this was the last chance I'd have for a long time to speak my mind freely.

'You have to follow your passion in this life,' I said. 'Only fools believe you get a second chance.'

'You're giving up everything to run off with a woman who enjoys humiliating you.' (Ha! she hadn't guessed the half of it.) 'Is that your passion?'

'What if it is?'

'It won't last,' she said. 'Then where will you be?'

She'd touched a raw nerve but I tried hard not to let her see it.

'Who knows?' I said with a casual shrug of the shoulders. 'There are no certainties any more. Half the staff in this building don't know if they'll still be working here in a year's time. Is *your* future so secure, Kim? Do you really think you stand a chance of winning that promotion?' I was trying to unsettle her but I did not succeed. She simply gave me one of her long-suffering, infinitely patient looks.

'Now you're no longer my boss I suppose I can tell you what I've always thought of you?'

'Go ahead. Be my guest.'

'You're an asshole, Matthew Crawley, an asshole.'

I had to hold onto my desk for support. The words could have flown from the mouth of Jasmine herself and I was thrown into a state of erotic confusion. Kim had badly insulted me yet I felt powerless to retaliate or even defend myself. On the contrary, I found myself intensely aroused. She had revealed a vicious streak in her nature – one I would never have suspected – and she was transformed before my eyes into something magnificent.

'You're an asshole, Matthew Crawley, and you made a lousy job of tidying my desk.'

She laughed out loud as I hurried from the office trying to hide my stiffening cock behind my briefcase.

By the time I got back to the flat I had regained my composure somewhat. Kim indeed! I set about packing everything I needed into a single suitcase, just as Jasmine had instructed. Then I sat down and wrote letters to my family and a few of my closer friends. I told them simply that I was going away for a spell and would be out of contact. People always seem to suspect the worst so I included a final paragraph reassuring everybody that I was in excellent health and had no financial or other worries. I asked them not to initiate any inquiries.

In the event I found it to be a surprisingly easy matter to disappear, leave one life and slip quietly into another. Nobody came looking for me – as far as I know – and I didn't see my face on any missing persons' posters.

When everything was taken care of, I drove the Volkswagen to a local dealer and offered it for sale. The owner checked it over like the great showman he was, rubbing his chin, sucking his teeth, and shaking his head solemnly. He sensed my urgency and at the end of his routine offered me barely half of what my car was worth, flicking through a wad of crisp notes as an incentive. After a moment's hesitation, I took the money and followed him to his office to complete the paperwork.

Evening was falling as I left the forecourt and I suddenly felt sick to the pit of my stomach. In a single day I'd resigned from my job and given away everything I possessed – my flat, my furniture, most of my clothes and now my car. These were the actions of a madman. Yet there were no laws against what I'd done. There were no policemen waiting to arrest me. And that was the most terrifying thing about it all. I was completely at liberty to continue my crazy adventure.

I needed a drink and wandered into the first pub I came to. It was busy and bright inside and I stood self-consciously among a crowd of rowdy office workers. The joy they expressed at being allowed to have a few pints before returning home was boundless. Some of them were planning to stay out all night.

'To hell with tomorrow,' one of them said. And they made this their toast and persuaded me to join in.

'To hell with tomorrow,' we shouted in unison and tapped our glasses together, slopping beer over our shirtsleeves. Then they fell into a discussion about the merits of the various clubs in town, the type of talent on offer at each one, the prospects of getting laid.

I used the phone at the bar and a few minutes later I was in the back of a taxi heading out to Jasmine's mansion. The driver was familiar with the address and eyed me through his mirror suspiciously. I was sure he knew what lay in store for me and my sense of foreboding increased throughout the journey. I was creeping into my late thirties, most of my friends had careers and families, and I had given up everything to be the slave of a cruel and beautiful young woman.

Eight

*'How about I make you go upstairs and clean
every inch of my toilet with your tongue?'*

My role as drudge was to be utterly subservient to
Jasmine's body. The very body that was denied to me
became the whole purpose of my existence. I dwelt in
the mansion it had paid for, ate the food it put on the
table and I lived only to perpetuate its dominance.
When Jasmine ventured out for the evening, dressed
in one of the stylish outfits I'd carried from her closet
and wearing the shoes I'd just shined, I felt in some
small way a part of her enslaving beauty.

Each day was different at Jasmine's house. I had no
schedule or routine to follow and, therefore, no sense
of independence. I simply responded to commands
like some dull unthinking brute. When Jasmine
called, I dropped whatever I was doing and presented
myself to her – on my knees, of course. She was
seldom satisfied. I could never get from one side of
the house to the other quickly enough for her.

'Don't make me wait,' she'd say, 'if you want to
keep your job.'

The birds were still yawning in the trees when I
began my day's work. I crept about in the twilight
cleaning, dusting and polishing, chores I'd have no
time for later in the day. I'd also try to make a start

on the ironing. (I never did get the hang of it and Jasmine slapped my face more than once for failing to press her clothes correctly.) If Jasmine was home, she would call me to her room around mid-morning and have me run her bath. I'd sprout an erection immediately on entering this warm, woman-smelling environment and I was thankful that she preferred me to be fully dressed at such times. I had precise instructions on how to run her bath and, if the water was not at the temperature she liked or I failed to mix in the right combination of oils and scents, I was certain to be punished. Bath ready, Jasmine would rise from her bed and shed whatever night attire she had on. (Unlike Marilyn Monroe, she wore silk to bed, not Chanel.) The curtains would be open by now, the room golden and bright, and she'd stand before one of the many mirrors and view her naked body. During these intimate moments, I'd be down on all fours, nose touching the carpet.

'I'll know if you're peeping,' she sometimes teased. 'That willy of yours will give you away.'

But I took the risk all the same. I'd sneak a look at her reflection in one of the mirrors and even raise my head slightly when she walked towards the bathroom. I caught many a glimpse of her splendid legs and ass stepping across that steamy threshold.

While she lay in the bath, I'd change the sheets on the bed and place her night attire in the laundry basket, along with any clothes she'd discarded the night before. I'd put away her shoes, straighten cushions and tidy her dressing table. She'd often interrupt my work.

'Bring me a glass of orange juice,' she might say, or 'Go fetch me the phone.'

Some mornings she'd stay in the bath for only ten minutes, on others she'd relax in the deep scented water an hour or more, chatting on the phone to friends and admirers. When she returned to the bedroom, wrapped in one of her fleecy bathrobes, I immediately set about rinsing out the tub and mopping the floor.

'Shoes,' she would often say while I was still working away – the oil she used to keep her skin in its perfect condition clung to the porcelain and was a bugger to remove. This meant I had to stop whatever I was doing and crawl across the bedroom to the closet.

'The white ones,' she'd say, as if I could read her mind.

From the dozens of white mules, stilettos, sandals and clogs she owned, I'd try to select a pair that I thought matched the outfit she had chosen to wear. Holding the shoes in one hand, I'd crawl as best I could over to where she sat on the edge of the bed.

'Not those,' she'd snap. 'How can I wear those shoes with this outfit? Get me the other ones.' She'd quote the name of a designer, cross her legs in vexation and swing her foot.

'Can't you move more quickly?' she complained once, as I struggled across the floor carrying a pair of bulky platform sandals.

'I'm doing my best,' I blurted out in sheer frustration. 'It's hard to crawl on one hand.'

'Well, from now on you can carry my shoes in your mouth.' She'd been in a foul mood since rising. 'That ought to shut you up too.'

From that day forth I brought her shoes to her swinging from my teeth by their straps. Those without straps I carried by the heels, one shoe jutting from each side of my mouth like a pair of bizarre fangs. The first time she saw me like this she fell back on the bed laughing and joked about sending me to the newsagent's to fetch a morning paper.

'You'd look so funny,' she said, 'carrying it in your mouth like a dog.'

When she was in a playful mood she'd put on the shoes and ask me how I liked them. She'd tell me to crawl up to the bed and take a close look at them. As a treat, she might say, 'There's dust on this one. Be a good boy and lick it off.'

On other days I'd be beaten because she found a trace of dust on her shoes.

Once she was dressed she'd go downstairs for breakfast. I'd serve her freshly squeezed fruit juice, brewed coffee, croissants, yoghurt and muesli. She'd flick through a magazine or read letters while she ate and, hungry or not, I'd stand silently in the corner until she told me to clear the table.

After breakfast anything could happen. She might receive visitors, and in that case I'd be at the beck and call of indolent young women who'd always contrive to have me punished. Or she might tell me to change into my chauffeur's uniform and drive her to an appointment in town. She'd leave me waiting in airless underground car parks or parked outside restaurants in the midday sun while she smiled over iced cocktails and signed lucrative contracts. As I sat in the driver's seat fanning myself, I'd start to fret about the housework that awaited me. I knew I'd suffer at some point for my negligence. Maybe I had still to take her favourite dress to the cleaners or scrub out her bath. God help me if she discovered her line-dry underwear had been left in the washing machine all day.

When I chauffeured her in the evening it was even more of a trial. I'd wait for hours in front of glittering bars, counting the minutes until I could return to the house and get on with my chores. While Jasmine and her friends were in their beds and being serviced by obliging studs, I'd be downstairs, ironing, dusting and polishing floors. There'd be no sleep for me on such nights, barely time to snatch a wank to the contented feminine moans that descended from the bedrooms.

But that was not the worst of it. Some of these slatternly beauties drank far more fizzy wine than was good for them and even fooled around with trendy drugs. (What can you expect? They were barely out of school uniform and their purses were overflowing with cash and credit cards.) It was not unusual for me to be summoned to one of the bedrooms to change soiled bedclothes or clean up vomit – but I won't go on about all that. You wouldn't believe they were capable of such things anyway, especially when you saw them the next day, freshly made-up, dressed in all their finery and smiling like angels.

To save time I cut corners and took chances. But this was a risky strategy as Jasmine usually found out if my work was not up to scratch or I'd failed to follow her instructions to the letter. I'll relate a trivial offence and its terrible consequences to give you an indication of the dog's life I led.

I had worked frantically since dawn, but it was already late afternoon when I got around to cleaning Jasmine's bathroom. I was in a state because I needed to prepare for a party she'd told me about at the very last minute. I started on the bath and before long the sound of running water had given me an urgent need to piss. To save myself the trouble of trotting downstairs to my pot, I decided to risk using Jasmine's toilet – something that she'd expressly forbidden. It was the most nerve-racking piss I have ever taken. My urine flowed in a cautious, narrow stream and I looked anxiously over my shoulder, truly expecting an enraged Jasmine to appear in the doorway, even though I knew she'd be away until evening. As I squeezed out the last drops I felt suddenly exhilarated. I shook my cock dry and surveyed the frothy yellow water. I grew proudly erect looking down at this scene of defilement. I had secretly violated my glorious Mistress – it gave me a tremendous sense of power – and I resolved to piss and even shit in her toilet on a regular basis. To christen what I expected to become a fine tradition, I jerked off into that hallowed place there and then. It was a short and intense experience and my knees almost buckled. I flushed the bowl twice and inspected the porcelain closely for any trace of piss or cum.

Later that evening, when I was in the lounge serving drinks to a crowd of lively young women, Jasmine asked cheerfully, 'Matt, did you piss in my beautiful toilet today?' My body froze and all the guests fell silent.

'No, Mistress,' I managed to say.

'Don't lie to me, creep. I *know* you pissed in my toilet.' The anger in her voice made me jump, as if she'd raised a whip to me. All the young women screwed up their pretty faces and one said, 'Yuck!'

'I should sack you right now,' she continued, fixing me with a level stare. I put down the tray I was holding and fell to my knees.

'How do I know you pissed in my toilet?' she asked. I shook my head blankly.

'Because like all dirty slobs you left the seat up.'

The girls burst into giggles. It never even occurred to me to make the obvious excuse that I'd forgotten to lower the seat after cleaning the toilet bowl rim. Instead, I begged for her forgiveness. I stretched out on my belly, utterly prone before her, and made my appeal. I watched her tap her platform mule on the carpet.

'How many chances does it take?' she asked.

I begged for just one more and told her I'd do anything she commanded.

'You do that already,' she said dismissively. 'What do you think, girls? Does this one get another chance?' None of them said a word in my favour. Some even seemed to find my distress amusing.

Jasmine laughed. 'That settles it then. Get out of my house.'

I was dizzy. I could not believe the words I was hearing. I implored her to give me one last chance.

'Didn't you hear me? Disappear.' Her toes flexed; if my face had been any closer to her shoe she'd have kicked it.

One of the guests, a vivacious tease with purple lips and a pierced tongue, made a suggestion: 'Why don't you have some fun with him first, Jaz? Punish him for us.' The others nodded and begged Jasmine to put on a show for them.

'What do you think, creep?' she asked indifferently. 'Shall I punish you instead of throwing you out?'

'Please, Mistress.'

'You really are pathetic.'

'Yes, Mistress.'

She tapped the front of her foot lightly on the carpet while she considered, then she spoke: 'How about I make you go upstairs and clean every inch of my toilet with your tongue? Would you do it?'

'Yes, Mistress.'

'But that wouldn't be a punishment for a freak like you, would it? If I told you I used it just ten minutes ago, you probably couldn't wait to get started, could you?'

I lay silently at her feet listening to the giggles. She knew the kind of creature I had become.

'I've got a better way to find out how desperate you

are to keep your job. Go and fill a pitcher with water and bring it here.'

I crawled off to the kitchen and returned carrying a large pitcher full to the brim with water.

'Now drink it, all of it.'

Without hesitation I gulped it all down.

'Now you stay here and wait on us. If you have to piss before we go out, you lose your job – it's that simple. Maybe this will teach you some self-control.'

I continued to wait on the women and before very long became aware of the growing pressure in my bladder. They, meanwhile, showed no sign of going anywhere and were still making up their minds about which nightclub to try. They chatted about new lines of cosmetics, the latest perfumes and tried on pieces of each other's jewellery. Some of them had yet to decide what to wear and discussed skirts and stockings, shoes and panties without reaching any conclusions. I fantasised about pissing. I could think of nothing else. The drink I poured into their glasses reminded me of streaming piss, and so did the silver and gold necklaces that were passed from one set of careful fingers to another. I willed the women to leave but they sat tight, pretending to be ignorant of my plight and looking right past my trembling thighs which I squeezed together for a little relief.

The pressure in my bladder soon became unbearable and I slumped against a wall with the effort to hold it all in. But they would not let me have it so easy and ordered me to stagger across the room to bring them appetisers and refill glasses. Their grins were especially wicked that evening, their make-up fierce. They left the room often, making it plain they were going to piss, even saying so out loud. They were going to spread their lucky cunts over the toilet bowl and let out long streams of lovely piss.

113

Jasmine watched me without much interest. She already owned my cock sexually. She sent blood rushing to its head whenever she was near and demanded the contents of my balls several times each day. Now she'd decided to take control of its other function. It was as if she were squeezing my bladder with her pretty hand, sending waves of sharp, paralysing pain through my groin. I fell down onto the floor ready to burst or rupture something.

'Will you use my toilet again?' she asked my grovelling form.

I shook my head, my whole body. She was torturing my insides. She let me lie there a long time, groaning and convulsing at her motionless feet. Then she slowly stood up and walked towards the other end of the room.

'Follow me,' she ordered.

I staggered after her on all fours, biting my bottom lip, delirious with the need to piss.

She slid open the French windows and pointed into the darkness.

'If you still want your job, crawl across to those bushes and piss like the dog you are.'

The girls crowded out onto the patio and Jasmine flicked on the garden lights.

I proceeded slowly and shakily over the grass, barely aware of the names they shouted after me. I collapsed twice before I reached the bushes. Once there I pulled aside the pouch, cocked my leg and released a fountain of steaming piss to the accompaniment of derisive laughter.

Then Jasmine called for the cane and beat her shameless hound.

Jasmine was fussy about the products she used and had her favourite brand of everything from tampons to toothpaste. I'd been her drudge for barely a week when I had my first hard lesson in how to shop for such a discerning woman. She called me from the top of the stairs shortly after I'd returned from Sainsbury's and I knew immediately she was not happy. Taking quick, angry steps and not speaking, she walked along the landing towards her bedroom. I crawled close behind her boot heels wondering what I'd done wrong. Had I left one of her hairs in the bath, a damp towel lying on the floor? My eyes travelled up and down her knee-high platform boots looking for dust, a spot where the leather did not shine.

She led me through her bedroom and straight into the bathroom. There I knelt in the middle of the floor, while she walked over to the toilet roll holder I'd just refilled. She flicked the new roll with her finger and watched it spin; a look of disgust spread across her face.

'Do you actually expect me to wipe myself on this?'

I really did not know what she meant.

'Didn't I tell you what brand to buy?'

She probably had, among a thousand and one other instructions. I apologised for my stupidity. 'Forgive me, Mistress.'

'You can't do anything right, can you?' She took a step towards me and raised her hand to slap my face. I braced myself for the blow but she slowly brought her hand down again. She went back to the toilet, closed the lid, and straddled it. She didn't care that her legs were wide open, that I was staring into the smooth crotch of her fashion jodhpurs.

'Crawl here,' she said pointing to a spot on the floor. I scurried forwards and knelt in the exact place she indicated, right between her knees.

'Now open your mouth . . . wide.'

Once more I obeyed without hesitation. I tilted back my head and offered her my gaping mouth. She ripped off a few sheets of toilet paper from the roll and forced them inside.

'Eat,' she said.

The tissue was highly absorbent and stuck to my teeth and palate as I tried to chew.

'Quicker,' she said, stuffing more tissue into my mouth. I worked my jaws frantically and forced myself to swallow. She pulled off six, eight, ten sheets at once and pushed them all into my struggling mouth.

'Your mouth's the only thing this paper is good for. I never want to see it again. Now swallow.'

I chomped on yards of the paper that wasn't good enough to wipe her pretty ass. It swelled, clogged in my throat and made me choke.

'You make a useless toilet,' she sneered, 'always getting blocked. Here, eat some more.' She fed me half the roll and made me eat the bile-soaked pieces that I coughed up on the floor.

After that she sent me back to Sainsbury's in search of the velvety paper her fine ass demanded.

I needed to pay meticulous attention to my work; Jasmine, on the other hand, was a total slut around the house. I firmly believe that most beautiful women are, as they can always find a fool to fetch and carry for them. Did I tell you how she kicked off her shoes when she came through the front door, especially if her feet were hot and tired? Or how she threw down her handbag or whatever else she was carrying right there in the hall? She left coats, jackets, scarves and even lingerie lying about for me to pick up. Each morning she'd litter the floor around her feet with torn envelopes and unwanted correspondence and then blame me because the room looked a mess. She never put away her magazines or threw an empty sweet wrapper into the bin. I never saw her so much as straighten a cushion.

When she was out by the pool or relaxing in the lounge she was in the habit of removing her jewellery; and although some of the pieces she owned – all gifts from admirers – were very valuable, she was careless and forgetful about where she left them. It was my job to see they all found their way back into the case on her dressing table. There would be serious trouble if she couldn't find a favourite pair of earrings or an anklet to match the shoes she was wearing. Dressed for a date or in some disgracefully sexy nightclub outfit, she'd root through her jewellery case and yell at me in frustration.

'Where is it?'

'I'll go and find it, Mistress.' (I soon learnt to be a pretty good mind reader at such critical moments.)

'Be quick,' she'd say, her anger rising.

I'd make a careful search of the bedroom and the bathroom and if I couldn't find the missing item in either of these places I'd run downstairs and search the dining room, the lounge, every room in the house except the kitchen. Then I'd go outside and check around the pool. I'd be sweating and out of breath when I finally found what I was looking for. Her bits and pieces slipped into the most unlikely places and, in my more desperate moments, I was sure they hid themselves deliberately because they liked to see me punished. I found them tucked between cushions, trapped between the pages of magazines and buried deep inside the laundry basket. And when Jasmine put on the piece of jewellery I'd finally recovered, it would sparkle slyly at me from the part of her body it was allowed to adorn.

I never received a word of thanks from Jasmine and was lucky not to get a slap when I presented her with the piece of jewellery she wanted.

'You've made me late,' she'd usually say, snatching it from my hand. 'Now go and get the car.'

Jasmine's needs and desires dictated my life and it never ceased to amaze me how much work a single woman could generate. Take her clothes, for instance, and her undergarments in particular – the patient care they required! You know already how much I'd dreamt of having access to a beautiful woman's used panties and for me that laundry basket was a treasure chest. But the truth is I was so busy I usually had time for only the briefest of sniffs as I sorted her laundry for a wash. I never managed to count all the panties she owned and I'm still not sure how often she changed them each day, but they came to me in an unending procession. No sooner had I washed, dried and ironed them, folded them carefully and placed them in the appropriate drawer than they were back in the laundry basket or discarded on the bedroom floor. Sometimes I felt submerged beneath her panties and bras and stockings. Her lingerie was the first thing I saw from my bed in the morning, a bright pile in a basket waiting to be sorted and folded, and the last thing I saw at night, sloshing noisily inside the washing machine on the gentlest cycle.

I don't think Jasmine had washed anything in her life. She'd perhaps taken a dress to the cleaners once or twice but that was my job now. She took her clean panties for granted, as a type of God-given right. She wore them with total disregard and cast them aside when she wanted a change. That fine ass of hers certainly was fussy. It accepted nothing but the freshest silk and cotton. She had her favourite pairs, too – and so it seemed did her studs. Of the countless pairs she owned there were a certain few she found particularly comfortable or sexy and it was imperative they were always clean and ready to wear, even if it meant washing them by hand late at night. Once I even had to fish a pair from under her bed, wash them in the bathroom sink and dry them with a hairdryer, while she watched me from her dressing table with silent loathing.

My name around the house varied according to Jasmine's mood. For the most part she addressed me as 'you'; but she had many insulting nicknames for me, which she would use without provocation and even in public. She took special delight in making fun of my Christian name, as she had that night at Apollo. When her friends were around she'd be sure to ask: 'Did you clean my bath, Matt?' Or, if the bell rang, she'd snap her fingers and say: 'Door, Matt.' These cruel puns on my given name stung me more than all the other insults as they expressed her innate contempt, not only for the man who now served her, but also the blameless child he'd once been. Yet it would have been fatal to protest. The slightest show of dissent would have earned me a swift punishment. I learnt that lesson after only a few days.

'Door, Matt,' she'd shouted at the sound of the bell, but I failed to crawl to the front door with the required enthusiasm.

'You really don't like being called "doormat", do you?'

I was stubbornly silent.

'But that's what you are to me, nothing but a doormat. Something to wipe my feet on.'

I searched her beautiful face for a trace of pity but found none. Her eyes were burning with a terrible passion, her lips were even redder than usual.

'What's your name?' she asked.

'Doormat, Mistress.' It was as if she drew the word from my mouth.

'Yes, that's exactly what you are. Doormat is what your mother should have called you.'

For the remainder of the evening she made me lie on my belly outside the front door. As each guest arrived she was invited to wipe her pretty shoes clean on my naked back. It didn't take much to encourage even the shyest among them to try me out. Such vicious behaviour came naturally to these rare and spectacular young women. I listened to them giggling as they dug their sharp heels into my spine, bruised me with their heavy platform soles and smeared dirt and grit all over my helpless body.

'How do you like my new doormat?' a proud Jasmine asked each of them. She tapped the back of my head with her foot as a sign of ownership. 'It talks, too. Hey, you down there, what's your name?'

'Doormat,' I said, spitting gravel from my mouth.

'What was that? I couldn't hear you. Speak up.' She kicked me in the side of the face.

'Doormat, Mistress.' There were tears forming in my eyes.

However, the most degrading name I had was invented not by Jasmine but her dearest friend, Jennifer. From the very start this cold beauty referred to me as 'Creepy Crawley' and nothing else. 'Creepy Crawley' was my nickname all through school and those two words, whenever they were spoken, took me back to the schoolyard and to deafening playtime chants, inducing a sense of fear and defeat that I felt deep inside my balls. Jasmine's friends loved to use the name and they pronounced it with a shrill girlish revulsion. 'Creepy Crawley! Creepy Crawley! Creepy Crawley!' they'd scream and lift their feet out of the way as I crawled around the room. 'Creepy Crawley' was merely one among the many games they played with me, but it responded to something deep in their nature and, I'm loath to admit, in mine as well.

I lived in hope that Jasmine would one day call me 'slave', as she sometimes did when she spoke about me to her friends. 'I've got a new slave,' she said over the phone, a few days after I was installed in her house. 'No, Carmen, not that one. He didn't have it in him.' She pronounced the word 'slave' complacently and with a sense of her own superiority that I found irresistible. She seemed to align herself with queens and empresses stretching back through history and I could easily imagine her sitting on a throne in place of Cleopatra, half of Africa kneeling at her feet. I was elated whenever she acknowledged me as her slave, the natural counterpart to Mistress. It placed me in a relationship – however unequal – with something illustrious and everlasting. From her lips that word felt like a caress and I prayed she would call me 'slave' whenever her dark eyes gazed down at me.

I never enjoyed the degree of intimacy with Jasmine that the former drudge had. I never sat at her table in a bar, for instance, or rubbed sun cream on her legs. And Jasmine's friends compared me unfavourably to him. I was too thin and bony, they complained, and I didn't look sufficiently enthusiastic when I chased scraps of food across the carpet. As well as trying to entertain these young women, I also served as their low-grade beautician. When they were preparing to go out for the evening it usually fell to me to paint their toenails. They'd either call me into the guestroom where they were staying and I'd carry out my work on bended knees, while they sat at the dressing table painting their faces in the mirror. Or else they'd assemble in the lounge and I'd crawl from one pair of waiting feet to another, doing my painstaking work while they gossiped, sipped their fizzy wine and chided me for taking too much time. 'Get a move on, Creepy Crawley,' an impatient voice was sure to say. 'Or do you want me to trample on you?'

There were so many hues and shades of varnish to choose from, they could never decide what colour toenails to have. Their eyes lit up at the selection I carried around and they wanted to try them all. Sometimes I would have to paint each toenail a different colour, wait for the exchange of opinions, then wipe them all clean again and apply the varnish the owner of the feet liked best. The little madams didn't do a thing to make my job any easier. Some kept their feet curled up on the couch and others placed them flat on the floor so I had to bend my poor back like a medieval supplicant to get at their toes. The meanest and prettiest kept their sandals on, crossed one leg over the other and casually swung their foot as I tried to work. After I'd carefully painted each nail, I was usually instructed to blow gently on the toes until the polish was dry. Some enjoyed the sensation of warm air on their feet and kept me blowing much longer than was necessary.

Painting a woman's toenails is an exacting task at the best of times. You have to apply the quick-drying lacquer in smooth, swift strokes if you want to get an even finish. It requires a confident and steady hand. But it's hard to keep from trembling when you know you might be punished for making the tiniest mistake. God forbid that I run the lacquer over a cuticle or inadvertently brush the end of a toe, especially if I were attending to Jasmine's royal feet. She'd point her slender toes and examine my work while I waited on my knees, trembling. If she was less than happy she'd say, 'Do them again, you useless creature.'

'Yes, Mistress.'

'Then you can go and fetch your cane.'

A set of painted toenails has always held an obscure fascination for me, even when the varnish is chipped or outgrown. I cannot say if I'm aroused by the sight, as some men clearly are, or faintly repelled. The idea of deliberately drawing attention to this part of the body strikes me at once as enormously childish and monstrously decadent. (Toe rings I find even more perplexing. Jasmine owned many but, surprisingly, seldom wore them.) I think a woman who regularly adorns her toes with varnish and jewellery is obeying a peculiarly feminine urge that few men will ever understand. Still, I felt a strange complicity with Jasmine and her friends as they left for an evening of drinking and dancing displaying hours of my work on the ends of their toes. I crawled among them as they tottered about in the entrance hall on their tall heels and high platforms. Their feet were raised inches above the polished mahogany tiles and their nails glistened like clusters of precious gemstones.

You might well think that after a day, a week, or certainly a month of this appalling treatment I'd have walked out, even though I had no place to go and no job to return to. You might call me insane for staying and refuse to accept that I could find a woman like Jasmine desirable unless I actually took a perverse pleasure from the abuse she handed out. I won't defend myself against the accusation of insanity, but I'll insist to my dying day that I never sought to be humiliated and beaten. I welcomed the slaps, the kicks and the canings Jasmine administered about as much as any man would in my place. I simply put up with all the violence and mistreatment for the chance of being close to the most beautiful woman I'd ever laid eyes on. There are countless stories of men who laid down their lives for the woman they loved. Why should the surrender of freedom and dignity be regarded as any stranger than that? Far more sensible, I say, to be whipped daily by your goddess than die in her name.

Yes, of course I loved her! Whatever that expression means, explains or justifies. And if my one-sided passion is hard to comprehend it's because you never saw Jasmine and can't know the wonder I felt in her presence. Women like Jasmine create storms. If she moved to a tranquil village the community would be in ruins a month later. I swear it. Old men would have heart attacks in the street, husbands would bankrupt their households, wives would shrivel up with jealousy and the children would run wild in the woods.

And I ask you, what man could grow tired of gazing at Jasmine's ass? That ass of hers will engross me until I die. The shape of it. The way it moved. I detected its unmistakable contours beneath whatever she was wearing. I could draw it from memory in all of its voluptuous detail and I once attempted a full-scale model in clay. I noted its every shudder and twitch when she walked. I observed it from the side, from the rear and from below. I watched it when she stood up and when she sat down and when she stretched out on her front in the sun. I saw that ass wet and dry and glistening with massage oil. I saw that ass in skimpy bikini briefs that had to struggle to cover its devouring cleavage and I caught glimpses of it, snug in the prettiest cotton panties, as she posed before her mirrors in high-heeled shoes. I saw it on dance floors shaking for men, watched it spread slightly as it settled over a muscular thigh and quiver when playfully slapped. Yet no matter how much of it I saw, I could never quite fathom it, never quite work it out to my satisfaction. Something about that piece of her anatomy always eluded me and left me gasping for another look.

Most nights I managed a wank or two before I passed out with exhaustion. I'd sniff a pair of her panties, which I'd kept to one side for this very purpose, and recall a particularly choice view of her legs and ass I'd stolen that day. (Occasionally the panties that were stretched over my face actually belonged to the scene I was reliving. That was pure magic!) Don't underestimate the pleasure these moments brought me. They were compensation enough for all I endured. But I also enjoyed other treats when Jasmine was in the mood to indulge me.

I remember vividly the first time I was allowed to kiss her feet. She noticed me staring at them longingly one morning as she sat at the breakfast table. If I was becoming a 'footman', then it was because her feet were the only part of her body I could look at with relative impunity.

'You like my feet?' She smiled and held one out towards me, wiggling the toes playfully.

'Yes, Mistress.'

'They are pretty, aren't they? Crawl over here and beg to kiss this pretty foot.'

I did so instantly. I crouched before her chair like a dog begging for table scraps. 'Mistress, please allow me to kiss your foot.'

'Pretty foot. Say "pretty foot".' She held it temptingly under my nose. It smelt strongly of the perfumed oil I'd added to her bath.

'Mistress, please allow me to kiss your pretty foot.'

'What's it worth?' She nudged my chin with her big toe. The sensation shot all the way down to my cock. I opened my mouth but no words came out. She'd taken the power of speech from me.

'Would you die to taste it?'

I nodded and felt a sharp, silver toenail scratch my bottom lip. By now my cock was a throbbing bulge in the black pouch.

'Is that little prick of yours aching?'

'Yes, Mistress.'

'I could make you come just by touching your face with my big toe.' She shook her head in pitying disbelief. 'You can't help yourself can you?'

'No, Mistress.'

'Go on, get down and lick it then.' She pushed my head down onto the carpet with her foot and, holding the sole above my face, continued to munch her breakfast cereal.

While she ate, I lay in rapture beneath her majestic foot, gazing up at the soft, private skin of the sole and worshipping it with gentle kisses. Timidly, I extended my tongue and began to lick the delicately wrinkled flesh. I began my journey at the pink heel and followed the rise of the tanned arch, savouring every millimetre of instep and sole as I licked my way towards her toes. To these I paid special attention. My lips pressed adoringly against the tender pads and the tip of my tongue fluttered for long delicious moments in the cleavage between each one. The skin here was very warm and slightly salty to taste and there was an addictive hint of musk beneath the perfume.

I don't know how long I paid homage to her hovering foot before I heard the words: 'Don't get greedy.' She lifted her foot away from my mouth, but my desperate lips followed their prize and were soon brushing soft flesh again.

'Hey, cut that out,' she said, glancing down at me for the first time. She kicked out and caught me hard in the jaw with her heel. 'Didn't you hear me? Don't get greedy.' She put her foot under the table again, where it wriggled its way back into a low-heeled mule, and resumed eating her breakfast and reading a magazine.

'Go and tidy my bedroom,' she ordered presently.

I got off lightly that time. She was in a good mood and did not beat me for the liberty I'd taken. But I had to wait a whole week before she gave me another chance to lick her precious feet.

Nine

When I carried the rod to Jasmine I never knew how hard she was going to beat me. She was quite arbitrary in choosing the severity of my punishment, often whipping me savagely for petty offences. Her eyes revealed nothing of her intention when she gave the chilling command: 'Go and fetch your cane.' Sometimes she took the rod but didn't actually use it on me. After slicing the air a few times, she'd pass it back to me and send me away again, her laughter ringing in my ears.

I was required to assume a low kneeling position when I presented the rod to Jasmine. I balanced it across my upturned palms, trembling in anticipation of the pain it would inflict. She made me participate in my own punishment to demonstrate how easily she could bend me to her will. She would have ordered me to whip myself had she not taken such delight in abusing my body herself. I fetched the rod at her command and was responsible for keeping it in its pristine condition. I polished it regularly so that it glistened in her hand and cleaned it thoroughly after she'd beaten me to her satisfaction.

When Jasmine lifted the rod from my palms, I had to thank her for the honour she was about to bestow upon me. If my praise satisfied her she'd give me permission to proceed to the next stage in the ritual. I'd crawl to the middle of the floor, crouch on all fours and, like some shameless primate, arch my bare buttocks high in the air. At her leisure my gorgeous tyrant would rise from her chair and take slow, menacing steps around my prone form, flexing the long punishment stick to test its suppleness. She'd tap my body in various places, hinting where I could expect to feel the first stinging blow, reminding me that she ruled every inch of my flesh.

Jasmine wielded the rod skilfully and with an instinctive disregard for her lowly victim. She could deliver a skin-slicing blow with a flick of her slender wrist and my flesh would be on fire before the blood had even risen to her cheeks. She'd practised on scores of men in her time and I think she often chose to beat me simply to improve her technique – on these occasions I considered myself lucky. When she was really angry she'd attack my body with a murderous passion. She'd beat me until I no longer felt the blows and curled up foetus-like and snivelling at her feet. These furious assaults only came to an end when she ran out of breath. My body would burn for days afterwards and the scars that appeared beneath the welts are still with me.

The first time Jasmine struck me with the rod, I instinctively moved away and scrambled to my feet. I'm sensitive to pain and the bite of the rod on my naked buttocks shocked me into an awareness of my wretched condition. It seemed absurd to submit my body to such violence, even for the chance to ogle the ass of a goddess. I stood before the woman I worshipped, trying to look defiant.

'Get back down,' she said calmly, confident I'd obey. She swung the rod hard against my thigh. I yelped and jumped back a step. I remained standing but had no idea what to do next. I glanced at the rod but the act of snatching it from her hand was beyond my power.

'Get down on the floor where you belong,' she said again. Her eyes were ablaze and faced with their challenge I stared down at the carpet. I'd grown so accustomed to kneeling and crawling in her presence I hardly recognised myself standing on my two feet like a man.

'On your knees now or I'll whip your balls as well.' She was pointing the rod at my crotch and I felt my balls recoil in terror. I stood dumbly before her, but she was without pity. 'Take off your pouch,' she ordered. 'You had your chance.' She prodded me between the legs. 'Take it off now.'

I backed away from her, shielding my balls with my hands.

'Either I whip your balls or I throw you out in the street.'

I begged her not to punish my balls.

'Why not?' She pursued me, poking me with the rod and laughing as I tried hopelessly to defend myself. 'What else are they good for?'

I pleaded but she shook her head. She was determined to make a cripple of me. In a last bid to save my manhood, I fell on my belly and grovelled at her feet. I let her see that I was utterly hers, her plaything, her whipping boy. I squirmed like a maggot before her red stilettos and she beat me without mercy, striking my head, my legs and my face with such savage intensity I thought she was trying to draw blood. My screams were those of an animal, not a man.

'Don't you ever disobey me, you little runt,' she said between blows. 'Next time you stand up to me I'll whip your balls *and* kick you out in the street.'

She beat my unresisting flesh until she was panting for breath, then she dangled the tip of the rod in front of my mouth. 'Kiss it,' she said. She smiled in triumph as my quivering lips reached up to do her bidding.

I suffered that first beating in private but Jasmine usually chose to punish me before an appreciative audience of her friends. Beating me was a more spectacular display of her power than ordering me to lick her salty feet clean or using me as a doormat for the evening. She gave off a special glow when she beat me. Her proud cheeks flushed red, her hair shimmered and her eyes glazed over as she swung the rod and left her mark on my flesh. Yet I lusted for her even as I felt the sting of her scorn. My cock would stretch the pouch, bending itself double in an effort to break free. Sometimes she'd roll me onto my back with her foot and tell me to show my dribbling erection to her friends.

'See how he likes it,' she'd say, striking close to my exposed cock and balls. 'I could whip the slime out of him if I wanted to.'

It was humiliating to be punished in front of Jasmine's girlfriends but truly emasculating to be beaten for the entertainment of one of her studs. This happened only once and was the price I paid for trying to steal a look at Jasmine's forbidden cunt. The events of that night are engraved on my mind.

I was awoken from a fitful sleep by the sound of Jasmine's tipsy laughter and a deep male voice, which seemed vaguely familiar, echoing from the hall. I pictured Jasmine and her night's catch moving slowly up the stairs, kissing, groping, unable to keep their hands off each other. But this image was quickly dispelled by the sudden clatter of high-heeled shoes on the wooden floor tiles. I grew stiff. Jasmine was leading her prize cock towards the lounge.

She would sometimes fuck an eager stud in one of the downstairs rooms before taking him up to her bed for a more leisurely screw. When she used the lounge I was in for a rare treat. From the kitchen, I would be able to hear her whimper and moan. And just to make sure I didn't miss a single sigh of her pleasure, I'd tiptoe out into the hallway and listen from there. If I felt especially brave, I'd position myself at the closed door, take my throbbing cock in hand and pump away, dreaming it was I who was up inside her, forcing that moaning tribute from her throat.

When I crept out into the hall that night, my cock already hard and leading me like a divining rod, I found the lounge door standing wide open. Was this merely the careless oversight of two fuck-focused individuals or had they intended to add the thrill of exhibitionism to their sport? Either way, as I approached the orange glow of the room, I felt I was walking into a trap and being lured towards the sad end of my time as Jasmine's drudge. Yet I could not resist. What sweet poison my Mistress laid!

I crouched nervously at the edge of the doorway. Holding my breath, I stretched my neck forwards and took a peek inside. What I saw almost knocked me off my heels. There was Jasmine, stripped down to her silky black underwear, kneeling between the open thighs of the basketball player from Apollo. He was sitting naked on a leather couch, a dark, muscular giant, and his attention was absorbed by her rhythmically bobbing head. I'd wanked to imaginary scenes of Jasmine fucking her studs before, but now I was actually seeing my divine Mistress down on her knees and gobbling cock.

She sucked him expertly and performed all sorts of fancy tricks. She had her ass to me (the thong panties cut a thin dark line between her tan cheeks) so much of what she did was left to my imagination. But I saw her spit twice, steadily jerk his saliva-coated cock with her hand and lower her mouth to attack his balls. From the way he dug his fingers into the leather cushions she must have given his nuts a good lashing with her tongue. She sucked on them, making obscene slurping sounds, and he closed his eyes and threw back his head. The sensations she was stirring in his balls put him in a trance and to snap him out of it, she slapped his heavyweight cock against her chin. Looking up at him now, straight into his glazed eyes it seemed to me, she nibbled the underside of his shaft as if it were a stick of salami then slowly swallowed a good half of it. She sucked hard, lifting her head steadily, trying to stretch his already oversized tool an extra few inches. She looked enormously greedy doing this. Her mouth gripped him firmly and she tugged on his root until his ass rose from the cushion. With a loud pop, the big purple cock head squeezed from between her constricting lips. She fished it quickly back into her mouth with her tongue.

She was too much even for this big stud. He seized her by the waist and lifted her onto his lap where his primed cock was quivering. She straddled his legs, pushing her breasts into his face, and thrust out her ass making a gift of it to him. Hungry for her cunt, he dragged the tight crotch of her panties to one side and after a few eager jabs found her slot and pushed himself into her. Jasmine gasped like a virgin bride so I knew it went in, but he selfishly covered her hole with his massive hands. His fingers were fastened together over the split in her ass and his cock pumped up and down behind them like a greasy piston.

I watched Jasmine ride her stud's cock while I rapidly worked my own and awaited that fleeting revelation of stuffed cunt that would trigger my orgasm. She took his whole length inside her and ground her ass around on his lap as if trying to squeeze his balls off. She rose up, released his juice-glazed pole inch by slow inch, but her cunt remained hidden behind its dark gates. She impaled herself once more and jerked her hips rudely, bending and stretching his cock until his hands were squeezing the blood from her ass cheeks. Impossibly, her cunt was still obscured. Eager to empty his balls, the stud encouraged her to ride him at his own rhythm. He held her firmly, blocking my view as that ass of a thousand wet dreams danced up and down for his selfish pleasure. He called her 'baby' and coaxed her with repetitive compliments about the tightness and temperature of her hidden pussy.

She was determined to keep the cum in his balls – and mine – for a while longer yet. She slid off his cock, cast aside her bra and panties, and got down on all fours in front of him. I caught a glimpse of a dark triangle of tightly trimmed bush but nothing more. She crawled to the middle of the room like a sultry she-animal and crouched down on her elbows. Shaking her tousled hair and waving her hindquarters in the air, she showed him what she had back there. The display did the trick and she knew it. She rested her cheek on the carpet, arched her ass even higher, and gazed back over her shoulder as her stud came at her. He was driven by the same crude urge that burnt within me. He knelt down behind her – all cock now. His hands seized her narrow waist, wrapped her like a dark harness, and he shoved himself into her. Holding her firmly in position, he delivered powerful, punishing thrusts. She kept her ass high for him and when he relaxed his grip she threw herself back to meet his plunging cock. She moved her whole body to his urgent rhythm, the most gorgeous and accommodating bitch imaginable.

Tossing her hair to one side, she glanced suddenly towards the open doorway where I knelt frigging myself. Obsessed by the hungry movements of her ass, I'd moved into plain view. She made no visible reaction when she saw me and kept herself in position for the thrusting cock and slapping thighs that were sending shudders through her body and shaking her dangling breasts. Her eyes were half closed, her strong cheeks twitched, and her lips were drawn back to form something between a snarl and a smile. She panted and moaned stupidly and even as she looked towards the open doorway, it was as if she didn't see me. But before she lowered her face towards the carpet again, driven back down there by the relentless force of pounding cock, she grinned with unmistakable malice.

I hurried back to the kitchen. A sense of dread hung over me as I paced around in my room. My cock, though, remained bone-hard and I lay down on the bed and began to stroke myself, more for comfort than pleasure. Listening to Jasmine's escalating moans, I awaited the inevitable and felt for a pair of her panties that were under my pillow. It consoled me a little to think I could take these with me, and other pairs too, if Jasmine threw me out on the street. A short silence followed her climax, which was louder and more aggressive than usual. Then I heard her cool voice summoning me to the lounge.

I didn't know what to expect when I presented myself to her, wearing only my pouch. Hoping to please her, and also to hide my still swollen cock, I crawled into the lounge on my hands and knees. I found Jasmine and her stud sitting on the couch like reigning monarchs upon a double throne. She had slipped back into her bra and panties and her stud had placed a pair of silk boxers over his cock and balls. The horny bastard was still half erect though, waiting for another chance to dig into his queen bitch. I sat on my knees at their feet and his eyes lit up in recognition. He snapped his fingers against his palm.

'Dayum! You really got this sucker pussy-whupped.'

'It was easy.' She was smiling and stroking his muscular thigh possessively. Her hand looked minuscule against its dark, solid mass. 'In fact, I "whup" him whenever I feel like it.' The stud stared down at me incredulously and slowly shook his shaved and oiled head.

'Straight up? You whup this fool?'

'What else is he good for?'

He let out a burst of laughter and eased himself against the back of the couch. 'Hell! You're mean, baby.'

'You want me to whip him for you now?'

His expression changed and he seemed less sure of himself. Had a sense of male solidarity come to my rescue? Would the sight of Jasmine whipping me also insult his own manhood? I tried to guess the thoughts that were passing through his mind as he looked from me to the magnificent woman he'd fucked senseless barely five minutes earlier.

Jasmine interrupted: 'I'm going to whip him anyhow. He deserves it and he knows why. You can watch if you want.'

His face became as wicked as hers.

'Whup this pussy's ass,' he said.

'You want to watch me do it in my black boots?' Her eyes glimmered mischievously.

'You're spoilin' me, girl.'

He slapped her bare ass hard as she rose from the couch and she yelped playfully and danced out of the room. He ignored me the whole time she was upstairs putting on her boots. There is nothing you can say to a big handsome man whose angry bitch is getting ready to beat the crap out of you, so I kept my mouth shut. While I knelt on the floor at his size 18 feet, he picked his teeth lazily and adjusted the position of his cock and balls that were now barely covered by the silk boxers. He sprung to life again when Jasmine reappeared and so did his cock.

She was wearing the shiny black boots, just as she'd promised. They climbed halfway up her thighs and their sheer extravagance made her thong panties look even tinier. She stood before the couch and did a slow turn, giving her stud – and me as well – the chance to appreciate how the high spiked heels lifted and shaped her faultless ass cheeks.

'You look phat, honey. You've even got me tremblin'.' He gave her tempting rump another spank. She glanced down at her feet where I was crouching in awe.

'What are you staring at, you little creep?' She stamped her foot angrily. 'Go and fetch your cane.' I scurried off to the kitchen before she had the chance to kick me.

I crawled back to the couch with the rod between my teeth. I knelt just in front of Jasmine's boots and raised the rod towards her, my palms glistening with sweat. She snatched it impatiently and ordered me to crawl to the middle of the room and hold up my ass ready to be beaten. She strode after me, eager to begin.

'Shall I make him lick my boots first?' she asked, planting a sharp heel in front of my lowered face.

'It's your show, baby.'

'Beg to lick them,' she said, her voice raw with loathing.

'Please, Mistress, may I lick your boots?'

'Louder, worm.'

I lifted my face from the carpet and repeated my grovelling request.

'Start with the sole.' She tilted her boot back on its heel, raising the sole an inch or so. I didn't waste a second. I pressed my cheek flat against the carpet, stretched my tongue into the narrow gap and began to lick the smooth sole with utter devotion. The stud yelled in astonishment.

'He'd lick your dirty butt hole clean if you told him to.'

'In his dreams,' she said charmingly, pressing down hard on my tongue, squashing it into the carpet. 'Only in his dreams.'

She made me lick each boot thoroughly. I dragged my tongue over yards of cool black leather as if I was trying to draw nourishment from it. She insulted me freely and told her stud that I was a worthless dog and useless even as a drudge. 'I'll probably kick him out in the morning and get a new one,' she said, while I worked down at her heels, sucking, licking, kissing, desperate to please her. She made me rise to my knees and lick the rim around the tops of her boots. I lapped away gratefully, my lips almost brushing her smooth, tanned thighs, my nose within sniffing distance of her panty-wrapped crotch. The V of black silk was quite mesmerising, hugging with a lazy familiarity the plump mound of her cunt. She stood like a proud huntress, one boot forwards, hands on hips, and let me drown in her scent.

She ordered me to stop and delivered a stinging blow across my back. I was getting greedy. 'Arch up,' she shouted. 'Arch up, you little creep, or I'll really hurt you.'

I forced my head down from her aromatic thighs and crouched at her feet, holding up my buttocks at the required angle. She took a step back and reddened my ass with a flurry of backhand swipes. Then she shifted position to get a good swing at the backs of my thighs. Releasing a girlish grunt with each brutal stroke, she drove me forwards across the carpet.

She came after me in her high boots, seething with rage. 'Don't you dare crawl away from me.' She landed the rod on my skull with devastating accuracy, making sure I understood.

'Better learn how to take a whuppin', boy,' advised the stud.

She struck me again and again to entertain him and he shouted encouragement.

'You want a turn?' she asked at length.

'You foolin'? Brothers would pay top dollar to watch this. A honey in boots whuppin' an Englishman.'

'A bitch in boots,' she said sweetly and brought the rod down hard between the cleft of my buttocks, stinging my balls with the tip. 'A bitch in boots.'

His voice rose three octaves: 'Holy shit! You're nasty.'

'But you like it.' She stung the back of my thighs with a few more well-aimed swipes. My screams excited her. I could feel an extra passion in her strokes.

'Why do you treat him so mean?' he asked. But it was less a question than an expression of his arousal.

'Because I can,' she replied.

He watched his bitch in boots circle her victim, striking at will. It increased her value in his eyes, I'm sure, to see how cruel she was to those beneath her, made her cunt especially appealing. She thrashed me because she could, because life had turned out that way, favoured some, condemned others – they took pleasure, I suffered pain.

'Look up,' she said when her assault was over. She was breathing heavily and her breasts were heaving in the lacy half-cup bra. Her skin was flushed and covered in a fine perspiration. The flogging had exhausted her like never before and left me striped from head to foot. I was a burning, aching mess on the carpet. Then something happened. As I crouched before her motionless boots, panting in unison with her own rushed breathing, I suddenly felt we were connected at a profound level, one that her stud could never reach, no matter how big and strong his cock. She held the rod at her side and my gaze climbed up that tapering tool, which had forged an unbreakable bond between us, towards her gorgeous glowing face. The moment was magical and I forgot my pain, or rather I welcomed it as the means of satisfying Jasmine's all-consuming desire for pleasure. I searched her eyes for acknowledgment, a secret sign of the complicity between an exalted Mistress and her abject slave.

She crushed me with her words.

'Up on your knees, you little freak. I want him to see how much you enjoyed that.'

Laden with shame and feeling a sickening sense of betrayal, I displayed my bulging pouch to her stud. His mighty cock was also hard, a dumb statement of lust rising from his lap. He started to stroke it with a deft hand, openly gloating. He was ready to pounce on his bitch.

'Get out of here,' she said and tossed the rod onto the floor. Administering a flogging, however intense, could not compete with stretching her cunt over a top-notch cock.

I bore the rod back to my bedroom and hung it clumsily on the wall, adding two more sweaty smudges to the plaster. Who would believe the story behind those dirty fingerprints? I could already hear Jasmine's cries as she enjoyed the thrusts of the cock that we had both excited. She was even louder than before, her moans deeper and more urgent. He was roaring, proclaiming his potency and triumph and the whole house echoed with their wild, animal sounds. I knelt down on the floor and pulled out my own cock. It was the only part of my body that didn't smart from the beating.

I had been abused and tortured to stimulate my gorgeous Mistress and her high-performance stud. Those prized bodies, model and athlete, were fucking over my sacrificed and discarded carcass. I wanked in envy of their boastful and selfish passion and climaxed silently over the cold stone, listening to the screams and grunts of a pleasure I could never know.

Ten

'Do not look around in the streets of a city . . .'

I never seriously regretted my decision to become Jasmine's drudge. Certainly things could have been better for me, but true to the earth sign under which I was born I regarded my circumstances in a pragmatic light. I simply judged between the life I led at the mansion and the one I'd left behind. I did not introduce could be's or should be's into the equation. That was Kim's way, always striving to transcend the working day, believing in corny dreams of love and success.

I asked myself two questions: What have I given up? The answer: a car, a flat, a job and a permanent sense of frustration. And what have I gained? Proximity to the ass of my dreams. Admittedly, my position was hazardous and uncertain; but then what is so unusual about that these days? I led a life of extremes, elated by Jasmine's unwitting indulgences one moment and trampled under her feet the next. But what more could I hope for? I was a man without resources, a man of average looks and ability, and I was cursed with a taste for beautiful women.

As the weeks passed and I grew more adept at my work, I managed to find a little time for myself, usually while I ran errands. If I was in the city centre I might grab a coffee and browse through a newspaper. Once an avid reader of the tabloids, I was developing a taste for the quality press now. Instead of poring over titillating pictures of pop divas and smutty exposés of Hollywood starlets, I rooted out reports of wars and atrocities. I especially liked the dispatches from the correspondents who were out there in the thick of things. I could fairly hear the bullets whistling past their ears and the shells exploding overhead as I read.

If you'd seen me sitting at a corner table in a city café, scanning the narrow columns of print through my reading glasses, you'd have taken me for an earnest fellow who wanted to get to the bottom of things. And in a sense you'd have been right – I have always been drawn to the bottom of things, as if I were especially sensitive to the pull of gravity. But you shouldn't think I read in the quest for greater knowledge or in the hope of acquiring an insight into this or that development. I turned to those tales of horror for self-confirmation, nothing more. To speak frankly, they put my own minuscule sufferings in perspective and strengthened my Old Testament convictions about the wrathfulness of God. I swallowed that day's news like the strong black coffee I always ordered, and when I got up from my chair and folded the paper under my arm, this convulsing world of ours was a gentle stimulus in my blood.

If the weather was fine I would plant myself on a park bench and watch the ducks and geese floating around on the lake. They didn't have a care in the world while the sun was shining and I envied them. Or I might take a stroll through the city streets, smiling at passers-by, savouring my few moments of freedom. My eyes still sought out pretty girls of course – force of habit I suppose – but I no longer felt my pulse race as one approached or the bite of disappointment when she all too quickly walked by. I could afford to be a more relaxed observer of these sirens now that I regularly saw their sisters at play and witnessed their most candid moments. Familiarity had bred in me a degree of contentment. Armed with my secret knowledge, I watched these cunning creatures parade their fine asses up and down the high street breathing a richer and sweeter air than the rest of us. But I always stayed alert. I was determined not to run into friends or drinking acquaintances whose questions would have been awkward to deal with. I kept my eyes peeled for familiar faces and ducked into many a shop doorway to escape. Often it was only luck that saved me. Sometimes I spotted friends of Jasmine coming my way and then my heart really jumped. Who would have believed it? Matthew Crawley suddenly found himself darting across the street to avoid pretty women.

There were certain pubs I could drop into during the afternoons without fear of meeting anybody I knew, and this I did when Jasmine was away. I have no hang-ups about sitting alone at the bar brooding over a pint; in fact, it is often preferable to dealing with another person's restless ego. If I did happen to be in a sociable mood there was always a Brylcreem-slicked old-timer or one of the eternally jobless willing to join me in a game of pool, providing I put up the money. When I looked around me at the mostly male faces and half-empty glasses, the dull walls and dark bar counter, I didn't think my present lot was so bad, even if I had to wriggle in my seat sometimes because my buttocks were still burning from a recent caning. I certainly had no deep longing for anything I'd left behind, least of all my so-called independence which was just something to drink and wank away as far as I could see. The world I beheld beyond Jasmine's high heels and delicately scented panties was a pretty crummy affair in my opinion.

As I sat in these pubs at the edge of town, identical in essentials to all the others I had come to know over the years – almost by accident it seemed, circumstance of birth – my only real worry was that my adventure as Jasmine's drudge would come to an end one day. Sooner or later I would be back among my own kind, back for good, grinning, grimacing and growing old. But I bore the bleak certainty of my fall surprisingly well. I took my life one day at a time and savoured every moment I was near the woman whose mere image drew a frothy tribute from a million cocks each day.

In the early hours of the morning, work over, wanking done, I'd sometimes dig around in the leather folder that my old rival had left behind on the bookcase. It was packed full of handwritten papers and I'd lie on my bed, squinting to decipher the frantic script. I'm a nosey kind of fellow and hoped to find letters or a journal of some sort. I was curious to know what kind of man my predecessor was and what he'd done to fall out of favour with Jasmine. But there was not a line of autobiography on any of the pages or a single detail about his relationship with Jasmine. Instead, every page in the folder contained the words of other authors, some he'd named, others he'd left anonymous, transcribed in his own distinctive hand. Only an occasional comment jotted in the margin or a word or phrase heavily underlined gave me an insight into his own thoughts and feelings.

My old rival had a one-track mind. The observations he made and the details he magnified all had to do with the same thing – female tyranny. He had as keen and eager an eye for its manifestations as I have for female ass. He saw female tyranny exercised as much by the playful smile of Vladimir Nabokov's Lolita as by the voluptuous dance of Oscar Wilde's Salome. He called himself a 'supersensualist' (this name, I discovered, he borrowed from Leopold von Sacher Masoch's *Venus in Furs* – a novel he praised highly) but he did not try to examine or explain his unusual predilection. He did not seek its origins back in his childhood or trace its development through puberty and adolescence. He had simply compiled illustrations of supersensual craving and the women who induced it in him.

The extracts came from many and varied sources. He'd copied down selected case histories of distinguished psychologists like Kraft-Ebbing, Havelock Ellis and Sigmund Freud that dealt with sadism, masochism, fetishism, exhibitionism and voyeurism. He'd collected myths that featured delightfully cruel women: Artemis, the exhibitionist and man-hunter; Venus, the cuckold maker; Circe, the keeper of men-swine; Brunhilde, the cocktease and ball breaker; and stories of fiery Hindu goddesses who trampled on their husbands or rode them like horses. Biblical females were featured too, scheming and vindictive temptresses like Judith and Delilah, and his clear favourite, Salome. There were countless vignettes of powerful women – Cleopatra, Messalina, Queen Constance, Catherine de Medici, Catherine the Great and Eva Peron, to name but a few – taken from biographies, history books and feminist studies. Surprisingly, there were also extracts from biographies and autobiographies of men, some of them quite amusing. I was consoled to learn that the esteemed French philosopher Jean Jacques Rousseau had been an incorrigible wanker and partial to sniffing panties,

146

and that Salvador Dali used to crawl under tables and bite the feet of his pretty models. He had also jotted down the juiciest details from anthropological research on goddess worship, matriarchies, Amazons, witches and succubae.

But most of the extracts came from novels and short stories. Here are the names of some that I remember: *The Sorrows of Young Werther* by Goethe, *Gulliver's Travels* by Jonathan Swift (only the Brobdingnag section), *Getting Married* by August Strindberg, *She* by Rider Haggard, *Of Human Bondage* by Somerset Maugham, *The Trumpet Major* by Thomas Hardy, *Mysteries* by Knut Hamsun, *Nana* by Emile Zola, *The Blue Angel* by Heinrich Mann, *The Idiot* by Fyodor Dostoevski (with uncharacteristic candour, my old rival expressed the wish that a Hollywood studio would buy the rights to this novel and cast Jasmine as the beautiful and tempestuous Nastasya Filippovna). He'd also delved into literary erotica in search of his illustrations. I found many passages from Pierre Louÿs's *The Woman and her Puppet* and Anaïs Nin's *Delta of Venus*. I even came across a few lines from Henry Miller's *Sexus* – the author's contemptuous portrait of one Bill Woodruff, a romantic fool who is denied sex by his vain and pretty actress wife and reduced to kissing her asshole in bed at night. And I also recall a paragraph from James Joyce's *Ulysses* dealing with a similar conjugal arrangement in the Bloom household.

The folder contained the essence of what seemed like years of diligent research. It was not something you'd be likely to forget to take with you, even if your face did bear the marks of Jasmine's high heels and her threat to call the police was hanging over you. I began to speculate he'd left the folder behind deliberately and for the same reason that Gideons leave their

Bibles in hotel rooms – he wanted to make a convert of me.

But what I find most odd about the whole thing is that having achieved his ambition to serve a cruel goddess, he should want to go on reading and writing about it. Life first, that's what I've always thought, and books last, at the very end of the day when you're too tired for anything else. Reading, I think, is like wanking, terribly addictive, but a sad substitute for the real thing. Rousseau made a similar point, if I'm not mistaken.

Yet I did read one extract that made me shiver; I have committed the words to memory and still struggle to heed their sage advice. The sheet must have slipped from the folder while I was reading one night because I found it staring up at me from the floor when I switched on the light in the morning. The lines were taken from the Bible, that much was indicated, but there was no clue as to their author – one of the Patriarchs, I guessed:

> *Do not look around in the streets of a city,*
> *Or wander about its deserted sections.*
> *Turn away your eyes from a shapely woman,*
> *And do not gaze at beauty belonging to another;*
> *Many have been seduced by a woman's beauty,*
> *And by it passion is kindled like a fire.*

I recognised a profound warning in these six short lines – so too had my old rival perhaps, back in the days when his supersensual craving was just a tremor in his limbs whenever a dark beauty passed him in the street. I reflected on their wisdom sometimes as I strolled through the city. I observed and I judged: men had learnt nothing in two thousand years. Like their ancient brothers in the sultry cities of the

Levant, their eyes lingered on the shapely women who paraded before them. And they were no longer content with merely looking at women in the streets. We'd erected a whole culture of the gaze that would be an old Patriarch's dream of hell. Painted women grinned down at us from towering billboards and seduced whole nations by means of television. We could buy women in magazines to meet any specification or take them home on videos or DVDs and animate and freeze them according to our desires.

Many months later I did encounter my old rival again. I discovered him in one of the city's forgotten back streets, the kind of place I never had to fear running into any of Jasmine's friends. From the look of him, the streets had been his home since the day he'd crawled away from the poolside. He seemed beaten and downtrodden and his lank hair and grisly beard had turned grey and lifeless like stone. Wrapped in a grubby overcoat, he stood before the boarded-up window of a breakfast bar and rattled a tin mug when anybody approached. I stared at him from across the narrow street, a giddy sensation rising in my stomach.

I asked myself whether Jasmine would take pity on her former drudge if she could see him now, driven to this by her rejection. I concluded that she might have thrown him a coin had she strolled by that afternoon, but only to tease him with her charity. I reached into my pocket for a few pound coins, aroused by the idea that my supersensual friend would eat his next meal courtesy of Jasmine's moneymaking ass. How good that food would taste to him if he knew! He glanced at my hand as I held it over his cup, nothing more. I was as invisible to him now as I had been in the queue in front of Apollo, at the window of the cocktail bar and by the poolside.

I saw him on several subsequent occasions. Most often he was sitting alone on a bench in the high street, as grim and dirt-encrusted as the pavement around him. Whenever I saw him, I went over and dropped coins into his cup. I felt the pull of gravity, a little stronger at each encounter. I knew it was only a matter of time before I would join him on the bench. When that day came, I would lay his folder of papers in the space between us and finally his eyes would see me. There was much we had to talk about.

Yet as much as I wanted to talk to him, I did not look forward to our meeting for it could only take place after I too had been cast out by Jasmine. This old tramp represented my future. My rival was always one step below me, one step nearer the bottom, which is never very far away.

Eleven

'You've never seen my pussy, have you, Matt?'

Jasmine was sitting at her dressing table, wrapped in one of the fleecy cotton robes she wore after taking a bath. Her hair was tied back in a girlish ponytail and her complexion was fresh and glowed with a youthful vitality. She was half turned towards me in the chair, her smooth legs crossed at the thighs and thrust out before her. The robe was loosely tied and seemed poised to fall open around her hips.

I dropped to my hands and knees in the doorway and crawled across the room towards her. I stopped at her feet and at a nod from her sat up on my knees and clasped my hands behind my back. She grinned at my swollen cock, a prisoner in its tight pouch. She was in a good mood that evening – she had a date with a rock star – and I was spared the usual taunts.

'You can tidy up in the bathroom later,' she said. 'First you're going to help me get ready. Start by painting my toenails.' She picked up a bottle of cherry-red varnish from the dressing table and held it out to me. 'Come on,' she said when I hesitated, 'I won't bite.'

I took the bottle and promptly set to work adorning the toes of the shapely, fragrant foot she held out to me. After many months of practice I had become quite adept at this job. Supporting her foot with one hand, I applied the bright varnish in smooth, fluent strokes, giving each perfectly shaped nail a flawless red coat.

'You're getting better at this,' she said, presenting me with her other foot. 'Maybe one day I'll have you trained to do pedicures as well.'

'Thank you, Mistress.' I blew gently on her toes to help the polish dry.

'Mmm, that feels good. I should have you blow on my feet more often. Especially when they're hot and tired. Would you like that?'

'Yes, Mistress.'

'I bet you would.' She allowed me to blow on her feet for a few moments longer then gently nudged my cheek with her toes, a friendly warning that I shouldn't get carried away. 'Later . . . maybe. Right now I have to put on something sexy for my date.'

She rose from the chair. 'Down, boy,' she giggled.

I dropped down onto my belly and buried my face in the carpet. I saw only darkness – even the bottoms of the mirrors were hidden. I listened for the whisper of the robe sliding from her body and felt a breath of sweet air as it landed beside me.

I lay perfectly still, pressing upon my hard cock, while Jasmine, utterly naked in my imagination and in fact, stepped gaily across the room humming to herself. I heard her go into the walk-in closet and root around in her collection of clothes, deciding what to wear. She slid open a drawer.

'I'll start with the panties, I think,' she said absently.

She tried on a variety, commenting to herself as she pulled each pair snug over her hips and let the elastic snap cheekily against her ass. It was some time before she found a pair that matched her mood.

'What do you think?' she asked me. 'Oh, I forgot, you can't see anything, can you? That's a shame because I know you'd like me in this pair.' Next she sought out a bra, but after trying on several decided that she would not wear one.

When she gave me permission to lift my face from the carpet she was already in her outfit. She had chosen a white tube top and a pleated tartan mini-skirt. With her ponytail, she looked like a precocious sixth former, the kind who sits at the back of the class, legs up on the desk, lazily chewing gum. She came back to the dressing table, the skirt swirling from her rolling hips. Smoothing it under her ass she lowered herself onto the chair, and then sitting with one leg crossed over the other she began to apply her make-up. From down on the floor, I watched the hem of the skirt ride up her thigh as she leant closer to the mirror – another inch and her panty-crotch would have been on show.

'You can't help me with this,' she said. 'Go and tidy up in the wardrobe.' I got up onto my knees and grimaced as my stiff cock buckled against the wall of its leather prison. But I knew better than to adjust it in Jasmine's presence. Yes indeed. I gritted my teeth and crawled with my stifled manhood all the way to the wardrobe. There, my cock still battling against the tight leather, I gathered together the pieces of lingerie Jasmine had left scattered on the floor. I straightened out each pair of panties, folded them carefully and put them back in the appropriate drawer (there was one for black, one for white, and two for the coloured pairs). The sight of all these panties, the wanton abundance of folded and ar- ranged knickers, concentrated my mind on the pair Jasmine had hidden away under her teasing skirt. I longed to be back in position at her feet and prayed the hem of the skirt had ridden that critical extra inch up her thigh.

I was almost done when she glanced away from the mirror and complained about my work. When it came to her personal belongings, she was as particular as any woman about tiny details.

'You're folding my panties too small.' Her tightly wrapped breasts were rising and falling as she scolded me. 'That's why I can never find the pair I'm looking for.'

I apologised and began to refold a slippery silver thong that I had in my hands.

'Let me see.'

I held up my work for her approval.

'That's a little better. Now do them all like that.' She turned back to face the mirror, sending a shiver through the pleated skirt, and continued brushing mascara onto her long dark lashes.

By the time I'd tidied away the last of her precious underthings she was putting the finishing touches to her face. She held a pointed red lipstick before her slightly open mouth and began to smooth on the gloss, first covering the upper lip and then the lower. I took care not to break her concentration as I crawled back to my place at her feet. From down on the floor I watched her pout as she studied her irresistible lips in the mirror. She seemed happy with the result. She picked up a cosmetic pad, kissed it lightly, and smiled at the faint imprint of her own lips.

'Here,' she said, tossing it down to me, 'a souvenir.'

Make-up complete, she shook loose her hair, letting it fall over her shoulders in magnificent dark waves. She was cock-hardeningly gorgeous and I was going crazy to get a look at her knickers – just her knickers!

She stood up and walked across to one of the full-length mirrors, twirling that skirt about her ass just for the fun of it.

'Fetch me some shoes,' she said, as she posed before her reflection.

I crawled quickly over to the wardrobe and selected a pair of elegant black mules with slender heels and open toes – the kind she liked to wear when her legs were on show. I placed them on the floor at her feet, fighting back the urge to stretch my neck forwards to sneak a peep up her skirt. Without glancing down, she stepped into them and admired herself in the mirror, turning to view her priceless figure from all angles. The delicate muscles in her calf flexed proudly as she pivoted one of the shoes on its heel. She looked down at her arched feet.

'Nice, but no.' She kicked off the shoes. 'Bring me something else to try.'

I scurried back over to the wardrobe and once more scanned the shelves of shoes. I returned with a pair of 60s-style calf boots made of white patent leather. It was currently the vogue for young women to wear these kind of boots in combination with short pleated skirts. I was rather proud of my selection.

'What are these?' she snapped, as soon as she saw them. 'Get me something that will show off my feet.'

I hurried away, grateful to have escaped a kick in the face, and for the next ten minutes I crawled back and forth between her feet and the wardrobe. She growled in dissatisfaction at each pair of shoes I brought to her but made no suggestions. My knees were sore and her patience exhausted before I laid something at her feet that took her fancy – a pair of tall white sandals with spaghetti straps. She stepped into them, using my shoulder to steady herself.

'Fasten them,' she ordered.

Even in her bare feet Jasmine was almost as tall as me; now, wearing the high-heeled sandals, she rose to an awesome height. My head was at the level of her calves and I was facing obediently downwards, attending to the intricate sandal straps. Her legs, two beautifully shaped columns of warm, lickable flesh, stretched upwards beyond the limits of my vision. Out of the corner of my eye I could see myself in a mirror, kneeling among the scattered shoes, while the long-legged Jasmine stood with hands on hips watching me fiddling down at her feet. I looked tiny and insignificant as I worked, on a par with all the rejected shoes. The tiny tartan skirt hovered high above me, still hiding her panties, which I now imagined to be red and very, very skimpy.

When I'd fastened the sandal straps and she was happy they were tight – but not too tight – I sat up on my knees and admired the glorious idol I'd helped to create. Now she was complete, set upon her tarty pedestals and ready to go out and send blood pumping into every cock she passed. She glanced down at me, at my own caged and excited manhood.

'I'll let you kiss my heels if you like.'

In an instant I was back down on all fours. I lowered my head towards the tapering white pillars that bore the woman who ruled my world.

'Don't you dare peek up my skirt while you're down there,' she teased.

She didn't give me the chance to try. She let me plant a single worshipful kiss on each of her cold heels and stepped away from my hungry lips. She laughed at my involuntary moan of anguish; my cock was ready to explode out of sheer frustration.

'There, that should be enough to keep you satisfied.' She walked back across to the dressing table, the pleats of the skirt bouncing happily against her ass. Lifting her hair she sprayed perfume on her shoulders and neck. 'You can go and mop up in the bathroom now,' she said after a moment.

Jasmine went off to meet her rock star lover while I scrubbed out the bath. Then I picked up all the shoes and placed them back on the shelves. I tidied her dressing table and put away the make-up she'd used. I did a hundred and one jobs too dull to mention before I returned to my room, fell on the bed and demonstrated to an absent Jasmine that the ration of heel she'd allowed me was indeed sufficient. I emptied my balls twice in quick succession and lay there in a contented daze.

Later I opened the folder and puzzled over a few pages of my old rival's notes. I find there is no better time to read than in the half hour or so following a wank and the blissful little doze that generally follows. The mind is clearer and more able to focus – the demon desire has been expelled . . . temporarily. The editors at *Playboy* are aware of this male peculiarity and that is why they provide a selection of middlebrow articles, unrelated to sex, in among the photosets of enticing naked ladies. After you've unloaded to Playmate of the Month, there is nothing so engrossing as a feature on the Stealth Bomber or an interview with a Formula 1 racing driver.

In the early hours I was woken by Jasmine shouting my name. She was summoning her houseboy to the lounge and sounded impatient. I sprang out of bed at once and automatically slipped on my pouch. This was not the voice of a woman who'd been fucked to satisfaction and I raced to the lounge expecting the worst. The door stood open, the lights were turned low and, as I'd feared, Jasmine was all alone. I found her sitting sideways in one of the leather chairs, legs slung over the armrest. The pleated skirt had fallen back around her hips and I could see, in profile, the swell of her golden ass resting on the dark cushion. What a spectacle she presented! I crawled into the room with my crazed cock beating its head against the walls of its cell, even though I knew she was in no mood to indulge me. Her eyes were narrow and her face flushed – the effects of whisky that I recognised only too well. Her stud had let her down somehow, and not for the first time I was about to suffer for another man's sins.

Halfway across the room I stopped and silently begged for mercy. She studied me coolly, slowly chewing something in her mouth. I could already feel the rod lashing my buttocks, hear the angry crack of cane against flesh. I waited for her to give the dreaded command.

'You've never seen my pussy have you, Matt?' she asked casually, still chewing. 'Would you die for a lick?'

I stared at her dumbly, mouth hanging open. I could not believe what she had said. She greeted my reaction with a burst of laughter and spat a piece of gum onto the carpet.

'Come on then,' she said, as if inviting me to rub her feet or eat an olive from her fingers. 'Get over here before I change my mind and whip you instead.' She swung her legs forwards and opened them wide and I bounded across the room like a hungry dog. She lolled drunkenly in the chair, hands clasped behind her head.

'I'll regret this tomorrow,' she said, 'and so will you – even more.'

The skirt had ridden up over her hips, at last exposing the panties she'd teased and tormented me with earlier. I'd expected to see something as red as her passion or dark as her mood, but discovered there instead an almost blinding innocence. The panties were dazzling white, like a sheet flapping in the afternoon sun. The soft cotton cut a clean triangle between her thighs and strained to contain the plump flesh there. She displayed her cool, panty-wrapped cunt with exquisite indifference and I knelt before the armchair, the most grateful man alive.

'Take them off,' she ordered presently. I hurriedly obeyed her command, wondering if this wasn't all a dream. Were my fingers actually touching her warm silky legs? Were the hands reaching up under her skirt really my own? I located the waistband of the panties and tugged gently, freeing her firm flesh inch by inch. As I eased the tiny garment over her hips, she lifted her ass from the cushion so I could peel the narrow gusset from her cunt. It resisted slightly, unwilling to give up its place of honour, then suddenly sprang loose and I saw her whole cunt for the very first time – but only briefly, not long enough to fix its image in my memory. She pressed her legs together as I slid the panties all the way down to her ankles. I guided them over one formidable shoe, then the other, and held them in my hands like a nun with her rosary beads.

Jasmine was looking down at me, an expression of perverse amusement on her passionately drunk face. 'Now your dream has come true. You finally get to taste the real thing.' With that she drew the skirt up over her waist, parted her legs and showed me what she had in between them. It lay there lazily, a dark pink gash, crowned with a trim black triangle of bush – a pussy, just as she'd said. I was enthralled by the rude simplicity of it.

'Yes, it's real,' she said. She clasped her hands behind her head once more and let me go on staring. She offered her cunt to my unblinking eyes as if it meant nothing to her, displayed it with something close to boredom.

'Now it's time to earn your keep,' she said. 'Lick me.'

But she was full of drunken malice. I stretched forwards on my hands and knees, like a beast at a watering hole, only to feel the sole of her shoe suddenly press against my shoulder and abruptly stop my progress. She held me within licking distance of her smiling cunt and watched my mouth dribble from the scent in the air around it.

'I should make you beg a bit first, shouldn't I?' she said, and began to rock my passive body back and forth. 'What would you do to lick the pussy of the woman who owns you?'

'Anything, Mistress,' I moaned.

'What does anything mean, you dull little creep?' She dug her heel into my collarbone and brought me out of my trance. I'd forgotten how volatile she was after drink. 'Say a prayer,' she said. 'Say a prayer to this pussy you want so much.'

I began to mumble words in praise of her cunt.

'Do it properly. Put your hands together like you're in church.' She pushed me back up onto my knees.

I pressed my palms together and worshipped the glistening gash of my vain goddess. Still she was not satisfied.

'Say the Lord's Prayer. Only, say it to my pussy.'

I couldn't remember more than the first few lines of the damn thing. It was years since I'd chanted it in school assembly. Besides, the sight of her yawning cunt was hugely distracting. I could hardly get a sentence out. The cunt of a beautiful woman will turn your brain to jelly. And to think, Jasmine carried hers around in public hidden by only a thin layer of cotton and a tiny bouncing skirt . . . and often even less than that.

'You're useless. Only fit to whip. Sing a song instead. Sing a song to my pussy. This is the last chance you get.'

Gazing into her shameless orifice, I began to sing the only song I knew by heart, 'Hotel California' by The Eagles. She ground her heel deep into my chest and all but drowned my voice with her laughter. She made me repeat the chorus over and over again. I sang as reverently as I could, my body twisting at the end of her heel, trying to ignore the pain. ' . . . Such a lovely place . . . Such a lovely face . . .'

'Go on then, lickboy,' she said at last. She pulled her foot away and I fell forwards and buried my face in her almighty cunt. A wave of satisfaction swept over me as I licked wildly at the freshly shaven flesh and plunged my tongue in and out of her crack. I was a starving man and this, the feast of a lifetime. I sucked at her warm lips and slurped up her precious juice with an insatiable hunger. But she did not tolerate my barnyard manners for long. She gave me a minute to snuffle in her crotch, then grabbed me roughly by the hair and tilted back my head. I could feel her sticky juice going cold on my nose and chin and all around my lips.

'It's time you gave me some pleasure,' she said. 'That's why you're here.'

She slammed my face back into place and held it there. She was as selfish in her pursuit of sexual gratification as she was in everything else. A bitch from the cunt upwards. I worked like a slave to please her but she had expected to ride a hard cock that night and my tongue was a pitiful substitute. I lapped at her insatiable hole only to feel it spread and swallow my entire tongue. I wriggled it about inside her quite uselessly while she rolled her hips, grinding her hot crotch against my face.

I was exhausted and gasping for air but when I paused for a breath she seized me by the hair again and used my tongue as a dildo.

'Stretch it right out,' she ordered. 'Further ... further.' I held out my tongue at full stretch while she rubbed it over her clit and plunged it in and out of her crack. From the musky darkness between her thighs I could hear her moaning. Her movements became more aggressive. She was using the whole of my face for her pleasure now.

'I told you to keep your tongue out,' she snarled.

She yanked my head into a new position, suffocating me between her ass cheeks as she mounted my face, and there she set my tongue to work. I existed only for her pleasure, a piece of warm, slithering flesh extending up from the cushion into her insatiable hole. I was hopelessly outmatched and my aching tongue was soon begging her cunt for relief. If she'd had another slave on hand, she'd have cast me aside like a broken toy and ordered the other wretch down between her legs. She'd have gone through a whole line of us on the road to her orgasm, leaving us all sprawled at her feet, tongues bent and useless.

If she reached climax that night I can take no credit for it. I provided a length of stiff flesh, that was all. When her moment came she pushed me deep inside her and crushed my face between her thighs. I felt her spasm slightly and she let out a moan, a tired sigh of pleasure by her usual operatic standards. She held me captive a few moments longer and then opened her legs. I fell to the floor, limp, beaten and rejected like a spent cock. She sat on her leather throne, eyes closed, legs still spread and I gazed up at the proud, dribbling cunt I had just serviced.

When she opened her eyes the first thing she did was cross her legs and smooth the skirt over her thighs. Then she glared at me, eyes intense with loathing.

'What are you hanging around for, creep?' she snarled. She kicked me square in the mouth with the heavy sole of her sandal. The pain was blunt and numbing. 'Do you think I'm drunk enough to let you fuck me?'

'No, Mistress,' I said rubbing my cut lip. I backed away from her shoes. She was preparing to kick me again.

Her eyes fell on the bright white panties lying crumpled on the carpet between us. She shook her head solemnly.

'You don't get to eat my pussy so cheaply, you know.'

I continued to rub my mouth. I was desperate for another sight of that cunt. I'd forgotten what it looked like now she'd hidden it away.

'Get out of here, you're making me feel sick.'

I crawled back to the kitchen in the knowledge that my life at the mansion would never be the same again.

Twelve

'How would you like to crawl at my heels, creep?'

Jasmine took her revenge the following morning. She appeared in my room dressed in thigh-high stiletto boots and latex shorts and basque. Her hair was pulled back and tied in a tight bun and her make-up – violet eye shadow, heavy mascara, scarlet lipstick – gave her face a severity I had not seen before. Most frightening of all, however, was the knowing, sarcastic smile on her lips.

She gave me no time to wash or shave or even comb my hair and told me to change into an old pair of canvas trousers and ripped T-shirt which I kept for outdoor work. I was allowed no underwear. She nodded approvingly when I was dressed.

'Perfect, now you look like the penniless loser you are.' She walked to the edge of my bed and kicked a pair of dusty worn-down shoes across the floor. 'Put these on too.' I stepped quickly into the shoes and stood for inspection. She looked me over critically and I felt myself wilting under her gaze.

'We're going shopping,' she said. 'There are some things you need.'

The blood drained from my face.

'What's wrong? Afraid somebody might recognise you?'

I fell to my knees and begged her to spare me the ordeal.

'Worried about your reputation?' she laughed.

'Please, Mistress . . .'

'It's too late to beg. Just pray I don't dump you somewhere. I'm in the mood to do that.'

Ordering me to follow, she left my room and walked through the kitchen into the hall. Her sharp heels struck the wooden tiles neatly, sounding her regal contempt for the creature that crept behind her. What a sensation we would create in the bright, window-lined walkways of the mall: a corny icon of female domination taking her good-for-nothing slave on a shopping expedition. All eyes would be on us.

'Get my handbag,' she said as we approached the front door.

I ran upstairs to her bedroom and picked up a Chanel bag that was sitting on the dressing table. I prayed it was the right one. She was already waiting at the car, tapping her foot, when I caught up with her.

'You're too slow,' she said. 'That's another good reason for getting rid of you.'

I held open the door and breathed in her perfume as she brushed past me and settled herself on the back seat. Her latex-wrapped ass squeaked against the leather upholstery. It was a sound I had come to adore, music to my trained ears. Need I describe how my cock leapt as she crossed one long, luscious leg over the other?

'What are you waiting for, creep?' She snatched the bag from my hand and pulled the door closed.

She sat in silence for the whole journey and I studied her face in the driving mirror, trying to read her mood as she gazed out through the window lost in her own thoughts. Her eyes were dark and intense at moments, bright and mischievous at others, her ultra-red lips sensual and sneering. I tried to disown my own appalling reflection as it stared back at me. The kick from the night before had left my face badly bruised and my lips were still swollen and sore.

I found a parking place in a side road close to the mall. Casting anxious glances at passers-by, I got out of the car and hurried around to Jasmine's side. I held open the door and watched her climb out and stand in the middle of the narrow pavement, a vision of mouth-watering curves rising from oil-black boots. She had come out today to play the dark and dreadful dominatrix of obsessive fantasies and wore her outrageous costume with obvious amusement. She glowered theatrically at a young couple who stopped to stare at her. I fumbled some coins into the parking meter and she shoved her Chanel bag at me.

'Carry this,' she said, loud enough for the astonished young couple and other passers-by to hear. With that she turned on her heel and set off towards the mall in the next street. I shuffled along after her, clutching her handbag. My eyes were alert and my heart beat anxiously. She walked at a slow, even pace, one hand resting on her hip, the other swinging at her side. I almost tripped over my own two feet trying to stay the required distance behind her. Heads turned at the sound of her clicking heels and it seemed we were passing through a tunnel of gawping spectators.

We entered the mall and rode the long escalator up to the second floor. Jasmine stood three or four steps above me, her engrossing ass level with my face and tilted slightly to one side as she held the handrail. I was aware that several men had jumped onto the escalator after me and I tore my eyes away from the glorious view in front to glance over my shoulder. They were lined up just as I'd expected, and all staring upwards in the same direction. I wondered if these were mere opportunists, compelled to follow the most amazing ass they had ever seen – really, those hot pants made you gasp over and over again – or if, like me in times past, some had been loitering around the entrance, eyes peeled for pretty women in mini-skirts and short shorts. I could sense the intense frustration of the man directly behind me when I moved a little and obstructed his view. I looked over my shoulder again and saw him stretching his neck in all directions, searching frantically for a clear line of vision. On the verge of exasperation, he raked his fingers through his thinning hair. I took a step closer to Jasmine, to that ass we each craved, that ass which made clowns of us all.

The second floor was always the busiest. Located here were the same two dozen shops you find in every British city. Jasmine led me slowly around the quadrangle of show windows, pausing to look at some of the displays. She'd rather have walked naked than wear anything that bore a chain store label and made no secret of her scorn for what she saw. I, on the other hand, would have given my right arm to exchange my humiliating rags for a shirt and pair of slacks from Burton's. At window after window I stood at Jasmine's side, clutching the handbag and glowing with shame; she shook her head at the proffered merchandise, proudly indifferent to the staring eyes around us. It was all a big joke to her to be out in public dressed like a fetish queen, exciting all manner of desperate cravings.

'Everyone can see what you are,' she hissed meanly as we came to a halt before Topshop. This had once been one of my richest fishing grounds and to be dragged back here as a pitiful handbag-carrying male submissive was truly gut wrenching.

'Stay here . . . lickboy,' she ordered.

She left me standing near the entrance while she went inside and looked around. Teens dressed up in their teasing Saturday clothes passed in and out giving me a wide berth and pointing in disgust. Some of them were so pretty it took all of my willpower to keep my cock under control. The trousers I had on wouldn't have done a thing to hide the bulge, the urgent visibility of desire that is the male curse. I dared not look down at my crotch; if I'd started to leak into the front of my pants I didn't want to know about it.

There were benches in the middle of the walkway and when Jasmine reappeared she went over and sat down on one. A man on the facing bench, who was holding his young son on his knees, turned deep red as she winked at him and crossed her legs. I was foolish enough to try and sit down beside her.

'On your feet,' she snapped. 'And give me that.' She took her handbag from me and with the toe of her outstretched boot indicated where I should stand. 'That's more like it. Don't you dare forget your place again.'

I watched her open a pocket in the bag and pull out a penny. She rolled the tiny object back and forth between her thumb and forefinger, as if trying to make up her mind what do with it. A devilish grin appeared on her bright lips. In front of the blushing father and his son and a host of distracted shoppers, she leant forwards on the bench and sent the shiny copper coin rolling across the floor towards Topshop. It steered a curved course through the traffic of shoes and struck the panel of tiles beneath the window. It rebounded, staggered in a small circle and finally came to rest behind the heels of two oblivious young women.

'Fetch,' Jasmine ordered.

I forced myself to smile as I went to retrieve the coin. I knew this was just the beginning. There were no limits to the games she would play with me, no humiliation too great to pay for those few minutes I'd enjoyed down at her sublime cunt. Yes, I did consider walking away, escaping to freedom in my loser's clothes. But where could I be free of Jasmine's ass? It sat astride my whole world.

I was careful not to get too close to the girls. I crouched down an arm's length from their Nike sports shoes and gingerly stretched out my hand towards the penny. The taller of the girls sensed something and glanced down at her feet, and then at me. She alerted her friend and they walked away quickly, shaking their heads. I picked up the penny and brought it back to Jasmine.

'Clean it.'

I wiped the coin on my T-shirt and placed it on her palm. To my horror she rolled it straight back towards Topshop.

'This time crawl like a dog.'

I had the sense that I was falling, that everything around me was receding into the distance. I felt the irresistible pull of gravity.

'Didn't you hear me?' Her voice seemed to come from far away and from another time. 'Crawl over there like the dog you are and pick up that penny.'

I remember the delighted (and delightful) look on Jasmine's face as I sank slowly to my knees. She was showing a crowd of strangers just how low my desire for her could bring me. As I have said, it was all a game to her, but the very guts of my being were on display as I played her obedient dog in front of a hundred strangers.

It must be quite uncanny to observe a grown man scampering on all fours across a busy shopping mall and people stopped in their tracks or jumped back to let me pass. I was aware of a blur of voices above me as I entered an arena of legs and feet and scraped up the coin. Finding myself suddenly surrounded, I panicked and lost my bearings until I spotted Jasmine's shiny black boots in the distance. I crawled all the way back without taking my eyes off them.

She was no longer interested in the coin.

'Get into position. I want something to rest my feet on.'

I got back down on all fours and arched my body for her. I felt her boots land heavily on my spine.

'Higher,' she ordered. 'Higher . . . That's better. Now don't move.'

She used me as her footrest while she took a mirror from her handbag and checked her make-up. She pulled out a pencil and touched up her scarlet lips. I let my head hang with the shame of it all. Then she decided to clean her boots.

'Hold still,' she said, and began to drag the soles roughly over my back, determined to remove every speck of dirt. She jabbed me with the spiked heels. 'Hold still, I said.' She wiped the toe of each boot on the belly of my T-shirt and held one, then the other up for inspection. 'Nope,' she decided, 'still not shiny enough. You'd better get to work with that tongue of yours.'

She sat with legs crossed and without a hint of self-consciousness let me polish her fabulous boots with my tongue. We had attracted a fair-sized crowd by now and as I sank deeper into degradation, I had the bitter conviction that the men and women pressing around me were essentially no different from the peasants who in times past assembled at the village stocks to pelt a neighbour with rotten fruit and animal excrement. Lying on my belly in that modern-

170

day village square and licking the dirt from the soles of Jasmine's gleaming boots, I was part of something primordial, something too strong to resist, too deep to comprehend.

Jasmine played the dominatrix to perfection. She cut a redoubtable figure, a dark and sexy Venus effortlessly controlling her infatuated slave. Yet she was laughing like a schoolgirl behind the hypnotic image she projected. She rose to her feet and told me to lick higher up her boots. She turned around so I could worship the back of each. I trailed my tongue up and down the long leather shafts, my eyes gazing upwards exploring the landscape of her ass.

'Kiss it, creep,' she said suddenly. 'Kiss my ass.'

I did so eagerly, gratefully, and as I pressed my lips against a firm round cheek, wrapped in its cool black skin, I could feel my own electric excitement spread through the gasping crowd. A few kisses and she walked away, displaying the damp traces of my servile lips like trophies on her rolling cheeks. The crowd parted like the Red Sea to let her through.

I followed Jasmine and I was not alone. My glorious Mistress had acquired a ragged entourage. Men, shadowy and nervous like those on the escalator, were cautiously trailing her, slipping from one shop entrance to the next and when necessary pretending to be absorbed in window displays. I stuck five paces behind her magnetic ass, clutching her handbag and sweating heavily. A damp stain was spreading under each arm of the T-shirt. My cock was hard and dribbling molten lust into my trousers. I was glad I had the handbag and could hide the evidence of my arousal.

Jasmine led me around to the other side of the mall. We came to the corner where the women's toilets were located and here she stopped. She pointed to a nearby bench and ordered me to wait for her there.

'Don't you dare move from this seat. Is that clear, creep?' She lifted her handbag from my limp fingers and strutted over to a department store, swinging her ass as if all the world belonged to her.

Once she disappeared from view I was assailed by oppressive thoughts. It seemed that half the city had watched me crawl after that penny and then lie on my belly and lick Jasmine's boots. I shifted around uneasily on the bench, my flesh revolting against the ragged clothes I was forced to wear. I was sick with worry that a friend or relative would come strolling along in my direction. Women on their way in and out of the toilets shot cold glances at me and I nodded back politely, desperate to convince them that I was not a degenerate, whatever my appearance might suggest. Cautiously, I raised a finger to my mouth; the bruises still stung and my lips remained swollen.

Time passed slowly. I tried to keep my eyes averted, but some of the women who passed by to answer the call of nature were so pretty that my cock started to get hard again. I crossed my legs tightly, wishing to God I still had the Chanel bag.

I soon became aware of a man in a navy-blue uniform standing several benches away. He made it very plain he had stopped there to observe me and kept on staring while he spoke into his walkie-talkie. Trying to appear calm – I had, after all, done nothing illegal – I waited for him to come over. Instead, he turned and walked away. I breathed a long sigh of relief as I watched him disappear into the crowd.

But he was not finished with me yet. I looked down the walkway again only to see him steering a path towards me. This time he had a colleague with him, a thick-necked thug who had no business wearing any kind of uniform. They marched over in a no-nonsense fashion and positioned themselves between the toilet entrance and me, as if they were protecting the privacy of the women inside. The gentler looking of the two spoke first. He had a strong local accent.

'Sir, I'll have to ask you to move from this bench.'

'Why?' I asked, sounding perhaps a little too indignant for my own good.

'These benches are for the convenience of customers.'

'Give me five minutes,' I pleaded. It was an entirely reasonable request I thought.

'As I've just explained, this bench is for the convenience of customers. You'll have to move.' His intransigence incensed me and so did the odious phrase about convenience and customers. Where had a man like him picked up such language?

'There is absolutely no law that prevents me from sitting here and you both know that.' I sounded more confident than I felt. The men glanced at one another; then it was the thug's turn to jump in.

'You're not very smart are you? You must be new at this dirty game. Now move or I'll have you run in for loitering with intent.'

'You've got it all wrong.' I was starting to shake. The thug screwed up his face and spoke into his walkie-talkie. He was giving the control centre instructions to put a call through to the police.

'Do yourself a favour, pal,' the other advised. 'Just fuck off somewhere else.'

At that moment Jasmine sauntered over. All three of us caught sight of her at the same time. The thug slowly brought his arm down to his side, ignoring the female voice bleating from the walkie-talkie. The pair of them licked their dry lips as the most gorgeous and

173

provocatively dressed woman they'd ever seen came and stood before them.

'Is he being a nuisance?' she asked sweetly. She placed her hands on her hips and let her body work its magic on them. 'I only left him for a few minutes.'

The security guards looked at one another and then back at Jasmine, as if all the answers lay in her dizzying cleavage and the creased latex that snuggled between her thighs. The voice on the walkie-talkie was shouting: 'Hello? Hello? Hello?'

With the eyes of the guards glued to her body, Jasmine spoke to me. 'Have you been sitting here ogling women's asses again, Creepy Crawley?'

I stared down at my dusty old shoes. Would this nightmare never end?

'Well?' She stamped her boot impatiently. 'I'm waiting for an answer.'

'Yes,' I said. I forced the word from my mouth, hoping that an immediate admission of guilt would satisfy her and put an end to this excruciating ordeal. She stepped forwards and gave me a fierce slap across the face.

'Yes, Mistress,' I cried.

'That's more like it.'

Jasmine was running the whole show; the guards had been reduced to a pair of supporting actors without lines.

'He's completely harmless really,' she said to them, as if discussing a troublesome pet. 'But sadly he's a slave to a sexy ass.' She gave me my cue. 'Isn't that right?'

'Yes, Mistress.'

'I want you to look at these two men and make a confession. Tell them what a pervert you are and what you were doing here, outside the women's toilets. And don't even think about lying to them.'

'I'm a slave to a sexy ass,' I said slowly, trying to focus my gaze beyond the chubby, incredulous faces of the guards. 'I was sitting here, on this bench, staring at the women on their way in and out of the toilets.' I felt distant from my own words, a complete stranger to the degraded figure sitting on the bench.

Jasmine was relishing every second of my humiliation. 'He really can't help himself,' she told the guards. 'If you ever catch him skulking around this mall, you can be sure he's got nothing but dirty intentions. But you needn't worry about him today. I'll keep him on a tight leash.' She squeezed my cheek possessively and dropped her handbag into my lap. 'He does have some uses, you know? Come on, creep. Up on your feet.' She led me away and the guards watched us go without a murmur. It would take their tiny minds a lifetime to comprehend what they had just witnessed.

Jasmine wanted to eat lunch and took me to a Mexican restaurant up on the third floor. It was a cosy place, atmospherically dark, and I could detect the soft strains of Latin guitar as we drew near. Dressed in my rags, I didn't feel at all confident about following Jasmine as she breezed inside, and sure enough a feisty young waitress blocked my path. I was ready to turn around and leave but Jasmine whispered something in the girl's ear. The result was a solemn nod and permission to proceed. The waitress showed us to a corner table and then brought over a basket of tortillas and a salsa dip as an appetiser.

'Thank the lady,' Jasmine said.

'Thank you,' I said dryly.

The waitress went away and Jasmine instructed me on how to behave.

'Just sit there. Don't move. And keep your mouth

shut.' Nibbling tortillas, she browsed through the menu.

When the waitress returned she ordered for us both.

'I'll have the taco salad and a glass of wine. Bring him some tap water and don't worry about putting in any ice.'

I watched hungrily as Jasmine's colourful lunch arrived. It smelt delicious. My water came without ice and without a single word from the plainly disgusted waitress. But these details did not matter to me. I was parched and reached for the drink immediately.

'How dare you touch that glass without my permission,' Jasmine snapped.

I slowly withdrew my hand.

'And keep your head down. Your ugly face will put me off my food.'

I stared at my place mat while Jasmine ate and sipped her wine. The sound of her crunching the crisp lettuce was giving me a huge thirst. I still had the bitter taste of her boot soles on my tongue.

She kicked me under the table. 'Do you need a drink, you disgusting animal?'

'Please, Mistress,' I mumbled between dry, swollen lips. Without a thought about who was watching us, she poured a stream of salt into my glass and stirred the water with her greasy fork.

'There, now drink. Drink all of it.'

I watched a strand of grated cheese spiralling through the cloudy liquid. Jasmine kicked me under the table again, even harder this time.

'Didn't you hear what I just said?'

I picked up the glass and brought it to my lips, wincing at the sting of the salt. Jasmine was smiling cruelly. I forced myself to swallow a mouthful of the disgusting brew and almost vomited.

Suddenly she snatched the glass from my hand. 'You've got a nerve to drink at the same table as me!' She poured some water into the half-empty bowl of salsa. 'There, now put it down on the floor.' She pointed to a spot with her boot.

I took the bowl and placed it on the floor where she indicated.

'Now get down on your hands and knees and lap it up like the dog you are.'

I did. I crouched at her feet and lowered my head towards the bowl. But no matter how much I tried, I could not bring myself to drink the orange soup she had made for me.

'If you don't drink it from the bowl, I'll make you lick it off the floor.' Her voice was calm, despite the people staring at us from the other tables. She casually nudged the bowl with her toe, slopping some of the contents over the side. I put my face in the bowl at once and began to lap up the foul liquid. I was relieved to see Jasmine place her boot back beside her chair.

After I'd drunk a few mouthfuls, a pair of feet in low-heeled black sandals appeared before me. Purple toenails ... recently painted. The incensed voice of the waitress broke my contemplation.

'Get out right now or I'll call the police.'

I lifted my head from the bowl and saw her glaring down at me with all the loathing her healthy face could express. Jasmine was sipping her wine, utterly composed. She took the glass away from her lips and spoke.

'Didn't you hear the lady? You're making a disgrace of yourself. Go and wait outside until I'm ready to deal with you.' She returned to eating her salad, ignoring me entirely.

I climbed to my feet and reached for a napkin to wipe my mouth.

'No,' the waitress barked. 'Don't touch anything. Just get out.' She was rubbing her bare arms in agitation as if the very sight of me gave her a rash. Keeping her distance, she escorted me all the way to the door. I saw grinning peasant faces looking up from every table I passed.

'Men like you shouldn't be allowed in public,' she said as I stepped outside. For a second her eyes fell on the damp patch around my crotch. 'You should be locked up.'

I paced around in front of the restaurant like a hunted animal. I was afraid to stay in the same spot for more than a moment in case I was picked up for loitering. Whichever way I looked I saw security cameras watching me, waiting for me to make a single mistake, reveal my nature. I walked past some of the designer stores but kept my eyes down and away from the elegant women who shopped there. It was no longer embarrassment or humiliation I felt but a chilling fear I might be arrested at any moment. I began to believe this was Jasmine's intention. Nothing would satisfy her more than to see me dragged away by the police and locked behind bars still dreaming about her ass. I kept glancing at the restaurant door, willing her to come and rescue me from this living hell.

Eventually she appeared.

'Still here?' she laughed. 'This is getting too easy. It's hardly fun any more.'

I chased after her clicking heels, dreading the implications of what she'd said. I could tell from her walk that she didn't care whether I was following or not; yet I'd have crawled across red-hot coals to keep her ass in sight. The Chanel bag swung from her shoulder and bounced against her hip as her buttocks swayed. Tucked between those proud, latex-stiffened cheeks was that maddening cunt of hers, the cause of all my suffering.

I scarcely paid attention to where she was going. We made our way down the escalators to the ground floor, and the next thing I realised I was following her into a pet shop. She walked along an aisle towards a young assistant in a white apron.

'I need a collar and leash,' she said.

The assistant took us over to where an array of collars and leashes were displayed on the wall. 'What kind of dog do you have?' she asked.

'This kind.' Jasmine snapped her fingers and I trundled forwards and stood at her side.

The young woman eyed me suspiciously but there was also a spark of mischief in her gaze. 'Leather or chain?' she asked, turning to Jasmine.

'Leather collar and chain leash.'

The assistant selected the items.

'Would you mind tying the collar around his neck to see if it fits?'

The assistant was not shocked by the scandalous request and opened the heavy studded collar with her pale fingers.

'Lower your head, stupid,' Jasmine snapped. I brought my neck towards the open collar and felt my balls recoil with shame as the girl fastened the cold leather around my throat.

'It might be slightly tight,' she said to Jasmine. The little minx had a stud in her tongue! I could see it clearly when she spoke.

'No, it's perfect. I'll take it.'

'Do you need anything else for your *dog*, Madam?' The assistant had adopted a disturbingly familiar tone. 'A rubber bone or some chocolate treats maybe?'

'No,' said Jasmine winking. 'He doesn't deserve any.'

We paid for the merchandise at the till (I was still wearing the collar) and left the shop.

She began to rattle the leash as soon as we were outside.

'Come here,' she said and attached it to the collar. 'Now everybody can see that you're no more than a dog.' She turned seductively and swung the leash over her shoulder. She tugged hard, causing me to choke. 'I should make you crawl behind me but you'd never be able to keep up.' She dragged me through the mall on the end of a chain, showing everybody that I was her dog.

She found a vacant bench not far from the entranceway and sat down, crossing one leg over the other as before. She held the grip of the leash against the seat, forcing me to stand before her with my head and shoulders bowed. She smiled at onlookers as I struggled to breathe in the tight collar.

'You need a nametag,' she decided after a minute or so. 'All dogs have a nametag.' She let me off the leash and sent me running to W. H. Smith to buy card, red ribbon and a marker pen.

'On your knees,' she ordered when I got back.

Tapping the pen lightly against her chin she thought for a while. Her dark eyes suddenly sparkled and, taking a piece of card, she wrote in thick black letters: CREEPY CRAWLEY. After a moment's further reflection, she added, SLAVE TO A PRETTY ASS. She was delighted with herself. She made me thread a length of ribbon through the top corners of the card and then she tied the card to the back of the collar so that it dangled between my shoulder blades. Happy with her work, she put me back on the leash. As she stood up she knocked her powerful thigh against my face just for fun.

'Walkies,' she giggled for the benefit of all those gathered around. I staggered to my feet as she pulled the leash, my cock growing hard against my will, against all reason, making a tent in the front of my trousers. People stood and watched us, dumb with amazement and shaking their heads in disbelief.

Jasmine paraded me slowly towards the exit, pausing to look at window displays and tugging the leash hard when she was ready to move on. In the row of windows I saw our reflection – a glorious bitch walking her aroused man-animal.

'How would you like to crawl at my heels, creep?' she teased at intervals. 'Or should I make you bark for them all?'

We came out of the mall and she dragged me through the street to the car, as if I were a piece of merchandise she'd purchased.

'Give me the keys,' she ordered when we reached the Mercedes. She snatched them from my palm, opened the driver's door and settled herself behind the wheel. She started the engine. 'You can walk back.'

I wondered how she'd work the pedals with those impossible boots.

'And don't you dare take off that collar and leash or the nametag.'

She pulled the door closed and I watched her drive away.

I set off on the long walk home. I kept my doggie things on every step of the way, just as she'd instructed. I'll admit that I was glad to be wearing the nametag despite the awful truth it revealed about me. It was a token of her recognition. I still had a place in her world.

Thirteen

'I told you, all men are dogs.'

The next morning, while she was eating breakfast, Jasmine glanced towards the corner of the room where I was kneeling with my hands over my pouch. She shook her head in disgust and said: 'Go and put some clothes on before my guest arrives.'

I took my shameful body off to my room and began to make myself presentable for the visitor. I scrubbed my neck and shoulders at the laundry sink, put on my best shirt and a pair of slacks, and then forced myself to look in the mirror while I attempted to tidy my lank and lifeless hair. The side of my mouth was still bruised and I had dark rings around my eyes which gave my gaze a sinister aspect. I stopped moving the comb and stared hard at my sallow reflection. It was not my own face that peered back at me but that of a ghoulish bogeyman from which children would run in terror. Yet truly I could not disown this face: it belonged to me just as my shameful desires belonged to me. My inner nature was making itself manifest, seeping outwards and infecting my physical features.

The voice of Jasmine calling from the hallway interrupted this anguished confrontation with the

Crawley within me and I scurried to my Mistress on hands and knees.

She stood at the foot of the stairs in a shaft of sunlight wearing a neon-pink halter-top and a matching miniskirt. Each item of clothing had one simple and enviable function: to cling jealously to the enticing curves of her body and excite the imagination. She tossed her hair exuberantly, but a glint in her eyes reminded me of my place and I lowered my gaze as I crawled across the tiled floor, heart pounding. Only her feet were in view as I drew closer, profoundly arched in open-toed leopard skin mules which had sharp, black, impudent heels. Her toenails glistened like talons dipped in fresh blood.

'My guest is here,' she said. 'I want to see the expression on your face when she comes in.' The bell rang and she stepped towards the door herself. She was enormously excited and looked at me over her shoulder, grinning, as she admitted the visitor.

How can I describe the horror which filled me as I watched my former assistant step into the hall?

'Kim!' I cried out in disbelief.

'No, not "Kim". Not any more,' said Jasmine, relishing every moment of my despair. She kissed Kim lightly on the cheek. 'What do you want him to call you?'

'Ms Lexington will be fine,' said Kim somewhat hesitantly, still not sure about the role she was supposed to play.

'Did you hear that, creep? If you forget her name, Ms Lexington has my permission to slap you as hard as she likes.'

'Yes, Mistress,' I replied, unable to take my eyes off Kim, who in turn was fascinated by the spectacle of her former boss, down on his knees, reduced to the status of a lingerie model's houseboy. She too had changed in the months that had passed, though she still had that shrewd, calculating look in her eyes. She seemed taller than I remembered and carried herself with an attractive confidence. Dressed sassily in a glittery T-shirt, denim cut-offs and a pair of black platform sandals, her toenails painted a light shade of blue, she resembled more closely one of Jasmine's teasing friends than the mousy girl who used to hide her figure beneath baggy cardigans and long spinster-skirts. My cock would have jumped to salute her were it not already raised in honour of Jasmine's barely covered ass.

Jasmine showed Kim to the lounge and I was instructed to crawl at their heels, which scuffed the tiles I'd polished earlier that morning. Kim glanced down at me, anxious I was getting too close and that she might kick me. Or maybe she sensed I was staring up longingly at her neat little bottom, that only now, in my bondage, was I allowed to see.

'Don't worry,' Jasmine reassured her, 'you'll soon forget he's there altogether.'

They settled on a couch and Jasmine sent me to fetch drinks for them. Kim accepted the cocktail I mixed for her without a trace of gratitude on her prettily made-up face, no doubt remembering all the times she'd brought coffee to my desk. When they had their drinks and snacks in front of them Jasmine told me to remove her mules and used my back as a footrest, inviting Kim to do the same. Mercifully my former assistant declined and kept her feet on the floor a cautious distance away from me.

Sipping their drinks the women chatted about work, about clothes and about men, while I crouched on the floor before them, disregarded and forgotten. Jasmine was quite restless and kept sliding her feet around on my back and neck; at one point she

184

pushed her naked toes against my ear and rocked my head back and forth without even realising it. She was quite careless about the way she let the skirt ride up her thighs and my thoughts were absorbed by the casual obscenity of her pose.

'I thought we'd go to the park,' I suddenly heard Jasmine say to Kim. 'We can have some fun with him there. What do you think?'

Kim was enthusiastic about the idea. 'He likes the park,' she said tipsily. 'Everyone knows he used to go there to spy on girls.'

I was astonished by that revelation.

'That settles it then.' Jasmine lifted her feet off my back and held them out, one at a time, while I carefully slipped the showy mules over her pointed toes. I did not dare look up at either of the women, though I could feel them both watching me closely. 'I should have got you to lick the insides clean while you were down there,' Jasmine remarked as she wriggled her foot about on its smooth vinyl platform and flexed the toes against the leopard skin strap. 'Never mind. Put on your collar and go and wait by the car.'

I waited in the garage, collar around my neck, and they came out much later, swaying their hips and giggling over a joke they'd just shared. As they approached, Jasmine began to twirl the leash in her hand, bringing the vicious chain closer and closer to my face until I was forced to jump away from the car.

'Get in the back, creep,' she said with sudden savageness, which may have been real or pretend, I could not tell.

I did as I was told.

'No, not on the seat. Get down on the floor. That's where dogs go.' She struck me hard across the shoulder with the leash as I scrambled off the seat.

'That's more like it.' She tossed the leash on top of me and slammed the door. The two women took their places up front and pushed back their seats until they were quite comfortable. 'Who needs a chauffeur?' Jasmine joked to Kim. 'I love driving this car.'

'It's to die for,' said Kim.

I heard a clatter as Jasmine kicked off the mules. She adjusted the seat again and started the engine. She asked Kim to put on the radio.

The park we were going to was at the other side of the city and Jasmine made the journey even longer by taking Kim on a tour of her neighbourhood and pointing out the properties of her celebrity friends. Squeezed into the cramped foot space behind their seats, I listened to snatches of their carefree conversation and the latest offerings from the pop charts. The smell of their perfume gave the air in the car a sweet, choking quality.

Jasmine found a place in the very car park I had so often used myself. She let me out of the car and told me to get the picnic mat from the boot. When I had done this she draped the leash around my neck and made me a promise.

'If you disobey me even once, I'll put this on and drag you around the lake on your hands and knees. Do you hear me?'

Kim was standing beside Jasmine and her face brightened at the idea of watching her former boss being walked like a dog in a public park. I'm sure her thighs were tingling in anticipation. My cock was starting to rise again and I wished I'd fucked the scrumptious Ms Lexington when she'd been plain old Kim; at least then I'd have known the shape and smell of her down there. I remembered my bumbling attempt to seduce her at Apollo and sorely regretted that lost opportunity.

The mean bitches didn't wait around for me. They set off across the grass in the direction of the boating lake, swinging their asses just as you'd expect, stirring cocks in a hundred-yard radius. A game of football was temporarily abandoned as the players whistled and watched them go by. I plodded after the gay pair, mat tucked under my arm, leash rattling around my neck, so obviously their sucker. I was in no mood to appreciate it but the afternoon was fine, not a solitary cloud tarnished the sky. The excited shouting of children and contented voices of parents echoed in the still, warm air.

Jasmine selected a spot on the side of a grass verge overlooking the lake. The area was popular with young people and I noticed, dotted about, several half-naked cuties soaking up the sun. Once upon a time I'd have been buzzing with excitement surveying such material, but now I found myself vainly wishing for a downpour that would send everybody running home, cuties and all. I unfolded the mat, laid it down on the grass and smoothed out the bumps; then I stood back. Jasmine and Kim sat down on it and kicked off their shoes. They leant back on their palms, lifted their faces towards the sun, stretched out their legs and wiggled their toes.

I squatted nearby and glanced anxiously at their bodies, scared of what they would see in my eyes if they caught me. I tried to be discreet but the temptation was too great. My gaze was drawn again and again to Jasmine's outstretched legs, which glistened beautifully in the sunlight. In the grip of a destructive craving, I began to manoeuvre myself into a position where I could look up her skirt. She soon realised what I was up to, however, and crossed her legs tightly and with genuine irritation. She gave me a withering yet gorgeous look.

'Get lost, creep! Go for a walk around the lake until I'm ready to do deal with you.' I stood up at once, ready to trot off before she decided on a worse punishment, but Kim spotted the bulge in my pants. Curses! Did nothing escape those sly green eyes of hers?

'You've turned him into an absolute animal,' she said, pointing with glee.

'I told you, all men are dogs. This one here, though, is a particularly horny breed. That's what makes him so easy to train. Isn't that right, Creepy?'

'Yes, Mistress,' I responded quickly. I backed down the slope, doing my best to hide the evidence of my arousal. I was in full view of a dozen onlookers.

'Wait,' said Jasmine. 'Stop where you are and put your hands behind your back.' I did so slowly and reluctantly, and glanced angrily at some nosey fools sitting on the grass beside me. My cock kept on growing in spite of everything.

'I'll show you just what a dog he is,' she said to Kim; and so saying she began to stroke her thigh. My eyes were riveted to the provocative caresses she gave herself. Slowly, she drew back her leg, raising her knee towards her chest, opening up the clinging skirt, inch by slow inch. Soon only the flesh of her inner thighs concealed her crotch.

'You know, Kim,' she said absently, as she brushed her fingertips over the silky flesh, 'I never wear panties with this outfit.' At these words, my eyes bore into the soft flesh wall, searching out her naked cunt. The sudden rush of blood to my cock made me dizzy. She had me ready to come in my pants. Another inch . . . Another . . . She was making me boil over with lust and all the while her face expressed nothing but contempt.

'There,' she said to Kim, lowering her leg and pulling the skirt straight, 'that's all it takes. He'll be stiff for the rest of the day.' Kim studied me without any sign of compassion. Her eyes rested on my provoked and humiliated manhood.

'He's worse than I ever imagined.'

'Oh this is nothing,' said Jasmine, starting to sound a little bored.

'I used to believe I could help him.'

'You're an angel, Kim, but you'll never change his nature. He's been waiting for this his whole sorry life.' She teased me with her eyes, daring me to contradict her. 'Isn't that right, Creepy Crawley?'

I nodded. My head felt light, insignificant compared to the weight in my groin.

'Now off you go. Walk around the lake, slowly, very slowly, and keep your hands behind your back.'

I did as I was told. I left the two smirking women and headed down towards the lake. I kept my hands clasped behind my back and ignored the sharp stares of those I passed. What a comical figure I must have cut shuffling along behind my rudely pointing fly.

I reached the lakeside and followed the path, walking past a café, toilets and a small pier where there were rowing boats for hire. Keeping a slow pace, I continued to the other side of the lake from where I could see Jasmine and Kim lying on the mat and chatting away like the best of friends. I was in a dreadful state of self-doubt. I had misread Kim's intentions all along, it seemed, and had never stood a chance with her. And just what had everybody at the company been saying about me all these years whenever my back was turned? My world, past and present, was collapsing around me.

At the far end of the lake the path led through a wooded area. I was grateful to be concealed and took the opportunity to adjust my cock so the bulge was less obvious. The idea that Jasmine had come out to the park in her tiny skirt without wearing any knickers was keeping me stiff, just as she'd predicted. I considered stepping behind a tree and beating off, but quickly gave up the idea as futile. I would start to get hard again the moment I zipped up my fly. I could never wank away my desire for Jasmine. I put my hands behind my back and walked on.

When I emerged from the trees and once more had a clear view of Jasmine and Kim, I saw they were no longer alone. Two guys about college age and wearing long shorts and athletic vests had approached them. I could scarcely believe they had the balls. The women were still reclining on the mat and a young jack squatted hopefully at the side of each. I kept praying Jasmine would shoo them away before I got back, but she appeared delighted by the attention and Kim was flirting outrageously. What kind of dogs did Jasmine consider these to be, I wondered? They weren't her usual studs, the rugged hunks, the big-cocked athletes. These were pretty boys, pooches who would yap excitedly at her feet.

I came slowly up the grass verge, hands behind my back, cock leading the way. With a satisfied smirk, Jasmine watched my approach.

'Look who it is,' she said, 'my horny lackey, Creepy Crawley.'

The two youths laughed nervously as an uncanny drama began to unfold before them.

'We've been waiting for you to come back,' Jasmine went on, and reached out a hand to stroke the knee of her fresh-faced admirer. 'Now you can trot over to the café and fetch ice creams for us all.' She invited Kim and the two pests to give me their orders. After much discussion they each decided what they wanted.

'Did you get that?' Jasmine asked.

'Yes, Mistress.'

'Well, off you go then. And make sure you wash your hands before you touch anything. We all know what you were doing over there in the trees.'

I walked away leaving behind the sound of their laughter. I obeyed Jasmine's instructions, scrubbed my hands in the gents, and hurried back balancing the ice creams. A terrible idea was beginning to take shape in my mind and I struggled to suppress it.

I distributed the ice creams and squatted at a distance while they ate. The two youths didn't give me a second thought; all their attention was devoted to the women who were licking at their strawberry cones with captivating self-indulgence. I studied the wide-eyed fool who was fawning over Jasmine, letting his own ice cream melt and dribble over his feminine hand. In any other circumstances I'd have taken him for a clean and wholesome kid, a bit of a sissy even. It really was impossible to believe that he'd approached a woman like Jasmine on his own initiative.

I could hold back the truth no longer. The afternoon felt suddenly chilly and a shadow seemed to fall across the park, as if rain clouds had seized control of the sky. Jasmine had summoned this pretty boy. She had summoned him to her just as once she had summoned me. There before me, young, handsome and innocent, was my new rival. It was hard to look at him and keep breathing at the same time.

I heard the voice of Jasmine, harsh but still enchanting. 'What's the matter with you, creep? You look as if you're about to faint. Are you hungry or something?'

'Yes, Mistress,' I replied, feeling enormous joy as she turned her attention from him to me.

'He's hungry,' she said to everybody. They could all hear the mischief in her voice and waited expectantly. 'Shall I give him some ice cream?' Before anybody replied she flicked a blob of pink ice cream onto the mat next to her leg. It began to melt immediately. 'There, that's for you,' she said flatly. 'Come and lick it up.'

'Yuck,' said Kim, turning up her pretty nose.

Jasmine's toy boy looked pale and seemed ready to throw up his hands in surrender. Things were going too far and he could not properly comprehend what was happening. He wanted me, Jasmine and Kim to roll on our backs laughing and tell him it was all a game, a big practical joke. I looked at his confused young face and felt vastly superior to him in knowledge and understanding. He was no rival at all. I crawled over to the mat, lowered my head and began to lap up the melting ice cream. My tongue dragged over the woven wool an inch from Jasmine's leg. I could feel her heat and smell the sweetness of her skin. Another blob of ice cream landed close to my nose.

'Eat that one as well.'

I lapped it up gratefully, showing Jasmine, the group, the whole park that no woman could hope for a more devoted dog. I heard Jasmine pick up the leash and rattle it above my head. 'I was going to walk him around the lake, but I'll only get sore feet in these shoes. I'd rather relax in a boat.' She made me crawl around the mat licking up more blobs of ice cream. Kim tut-tutted loudly as I followed Jasmine's feeding fingers, but the toy boys remained silent. I was shameless and would have gladly eaten ice cream from the grass if Jasmine had smeared some there.

When she decided I'd eaten enough she sent me to get a boat for them all. Once I had the boat ready they came down to the pier in a group. They climbed in and I took my place at the oars and rowed them around the lake.

'You're our personal galley slave,' said Jasmine who had her toy boy's arm around her slender waist. 'Take off your shirt.' They all gasped when they saw the welts and scars Jasmine had inflicted with the rod and I displayed these marks, her marks, with a new sense of pride. The toy boy had turned pale again and could not bring himself to look at me. He was no rival, even if he did have his arm wrapped around my Mistress.

I strained at the oars for a good half hour before pulling up at the pier again and running to fetch drinks for them all. As soon as I got back into the boat I rowed out onto the lake once more. I was fatigued; my shoulders and back were aching and my throat was sand dry. They sipped from their bottles of chilled Coke and watched me work. How often had I dreamt of rowing on this lake, showing off to envious guys one of the pretty women I used to see lying on the grass? What bitter irony! Here I was, my rod-marked body glistening with sweat, a human engine for a sexy model, my former assistant and their afternoon's catch.

Jasmine struck me with the leash if she judged I was rowing too slowly.

'You know the punishment for slacking,' she warned. 'He's just so scrawny,' she said to the others.

When the boat ride was over and we were on land again, I begged to be allowed to go to the toilets and drink some water.

'No,' Jasmine said sharply, 'we don't have time.' I staggered back to the mat, faint with exhaustion.

The afternoon was drawing to a close and the park was emptying. Jasmine and the others sat around and discussed where they should go for dinner. The toy boys saw me as only a minor inconvenience now and were becoming bolder and more suggestive, even pawing at the women's bodies. Jasmine slapped her puppy's face playfully, but hard enough to leave red finger marks behind. At length they set off across the grass back to the car laughing and joking like the young people they were. I folded the mat, picked up the leash and trotted after them.

'Ms Lexington wants you to clean her shoes,' was the first thing Jasmine said when I reached the car. I looked over at Kim who was sitting in the passenger seat with her legs dangling from the open door. Her admirer was standing proudly beside her and she had an insolent expression on her face, which I now realised had always been there, lurking behind her obliging professional demeanour. She was using my enslavement to Jasmine to enact her own personal vendetta and though raging inside I could not utter a single word of protest. She began to bob her feet impatiently. The soles of her sandals were caked in mud and grass, and I could feel the bile rising to the back of my throat as I walked slowly towards her.

'It's all right,' Jasmine said, 'you can use your shirt.' I was grateful for this small mercy; but, as I began to unfasten the buttons she spoke again, and for a dreadful moment I thought she'd changed her mind. 'No! Keep it on for God's sake. You'll make us all lose our appetites.'

I knelt on the ground in front of Kim and took one of her sandals in my hands. She had lost all her inhibitions now and was determined to enjoy humiliating her old boss. She leant back in the seat and let me support the full weight of her leg while I busied myself with my lowly task.

'This is for the time you tried to kiss me,' she said grimly.

Thinking only of pleasing Jasmine, I wiped all the

muck from her sandal and watched the front of my shirt turn black in the process.

'And this is because you like it,' she said, pushing her other dirty sandal into my hands. I ignored her taunt and the bitter look in her eyes, twisted around my shirt to an unsoiled section, and set to work once more.

'That will do,' was all she said when she was satisfied. She pulled both feet away from me as if I were now a source of contamination. I made to stand up but Jasmine was not finished with me yet.

'Stay where you are, my shoes are dirty, too.' She stepped over to where I was kneeling and proceeded to wipe the filth from her fancy mules all over my trousers.

'Is it all off?' she asked casually, holding one shoe slightly above the ground. I lowered my head until I could see the underside of the sole.

'Yes, Mistress.'

She dragged her shoe roughly over my cheek to make sure.

'Yes, I guess it is . . . now.'

She checked the other shoe in the same manner and then pressed my face down into the gravel.

'How about you guys?' she asked, pinning me there. 'Did you step in anything nasty walking across the grass?' She pressed down harder on my head as she said 'step' and 'nasty'. To my relief the toy boys declined the invitation to clean their shoes on me. They sounded embarrassed by the suggestion. Even now, after all they'd witnessed, it was not easy for them to watch Jasmine abuse a man in such a crude and direct fashion. They shuffled about showing their discomfort, but this was the only stand they were prepared to take, as far as their commitment to masculine pride, or even basic human dignity, extended. They were being led by their excited young dicks and would let a fine bitch like Jasmine get away with murder if there was even the slightest chance of a fuck.

Jasmine took her foot off my face and let me get back up on my knees. She began to walk around the Mercedes.

'When did you last wash my car?'

'The day before yesterday, Mistress,' I answered, wiping pieces of gravel from my lips. The bodywork was gleaming; the car looked like new. Smeared from head to foot with mud and grass, I was the only thing in need of a wash. All the same, she paused to run a finger over the bonnet, checking for any trace of dust.

'Not bad,' she conceded. 'It seems you are good for one or two things. But, you know, these tyres do look a bit grimy. What do you think, Ms Lexington?' The two women exchanged a playful glance through the windscreen.

'Oh, yes,' Kim agreed suppressing a giggle, 'they're terribly dirty.'

Jasmine came back around the car and stood in front of me. She was glorious to behold in the late afternoon sun and I was in love with every particle of her deliciously tanned flesh. Yet I knew better than to expect any mercy from my omnipotent goddess. Her scarlet-crowned toes were an instant reminder of her cruelty, poking rudely beneath the leopard skin straps as if the animal had died just for them.

She pointed down at the tyre. 'Lick it clean,' she said. I crawled forwards and set to work at once, rasping my dry tongue over the warm, bitter-tasting rubber. My only thought was to win her contempt, to show her that no man on this earth was prepared to sink as low as I for the privilege of being her slave, her dog, her doormat or whatever else she required.

She stood behind me with her hands on her hips and supervised my work, watched me as I struggled to cover the side of the tyre with my scarce supply of saliva.

'Now get the grit out of the tread.'

'Yes, Mistress.'

She left me to work my tongue into the tight grooves while she spoke to Kim. After some time she asked: 'Does the tyre look clean to you?'

'It'll do,' said Kim without even bothering to check.

'Follow me,' said Jasmine. She walked around to the driver's side, crunching the gravel beneath her shoes, and I crawled after her like a beast, gazing up at that ass which so effortlessly enslaved me.

'Now clean this tyre.'

Once more I set to work licking the filthy rubber, as if this were my supreme purpose in life. I had long ceased to care that I was disgusting the two toy boys and terrifying unsuspecting families who were returning to their cars after a day of wholesome fun at the park. I saw a mother shield her child's eyes as they passed by. It would have been more acceptable if I'd been holding my cock and taking a piss. The need to piss is a natural urge after all. But this show of absolute devotion to a gorgeous woman, this love that had no name, the world could not bear to witness.

Jasmine soon grew bored of watching me and climbed into the driver's seat and closed the door. She wound down the window and in her rich, seductive voice invited the two puppies to come along for a ride. They jumped into the back seat as if it were the last place available on a shuttle to paradise. My eyes filled with tears as I continued diligently to lick the dirt from the tyre. I had never felt such hopelessness, such absolute despair. The moment I'd dreaded had finally arrived – Jasmine was about to dispose of me, drop me back into the hole from which I'd briefly emerged. She fastened her seat belt and kicked off her mules ready to drive away forever. She started the engine and I heard her speak to Kim.

'I should have got him to lick these pedals clean . . . and my foot mat, too.'

How I longed for the chance to clean those places that came into contact with her bare soles, for one final opportunity to show all my grovelling devotion. But it had been merely a passing thought for her, nothing more. Without warning she rolled the car forwards over the gravel, crushing one of my hands. I yelped out in pain and fell on my backside. Jasmine poked her head through the window and laughed.

'Did I say you could stop?'

'No, Mistress.'

'Well get up and clean the back tyres now, you useless object.'

She didn't stop the car. She drove just slowly enough for me to crawl after her like the desperate dog I was. I cut my hands and knees trying to keep up and the revolving tyres shot gravel into my face whenever I got close enough to touch one of them with my tongue. She made me crawl behind the car for the whole length of the car park. She honked on the horn to make sure nobody missed the grotesque sight of a mud-smeared maniac chasing after the tyres of her dazzling Mercedes. Then she accelerated and left me kneeling on the ground, panting breathlessly.

Fourteen

*'All I have to do is snap my fingers and he'll
crawl to my feet and die for me.'*

There was no question in my mind about what I
should do. I soberly gathered up the picnic mat and
leash and set off back to the house at a quick pace. I
arrived late in the evening to find the place dark and
deserted. Once inside my room I stripped off the filthy
shirt and pants and collapsed on the bed. There I lay
wondering at my fate until I passed out, exhausted by
the day's events.

I awoke late the next morning to howls of feminine
laughter and the clatter of high heels in the hall.
Excitement had never sounded so alien or felt so
brutal and I pulled the pillow over my ears in an
attempt to blot out the hysteria that seemed to be
rising all around me. The voices became dull and
blurred but I could still hear Jasmine, louder and
more punishing than all her friends. I waited for the
door of my room to fly open and reveal her menacing
form. Then, all at once, there was silence.

Much later I ventured out of my room and walked
around the empty house. Nothing had changed.
Everything was as it should be. It was I who did not
belong here any more. I wandered from room to

room, trailing my fingers over the furniture, touching familiar objects, picking up ornaments, wanting to regain my former sense of belonging. Then, unable to contain the urge any longer, I dropped the cushion I was holding and bounded upstairs to Jasmine's room.

Heart pounding, I inhaled the rich womanly scent of the place and let my eyes feast. The bed was unmade, the pink satin sheets turned back in a graceful diagonal. I pictured Jasmine sweeping them from her sleep-warmed body and rising naked, along with her hundred reflections, to meet the new day. A damp towel lay on the carpet before the bathroom door and draped over the back of a chair were the pink skirt and top from the day before. I inspected them and found no sign of any panties. The leopard skin mules were in front of one of the mirrors, the right shoe lying on its side, dusty sole exposed. The disarray delighted me, gave me reason to hope, and I set to work putting the room in order. When I'd finished, I went for the laundry basket. I carried it to the bed, emptied out the contents and rolled myself in the scent of my Mistress.

In the thick of this indulgence the phone in the hall began to ring. I ignored it at first but it would not stop, so cursing I let go of my cock and went downstairs to deal with the caller. I picked up the receiver and, to my horror, found myself talking to the young fool from the park. In a nervous voice he asked to speak to Ms Del Ray and, when I did not respond, he repeated his request more forcefully. Pulling myself together, I explained that Jasmine was not at home and wrote down the message he dictated, just as a faithful drudge should. I hung up and pinned the message on the board above the phone, on top of all the other long-forgotten requests. What a pitiful mosaic those curling slips of paper made. A sadder testament to male desire you could not imagine.

He called again later that afternoon and twice in the evening. More questions. More messages. He simply refused to believe me when I told him I had no idea where Jasmine had gone or when she'd return. What games had she played with his excitable puppy prick, I wondered? A bit of dirty talk on the way to the restaurant, a little footsy while they ate, a thigh between his thighs at a nightclub. His young world would be reduced to the circumference of her ass by now.

I was not surprised to have him on the phone early the next morning and to hear from him at regular intervals until late at night. It went on like this day after day and when he suddenly erupted in a flurry of unforgivable insults, I had a hard job controlling my own temper. But I reminded myself that the lad was behaving just the way I once had. In his mind I was the same detestable figure that Jasmine's old drudge had been to me.

Jasmine returned after eight days, suddenly and without warning. I can still see her walking across the hall towards me, legs deeply tanned, feet in fashion clogs, a slip of a dress swirling around her hips. There was a rush of sweet air as she approached, the scent of the tropics and her body's own unmistakable perfume.

'Get my bags,' she said.

I fetched the suitcases from the car and dragged them up the stairs to her bedroom. My head was spinning with the exotic scent that now filled the house making it her territory once more. I found her sitting at the dressing table, gazing into the mirror. She was utterly absorbed in her own reflection – in love with the self-love she saw in her own eyes. I put down the cases and stood watching, captivated by this spectacle of endlessly rebounding narcissism. The beautiful eyes in the mirror focused on me for the briefest instant, detecting a flaw in an otherwise perfect universe.

'Get out of my sight,' she said.

I avoided her during the long days that followed. I crept around the house full of dread and darted like a roach at the sound of her approaching heels. For the most part I hid in my room, coming out to do my chores only late at night or when she was not at home. She had taken to locking her bedroom whenever she left the house, and in desperation I'd stand outside and rattle the handle. Then, feeling utterly desolate, I'd lie down on my belly and press my nose into the half-centimetre gap beneath the door. A whole week passed before she spoke to me again.

'I'm having a party this evening. Make sure everything is ready.'

I did as instructed while she prepared herself for her guests. She began with a leisurely bath and I did not see her again until evening, when she descended the stairs wearing a black evening dress with a high slit up one side, sheer stockings and a pair of steel-tipped Gucci stilettos. These shoes, the pride of her collection and a gift from the designer himself, captured my gaze. She'd worn them just once before, when she'd attended an awards ceremony as the guest of a distinguished actor. A picture of her arriving at the venue had appeared in all the Sunday colour supplements. The photographer had caught her in the act of swinging her legs out of a limousine and the attention-grabbing Gucci shoes were suspended above a red carpet, the silver heels sparkling in the flashlights of the surging paparazzi. I lowered my head as the shoes reached the bottom of the stairs and resumed buffing the tiles around the front door. I waited for an order, a word of reproach, even an insult – my soul cried out for it. But she stepped past me as if I were invisible and walked to the lounge, her long heels reflecting in the freshly polished floor tiles.

Jasmine's guests soon began to arrive and I opened the front door to a succession of young women dressed in fiendishly sexy outfits. Each one carried herself across the hall with a sluttish swagger, aware of her body's enormous value in this world. I shrank before them all, even the shyest, dragged down and rendered impotent by the awful cravings they excited in me. Some pointed to the floor and let me grovel like a worm at their shoes before proceeding to the lounge, where Jasmine planted a girlish kiss on their bright cheeks.

Some settled into sumptuous armchairs, crossed their legs and purred in contentment. Others kicked off their shoes and curled up on the couches. Dressed only in my pouch, I crawled around pushing a trolley of drinks and snacks, careful to avoid legs and feet and scattered shoes. Stopping before each woman, I lay prostrate while she made her selection and commented on the scars on my back and buttocks. Carefree voices floated in the air above me as I crawled from one pair of spoilt feet to another, hating my degradation but feeding off my proximity to these exalted beings.

Last to arrive was Jennifer, wearing a pale-blue dress and matching shoes. She always took place of honour among the guests and settled on the couch next to Jasmine. Side by side they were awesome to behold and my eyes ached as they darted back and forth trying to decide which woman was the more devastating in her archetypal beauty. Each was the queen of her kind, the pride of her race, and I was at a loss on whom to bestow the allegiance of my lust. I pushed the trolley across the room and fell on my belly at the feet of these two contrasting models of female perfection. I was glad of the chance to bury my nose in the carpet and free myself momentarily from the demands their bodies made of me. They sipped their drinks and left me to stare at their feet – I could see no higher than their ankles. Jennifer idly tapped the toe of her blue stiletto on the carpet just in front of me. The shoe was made of the softest leather and moulded itself to the contours of her foot, creasing like skin when she flexed her toe muscles.

'I want you completely naked,' Jasmine said to me suddenly.

I tried to wriggle out of the pouch, while lying belly-down at their feet.

'Get up and take it off, stupid! And stand in the middle of the room so everybody can see you.'

I rose to my feet and, crippled with shame, removed the pouch before a giggling audience. My cock betrayed me. It reared up at the women and they pointed and shrieked as it bobbed up and down, dribbling its disgraceful lust.

'Turn around and show everybody what a dog you are,' Jasmine ordered.

I turned around slowly, like an overwhelmed savage on an exhibition block at a fairground. My cock remained thrust forwards and upwards in a stiff salute to the assembled women. Jasmine then instructed me to walk to each of her guests in turn and allow them to inspect my treacherous appendage and amuse themselves with it if they chose. They were surprisingly timid at first and, squealing with embarrassment, recoiled from the throbbing male organ that was obediently presented to them. Naked male lust at such close quarters they found an absurd and revolting thing and it took a little encouragement from Jasmine to get things started. She assured her guests I was harmless.

'He's a complete slave,' she said. 'All I have to do is snap my fingers and he'll crawl to my feet and die for me.'

The bolder women reached out and gave my cock tentative flicks with their painted fingernails. Some of them pinched the skin around my balls, so viciously that my eyes began to water. I accepted their abuse without a murmur of protest and, encouraged by my passivity, the others soon joined in. They blushed and gasped at their own audacity, but couldn't resist the opportunity to molest a slave cock. Soon they were crowded around me prodding, pinching and squeezing, and they reached a state of near hysteria realising I stayed fully erect whatever they did. My lust-drunk cock was an unequivocal sign to them that I enjoyed pain and humiliation and they gave free rein to their vicious imaginations.

An auburn-haired delight, fresh out of finishing school, decided to up the ante. She removed her pretty hair slide, clipped it to my ball sac and slowly twisted the tender flesh, increasing the pain she inflicted with an engineer's precision. The vixen didn't take her eyes from my face and studied my contorted features like the proud inventor of a new machine.

Two Americans, both blonde and with eye-popping Californian tits, took over from her. One of them snapped off a length of dental floss and looped it around my shaft. Pulling hard so that it snagged beneath the head, she joked she'd caught a one-eyed snake in a noose. The other used her dental floss like a garrotte wire and was on the verge of decapitating the weeping reptile before it snapped. She quickly attached another length of floss, winding it tightly from the balls to the head, and they took turns walking me around the room, tugging on the biting cock-leash without mercy.

There was no respite, and the next thing I knew I was in the hands of a doll-pretty oriental girl who'd been licking her tiny bow-shaped lips in anticipation. She took a lighter from her handbag, ignited it and brought the flame swiftly towards my balls. The others fell silent as they watched this delicate creature calmly torture her victim and bring tears flooding from his eyes. The searing heat beneath my balls forced me up on tiptoe and I danced before her, groaning and pleading. The expression in her wide eyes was unchanging and unreadable and I sensed there was no limit to her cruelty. She would have roasted my balls like chestnuts if the smell of singed pubes hadn't finally turned her stomach. She cursed me in her own harsh language and pushed me away with a dainty foot.

She had inspired them all to greater wickedness and next a curvy number with copper-coloured ringlets had me crawl over to her chair and present my cock, which, though brutalised, remained swollen with lust. The minx lit a candle and boasted she could make me come merely by dripping hot wax over my shaft and balls and telling me what a dumb animal I was. How knowing and confident she sounded! And how bountiful in her wish to humiliate me! There was nothing I desired more than to empty my throbbing balls, even if this would mean acknowledging the fullness of my contemptible craving and the relief only temporary. My eyes pleaded for her cruel indulgence as she rolled the candle between her teasing fingers and gazed smugly around the room. But none of the other women was prepared to take up her challenge. They wanted to keep my cock primed and my balls bursting. She dribbled the scalding wax over me all the same, but in a strict voice warned me not to come.

Every last one of them had their way with my helpless cock. It was pinched and poked, squeezed and strangled, battered and burned, decorated with hair clips and earrings and bedaubed with lipstick and mascara. Throughout the ordeal it remained hard for them, a bone-headed appendage wallowing in abuse.

Finally Jasmine addressed me. She held a glass between her fingers, absently swirling the amber contents.

'You want to fuck me, don't you?' she said in a strangely candid tone. All the others fell silent. 'Tell the truth.'

'Yes, Mistress.' Was there any point denying it? My cock was stretching across the room towards her, dribbling its passion.

'But you know I'll never let you, don't you?'

'Yes, Mistress.'

'And do you know why?'

'No, Mistress.'

'Because you're just a dog to me. Just a dog.'

I fell down, crushed and yet elated by the undeniable truth of her words. Jasmine continued to speak in the same slow and reasonable manner. Jennifer, at her side, looked on with complete detachment.

'I told you at the very start you'd never fuck me but there was one thing I didn't mention. Have you any idea what that might be?'

I waited expectantly.

'I forgot to say that *I* might decide to fuck *you*.'

The whisky had put a shine in her eyes. For a mad moment I thought she was going to come across the room, sit astride my cock and ride me half to death.

But she had something else in mind when she spoke about fucking me.

'I'm going to show everyone here that you're not even good enough to be my dog.' She was spitting her words at me. 'I'm going to show them that you're nothing but my bitch. A bitch's bitch.'

The eyes of each woman were trained on me. I felt like a fox surrounded by hounds waiting to taste its blood.

'You once asked me what women do with their fashion shoes,' Jasmine went on, drawing sniggers from her friends. 'Do you remember?'

My thoughts raced back to the day she'd first taken me shopping – a far-off time when I used to walk in her presence and call her Jasmine. I recalled quite vividly the outrageous shoe that had provoked the now incriminating comment – the wooden-platform mule with the chunky heel and black suede strap. An admirer had bought Jasmine a similar pair some weeks before, though I had yet to see them on her feet.

'I'm going to answer your question with a personal demonstration,' she said. 'Crawl over here and find out how we use our shoes on creeps like you.'

To a chorus of giggles, I crawled across the room and prostrated myself at the feet of my Mistress, unable to guess her intention but anticipating something abominable. She crossed her legs bossily and twirled a Gucci shoe in front of my nose as if it were the most delicious bait, driving me into a frenzy of desire for her.

'Suck the heel,' she said.

I slithered forwards, lifted my head and cautiously swallowed the long tapering stiletto. I could feel the cold metal tip scraping the back of my throat as I took it deep into my mouth. I choked involuntarily and tried to cough it out, but she held it firmly in place, indifferent to my spluttering.

'Suck it properly. Get it nice and wet for your own good.'

I lay with my head under her suspended shoe and sucked at the exquisite heel as if I were nursing at a teat, making it glisten with saliva. Jasmine observed me sternly but with a trace of a smile on her lips.

'Cocksucker,' she taunted as she thrust the heel in and out of my mouth, careless about what she jabbed or scraped with the metal tip and slapping the sole against my face. After she'd made me gurgle all kinds of nonsense she withdrew her long designer cock.

'Turn around,' she ordered, 'and show me that scrawny backside of yours.'

I presented my rear end to her, gripped now by the realisation of what she intended to do. I arched my buttocks upwards into the wanton position I adopted for a beating and stretched my arms out in front of me. I buried my face in the carpet, consumed with self-loathing for the outrage I was prepared to accept.

'Lift up your head,' she said. 'They all want to see how much my bitch loves to be fucked.'

I was surrounded by adorable, cock-rousing females and the face of each one was flushed with excitement. For the first time in my life I had that rarest of experiences – the breathless attention of supremely fuckable women. But it was being bought at a terrible price. A rude prod in the buttock from Jasmine's heel reminded me of this. I felt all the power of her spectacularly toned leg in that single jab and begged her to have pity on me. She merely mocked my whimpering tone and laughed acidly. She dragged the heel up and down the furrow between my cheeks, prodding at intervals with a lazy curiosity.

'Hold it open,' she ordered.

I reached my hands around and spread my buttocks for her, still holding my head up so her guests could see my bloodless face. She located my innocent hole and stabbed it experimentally a few times.

'This is so easy,' she said. 'You can't resist me, can you?'

It yielded to her with a shameful eagerness and she inserted the first inch of cold steel. She stirred it around in there, stretching the shocked virginal muscles, threatening to rip me wide open. Then she slid the rest of the heel into my passage in a single steady movement, penetrating me to the hilt. I felt my insides freeze. I groaned but held myself steady – I took that length of icy metal like the Crawley I was.

Making herself comfortable on the couch, she proceeded to sodomise me for all her pretty friends. She started slowly, twisting her heel cynically to loosen me up; but before long she was pumping away with gusto, poking the very guts of me. Shuddering each time her sole slapped against my buttocks, I lowered my head and bit into the carpet, delirious with pain and shame.

She paused briefly to speak to her audience, leaving her heel embedded in my aching passage.

'Shoes like these are a real pain in the ass to wear, don't you agree, girls?'

The women were delighted by her wit.

'I've had them on for just a few hours and my right foot is absolutely killing me.' I felt her slip her foot out of the shoe, careful to leave the heel buried inside me. She sighed pleasantly. 'That feels so much better.' I heard her lean back on the couch and stretch contentedly, before she commanded me to crawl around the room and suck the heels of all her friends. She warned me against dropping the precious Gucci.

'If you let it fall,' she said, 'I'll put on my other shoes, you know the ones I mean, and I'll fuck you with them instead.' The threat made my bowel muscles slacken with fear. I had a vision of that platform mule up on its spot-lit pedestal, the blunt wedge heel, outrageous in its conception, waiting to serve its Mistress.

I crawled from woman to woman, clutching the slippery steel in my trembling rectum as if holding onto life itself. The blinds had not been lowered and I saw my reflection in the dark French windows at the end of the room. The Gucci was wedged between my buttocks, toe pointing up in the air, and bobbed like a poodle's tail as I shuffled around the room on my hands and knees. The women knew instinctively how to treat a man forced to grovel at their feet. They sat prettily and made me stretch my neck to get at their neglected heels. They dangled their shoes just above the carpet and when I had managed to swallow the heel, they wriggled it around inside my mouth until I was forced to release it and start all over again. Filthy words flew from their mouths and one of them spat on me repeatedly as I lay at her feet. They called me their 'cocksucker spaniel' and sniggered at my frantic efforts to perform such a degrading service for them.

I was confronted with a dizzying variety of heels. Some of these women walked about on things too big to fit inside my mouth, no matter how wide I opened it for them. As a last resort I licked these freakish creations in a great show of devotion, terrified that one dissatisfied owner might ask Jasmine for permission to shove her monstrosity all the way up my ass. Only when each woman's heels were glistening with saliva was I permitted to crawl back to my Mistress.

By this stage the sly heel had worked its way up to the opening of my passage and I had only a pinch of a hold on it. Smiling at the effort it took me and bobbing her waiting foot, Jasmine watched me pad my way stiffly across the room. She curled and uncurled her toes sensually, the red nails glowing like hot coals through the sheer nylon stocking.

'Turn around,' she said as I drew closer.

I rotated myself slowly, straining every muscle in my ass to prevent the Gucci from popping out.

'Now put my slipper back on, Prince Charming.'

To another wave of wild laughter, I reversed towards the dangling foot of this vicious Cinderella, my rectum grasping at the very tip of the heel. I could feel the shoe wobbling, tearing away from my tired hole.

'Don't you dare let it drop,' she warned me. 'You know what will happen if you do. Your little hole will be stretched until it rips.'

Somehow I managed to manoeuvre the shoe to her impatient foot. But even now she did nothing to help. She seemed determined to wear those mules. She let me brush the Gucci against her toes without reacting and pointed her foot at an awkward angle making the task of replacing the shoe quite impossible. Straining my spine to elevate my rear end and clinging to the heel for all I was worth, I stroked the rim of the shoe against her sole, tickling the nylon-sheathed flesh, coaxing her like the lowest slut on earth, begging to receive her foot. There was nothing more I could do. She could choose whether to accept the fabulous slipper I offered to her foot with my whole body, or wait for it to fall and bugger her bitch with a fist-sized wooden heel.

She finally slid her foot into the shoe. Once again I felt the strength of her leg as she shoved the steel deep inside my passage. The force of the thrust sent me flying forwards onto the carpet.

'Get up, you little runt, or I'll send you upstairs to fetch my mules.'

In a red panic, I scrambled back up onto my hands and knees. I wasted no time and impaled myself on her waiting heel like a piece of cheap meat. She buggered me again, more cynically this time, scraping away at my insides while she sipped her whisky and told Jennifer that this was all I was good for.

The pain was intense but in some awakening part of me, I longed for her to continue, to never stop heel-fucking my ass. I felt more connected to her than ever before, even more a part of her world now than the night I'd worshipped at her cunt. I was an extension of her fabulous heel, part of the earth that bore her, the dirt beneath her sole. She prodded away at me as if she had her heel in a nest of ants and was intent on killing them all.

'He loves it,' she laughed.

'You shouldn't be so kind to him,' said Jennifer coldly.

My cock had swollen to an enormous size and Jasmine was using her heel to stab the last scraps of resistance out of me. She had me white-eyed and grunting like a baboon.

'What a racket,' she said, fucking me even harder. 'Come on, get it over with.'

I begged her to stop but my lying voice was drowned by the laughter that now engulfed the room. Jasmine brought her heel right out of my slack hole and slipped it in again, up to the hilt. She did so repeatedly and with disgusting ease.

'This is the best you'll ever get, creep.' She pressed down hard and I caught sight of myself in the dark glass window, skewered on the celebrated Gucci. The heel that had been the target of a hundred zoom lenses was now buried deep in my arse and lent my whole body its sparkle. I was an object, a receptacle, something lower than a shoe but at the same time fabulously desirable because of my connection to Jasmine's foot. I shared in the eroticism that extended from her designer heel, along her priceless leg, and up to the brutal smile on her lips. The image in the glass sent a shiver through me and made my balls erupt. Crying out her name, I splashed streaks of cum onto the carpet. I slid from the heel and collapsed, fulfilled as never before.

'Lick it up, every last disgusting drop of it,' she said, waking me with a kick.

I set about licking my own cum from the carpet, already growing hard again, my ass wide open and begging for the magic of her heel. After swallowing it all down, I glanced up hopefully at my Mistress.

'He's yours if you want him,' she said to Jennifer.

Jennifer nodded.

'What are you looking at, creep!' Jasmine snapped. 'Go and fetch your cane.'

Fifteen

*'If you step out of line even once, I'll make you
lie in the dirt and piss all over you.'*

Imagine a blonde debutante sitting at the wheel of a
red Porsche convertible, driving south in the afternoon sun. The car's gleaming bodywork matches her
cherry lip-gloss and the polish on her fingernails. Men
honk their horns in crude mating calls as she sails
past them, serene, hair blowing in the wind. None of
them dreams that locked inside the boot is her new
slave.

I lay in total darkness, the cramped companion of
travel bags, tennis rackets and a jumble of sports
shoes. The chamber was hot and airless and heavy
with the salty-sweet scent of female belongings. Face
buried in a pair of running shoes, I inhaled deeply,
massaged my throbbing cock and contemplated my
future. Jennifer Bond was taking me to her country
estate to clear land for tennis courts. This was all I
knew. I thought only of pleasing my new Mistress
and winning my place back at Jasmine's feet. Failing
that, I hoped to be retained by Jennifer as her drudge.
My life had no other meaning.

We arrived at our destination sooner than I
expected. I quickly tucked away my cock and braced

myself for the flood of light and the dazzling face of Jennifer. But I waited for what seemed like hours before the boot was lifted open.

'Out,' she said, 'and follow me.'

I clambered out of the boot and found myself standing before a stately mansion house. I had been brought to a part of England that I thought existed only in costume dramas and Jane Austen novels. Stone lions guarded the pillared entrance way and behind me was an ornate fountain, complete with marble nymphs and water lilies. All that was missing was a horse-drawn carriage and ladies strolling with parasols, their dainty slippers hidden under long dresses.

Jennifer was already some distance away, heading towards a stone pathway which skirted the front of the house. She'd changed from the light summer dress she'd left Jasmine's in and now wore a suede waistcoat and pink corduroy pants tucked into calf-high boots. Her hair, tied back in a long ponytail, was a cascade of white gold. I scampered after this young aristocrat feeling like an urchin she'd brought from the city.

Walking briskly, arms folded bossily beneath her breasts, she led me around to the back of her property. Here the land sloped gently downwards from a wide terrace to level out in a manicured lawn far below. The grounds were bordered on all four sides by tall trees and through the thick foliage a neighbouring estate was just visible.

Jennifer steered a course away from the terrace, where a liveried servant was placing platters of food on a long table, and took me down a stone stairway that was set into the grass slope. We descended in silence, passing an endless variety of shrubs and a multitude of bright flowers, most of which I could not find names for. The air was thick with pollen. Bees buzzed and birds chirped in the trees. From some-where came the burble of running water. Striding ahead of me, Jennifer seemed indifferent to it all, the sway of her pink ass steady and proprietorial.

From the slope, I had a view over a tall privet hedge along the lawn's edge and into a neglected patch of land that was heavily shaded by trees and overgrown with wild bushes and weeds. When we reached the bottom of the slope we proceeded in a diagonal line across the lawn towards a gap in the hedge and it was then I first realised what my work would entail. I glanced back up at the house and saw the servant standing on the terrace holding an empty silver tray. I wondered what he thought as he looked down at us. Did he simply see two abstract figures moving across a blanket of green felt? Or did he recognise a drama that had been enacted on this land for countless generations – a Bond leading a Crawley to his work?

Jennifer halted abruptly when we reached the gap in the hedge. She planted her hands on her hips making it clear she did not intend to go a step further.

'Do you understand what you have to do?'

'Yes, Mistress.'

'I brought you here for one reason. You work, that's all.'

'Yes, Mistress.' I looked through the hole in the hedge. The ground was stony; fires had been built here and rubbish dumped. Hit by the smell of something foul, I turned my head away.

'If you step out of line even once, I'll make you lie in the dirt and piss all over you. I'll make you stay there until it dries. Is that clear?'

'Yes, Mistress.'

She had nothing else to say to me. She turned around, almost whipping my face with her ponytail, and set off back towards the house. I watched her go. Her ass had none of the flirtatious charm of Jasmine's; she rolled her luxurious yet firm cheeks with a frightening display of purpose, pulling the corduroy taut. I was in no doubt that given the least provocation she'd punish me in the manner described. She'd do it very calmly, keeping her gaze level and lips pursed even as she squatted over my prostrate body and released the contents of her bladder.

In the weeks that followed, I started work at sunrise and didn't quit until it was too dark to see. First I had to hack down all the small trees and bushes with only a blunt axe to help me. Then, sitting in the stony earth, I pulled up weeds and roots with my bare hands. Next came the endless task of picking out rocks from the soil and burying the rotten matter that had been left behind by man and beast. At the end of each day, I built a fire to burn the pile of debris I'd assembled. Choking in the thick smoke, I'd use my shirt to fan the pale, protesting flames.

A hose served as my shower and I went to bed still dripping, as there were no clean rags to dry myself on. I slept on a mat inside a shed, in among clay pots, buckets, bags of plant feed, and gardening tools that were brown with rust. My home soon became a refuge for the many insects whose natural habitat I was destroying.

Life up at the mansion went on with a practised disregard for the world of toil and dirt beyond the hedge – though doubtless there were impatient inquiries about when the tennis courts would be ready. When she was home Jennifer entertained friends out on the terrace, young men and women of her own type who oozed breeding and privilege. In the hazy afternoon sun they looked like figures in a delicate watercolour – poised, hardly moving and insipidly elegant. The sound of a piano playing or the murmur of contented laughter occasionally drifted down to the bottom of the garden.

If the weather was fine they sometimes played tennis on the lawn, their carefree voices ringing out beneath the blue sky. The women looked ravishing in stiff white skirts that lifted from their asses as they chased after the ball. I tried to position myself close to a gap in the hedge when a pretty one had her serve, hoping for a flash of panties as she jumped forwards with her swing. (Eventually, my cock would grow hard without my needing to watch the game – the hollow clap of ball against racket was sufficient.) The asses of these women, snug in immaculate white cotton, tantalised me long after the players had packed away their equipment and returned to the house. These asses inhabited a world I could not enter, but a world whose border I was working to extend.

One hot afternoon Jennifer stepped out onto the terrace in a glimmering silver bikini. I was shovelling manure over a section of soil at the time and from the moment she appeared I had to struggle to keep my dirty hands off my cock. Standing with her back towards the house, she slipped her long hair into a headband and proceeded to rub lotion over her body until her fair skin glistened down to her painted toenails. Then she spread a towel over a chaise lounge, adjusted the parasol and laid herself down. A servant came from the house, placed a cocktail and some magazines on a low table beside her and crept away again.

She lay on her back, reading and sipping from her drink. She did not once glance down towards the bottom of the garden, knowing by instinct that I was toiling away for her, even if my unruly cock was begging for relief. There was no need to check, monitor or supervise me; to her kind I was obedient by nature, my behaviour absolutely predictable. Continuing to heave the heavy shovel, I watched her with an enhanced sense of longing. Her cool self-assurance and natural indolence were irresistible. Jasmine had turned me into her dog, her begging bitch; Jennifer had made me her labouring brute.

With each load of muck I lifted from the barrow, I found myself wishing with increasing intensity that Jennifer would descend from her lofty stage and order me to lie prostrate here on the ground while she doused me with her golden waters as she'd threatened. I was crazed with the desire to be drenched in her steaming piss, to drown in her hot and salty scorn. My soul was wilting with the arid experience of impersonal daily labour and I needed her urine like life-giving rain. I wanted to be scented by this pedigree bitch and feel the intimate heat of her ownership. But my wish was not granted. Insensible to me, Jennifer lay on her back and continued to read and sip her drink. It did not matter to her who or what was clearing the land down at the bottom of her garden, only that the job was completed on schedule and in keeping with her specifications. As if emphasising this fact, she rolled onto her side, turning her back towards me.

The nonchalance of that simple act! The sheer indifference of those creamy ass cheeks, tantalisingly split by the narrow triangle of bikini briefs! It was truly annihilating. I wrenched out my cock there and then and worked myself off to the far-away image. It took only a few short tugs before I felt my knees give way. Leaning on the shovel for support, shaking and panting, I pumped a trail of cum onto the shit at my feet.

When I opened my eyes again and looked up towards the house, I saw that her pristine ass was in the exact same position. It had not moved an inch though my whole body had convulsed in ecstasy. Those perfectly composed cheeks gave me a crushing sense of insignificance and in an instant had my cock standing to attention once more.

I lost count of the days I toiled down at the bottom of Jennifer's garden – out of mind if not always out of sight. I received a few additional instructions regarding my work from a servant with sagging cheeks and heavy eyelids, who relayed them through the gap in the hedge and scurried away again. But that was my only human contact. I caught precious glimpses of Jennifer when she appeared on the terrace, but only then and never again in a bikini. She seemed more distant, more aloof and more magnificent on each occasion. The mere sight of her blonde hair sent me into a frenzy of longing and her proud disregard for the vast world beneath her feet only intensified my passion for her.

Eventually, the day arrived when I could rest on my spade and survey an expanse of dark, fertilised earth. There was not a weed in sight, not a rock or stray leaf to disrupt the smooth harmony of soil. The view filled me with a sense of pride and I was eager to begin laying the grass.

That same afternoon the servant appeared and informed me I was to present myself to the Mistress at the front of the house. His face, as usual, gave nothing away. I took as long as I dared preparing myself for the meeting. I washed thoroughly and shaved the best I could with a much-used razor, entertaining a timid hope that I was about to be rewarded in some way.

But as soon as I started across the lawn such

fanciful notions took flight. The garden with its joyful abundance of vegetation was too rich for my unaccustomed senses and, as I neared the flowerbeds, a nervous sweat began to form under my arms. I had to force myself to climb up the steps; my feet in their heavy boots felt as clumsy as hooves. I wanted to return to my work tools and the musty shed I shared with insects. The house gleamed in the distance like a holy place that was forbidden to me. I feared the worst, the very worst.

Jennifer was waiting for me at the front of the house, dressed in a black pantsuit. Her golden hair was fashionably tousled and diamonds sparkled on her fingers and wrists. She had her back turned to me, one hand resting on the Porsche, and was in conversation with a woman who, while not especially pretty and forty years old at least, was very elegantly attired. This stranger was the first to notice my creeping approach and raised her eyebrows quizzically. Jennifer glanced over her shoulder, flashing a diamond earring, but showed no further interest in me. Soon I could hear what the woman was saying. She spoke like a Radio 4 presenter.

'I say, your new man has done a splendid job down there.'

'Thank you.'

'How much does he charge?'

'I don't pay him. He does it for free.'

'Really! Why's that?' The woman was studying me keenly.

'Because he's a slave.'

'A slave?'

'Yes, a born slave.'

'Well I never . . .'

In a few terse sentences Jennifer told her curious neighbour the story of my enslavement by Jasmine.

'But why does he do it?' the woman wanted to know.

'Some people have it inside of them. They inherit it, I believe. His ancestors were probably among the slaves who were crushed to death building the pyramids.'

With a series of quick nods the woman signalled she found the explanation entirely reasonable. She licked her lips salaciously and pressed Jennifer to say more about my life as Jasmine's slave. What work did I do? Was I really whipped? Did I kiss everybody's feet? Jennifer answered each question patiently, giving a dry account of my degraded existence. She offered no insight into my character or motivations and I felt betrayed. She portrayed me as a ridiculous and mildly repulsive figure.

Suddenly I heard the woman ask: 'Can I borrow him?'

Jennifer was only too happy to oblige. 'Certainly, he's finished here. Keep him for as long as you like.' She ordered me to come forwards and passed me on to her neighbour with the simple command: 'Do as you're told, or else.'

The woman marched me away like a headmistress leading a naughty schoolboy to her office. But when we reached the entrance of her house she became apprehensive, worried that the whole thing was a joke at her expense.

'Are you really a slave?'

'Yes, Mistress.'

'I still don't believe it.'

I stood before her, shoulders drooping, gaze cast downwards.

'If you're a real slave, get down on your hands and knees and kiss my foot.'

I dropped to the floor and pressed my obedient lips

223

against the toe of her low-heeled shoe. She gave a shriek of delight.

'Oh heavens, you really are a slave.' She pushed her other shoe to my lips. 'What a waste to use you in the garden.'

Bubbling with excitement now, she took me through her front door, up a sweeping staircase and straight into her bedroom. There she instructed me to wait while she went into an adjoining room to change. I was overwhelmed by the room's proportions and dazzled by the glitter of silver and sequins. I was still blinking when my new Mistress reappeared, now wrapped in a thick sable coat and wearing high black boots.

'I'm Catherine the Great,' she announced in a majestic voice. 'And you are a lowly serf called Gregor.' She pranced around the room narrating a preposterous scenario. 'You were caught trespassing on imperial land and stealing potatoes and now you've come before Russia's mighty Empress to beg for mercy. Miserable peasant! I could have you flogged to death.' She scowled at me as if I really were guilty of the crime and I crouched trembling in the middle of her chamber. 'Poverty drove you to this desperate act. You were evicted from your hovel and you've been tramping from village to village. Poor, wretched creature! You've been feeding yourself on rotten potato skins and you're starving half to death.'

An antique chair served as the imperial throne and to this I crawled and told the Empress my woeful story with all the conviction I could muster. Real tears fell from Gregor's eyes onto the tall ebony boots at which he knelt. My Empress regarded me in silence, palms resting upon the carved armrests, regal and unmoved.

'You dare to trouble me with your trifling woes, you miserable cur!' she finally interjected. 'Princes have knelt where you now kneel and offered me all the riches of their kingdom.' She surveyed an imaginary court of retainers and lackeys. 'Yet the Empress is feeling gracious today,' she announced. 'She will spare the life of this lowly subject. But he must be punished for his crime. He will work in my fields for the remainder of his days. He will labour from sunrise to sunset and for his sweat he'll earn a ration of potatoes and water each evening. He will own nothing, not the hair on his head, nor the skin on his back. And he will sing my praises or die. Such is my decree.'

To show my gratitude I had to remove the tight boots and lick her bare feet.

'Clean them thoroughly, peasant.'

Her feet were hot and clammy from the excitement and they had a vinegary odour that mingled with the scent of the old leather. My tongue recoiled at the first taste of them and I felt my bile rising as I forced myself to start licking. The feet of the Empress were not shapely and sweet like Jasmine's, or pale, flavourless abstractions like Jennifer's.

'Put your tongue between the toes and get it all out.'

I closed my eyes and did her bidding, almost fainting from the intensity of the smell. I moved my tongue from one tight toe cleft to next, licking it clean of the accumulated sweat and scum. Her feet were sensitive and she occasionally giggled while I worked.

'Good peasant,' she said. 'Good peasant.'

Soon she began to moan. I wriggled my tongue with increasing vigour, hoping to accelerate her climax. The moans became deeper and I sucked her fat big toe into my mouth and fellated it noisily, eager to finish the game. I was servicing a Mistress I did not desire and who ruled me by privilege alone. I took no pleasure in her mounting cries or her climax when it arrived. I only wanted to keep her content until I could be with Jasmine or even Jennifer again. She fell back in the chair and let out a long happy sigh. I sat on my knees wondering what her next command would be. There was something depressingly familiar about the sour taste her feet had left in my mouth.

She left me to go and change into a new costume and then another game commenced. This time she wore a blazing red skirt suit and matching court shoes with tiny bows at the front. The outfit did not flatter her; the narrow skirt hugged her ample hips obscenely and her feet bulged in the finely made shoes. I breathed in deeply and braced myself for more abject footlicking.

In a great hurry, she took me downstairs to a walnut-panelled study that smelt strongly of expensive cigars. She sat in a leather chair behind a commanding desk and, puffing on a Havana, outlined the next scenario.

'I'm the First Lady and you're the leader of an impoverished third world country. You have come to my office to grovel for aid . . .'

I was soon on my knees.

'You want money to build a hospital, Dr Bongo?' she sneered. 'You'll have to earn it.'

Dr Bongo was required to crawl under the desk and remove the First Lady's pumps and sheer stockings. She blew smoke down at him while he carried out his demeaning task.

'Sniff it,' she ordered, lifting up one of the stockings with her toes. I took the rolled-up nylon, pushed it against my nose and inhaled loudly for her benefit. Fortunately it had absorbed only a trace of her foot odour. 'Put it over your head,' she said after a few moments. 'Wear it like a cap.' Thus attired, I negotiated with a contemptuous First Lady, who used my outstretched palms as her ashtray. 'Time to grovel,' she announced, raising a foot towards my face. Without delay I began to kiss her supreme toes. 'You get a million dollars for each one you do properly.'

Dr Bongo earned 10 million dollars for his afflicted people but it took many hours and his mouth was burning with ulcers before a contented First Lady would sign the cheque.

She ran back upstairs and changed again, this time hiding her chubby legs beneath a grey pantsuit, though she insisted on wearing high-heeled sandals. Lord above! Hadn't anybody told her what unsightly feet she had? We went to a dining room where she sat at the head of a long table and I perched on a low stool at her side. While servants carried in food and drink, she briefed me on our new roles.

'I'm the president of a multinational company and you're a trouble-making union leader who's about to learn his place. I've summoned you to my country retreat ... Look at you! You barely know which cutlery to pick up with your clumsy proletarian hands.' She paused to eat a truffle and sip some wine. I kept my hands on my lap.

'I've called you here to say you can't threaten me with strikes any more because we're moving our operations to southeast Asia. Everything's ready. It just takes my signature.'

I appeared appropriately mortified.

'What do you say to that, you old dinosaur? Not so loud now, are you? But you know, I might be prepared to reconsider my decision. Just maybe.' She drank some more wine and pressed a napkin against her lips. They had begun to quiver with excitement. 'Show me you can grovel for work like those desperate masses waiting overseas.'

I was down on my knees in a flash.

'Now lick my shoes clean, worker, while I finish my meal.'

I licked her shoes to save the livelihood of thousands of men and women.

'That's more like it. At last you've found a good use for that crude tongue of yours. Lick right down to the bottom now. Yes, and under the sole too. Good boy.'

The servant came in and popped open a bottle of Champagne. The company president raised a toast to her own victory: 'Here's to bringing the unions to heel.'

I spent countless days locked in the house beyond the trees. My Mistress donned one costume after another and we ran up and down the stairs and from room to room, passing back and forth through the ages. Our games were staged in the deserts of Ancient Egypt, at the Colosseum in Rome, on cotton plantations in the Old South, in war rooms and in boardrooms. We rearranged furniture, added lights, music and sound effects, and with the help of servants and props we had scenes of famine, massacre and despair in which to act our parts.

Wherever we went I played the oppressed, the downtrodden, the utterly wretched, and she the tyrant, now man, now woman, the heavy-footed monster who kept my neck pressed to the ground, my nose in the dirt. She was possessed, her lust unquenchable. She shouted obscenities and held out her sexless foot for me to worship and adore – and all through the ages, wherever we went, whatever costume she wore, that foot tasted rank. She would shove all her toes to the back of my mouth and wriggle them like maggots, push them so far down my throat that I'd cough and splutter. But even on the verge of vomiting, I had to continue sucking her toes and licking her soles, while she frigged herself into oblivion.

One freezing morning, laden with rocks, I staggered towards the Great Wall of China; by the time evening arrived, I was waist-deep in mud digging the Panama Canal. We played on through the night until the blue light of dawn, when, naked but for a loincloth, I gazed out from an upstairs window across the land of my conquered people. I was kneeling and standing sternly at my side was the Empress of India, her feet freshly licked clean but soon to be stained with more blood. The moon stared back at us, pale with horror.

But this carnival of the perverse could not go on forever. One morning, as she was dressing to play Imelda Marcos, my Mistress received a phone call from the man of the house announcing his imminent return. I watched her knuckles turn white as she held the receiver against her ear. His business negotiations had ended in wide smiles and firm handshakes and his plane was flying overhead even as they spoke.

Down below, we danced around in a panic among a hundred pairs of shoes. Order needed to be restored at once. Everything that had been used for our orgy had to be put back in its proper place. Even with the help of servants we were almost too late. Her husband's Jaguar was rolling up the driveway as the last prop was stashed away and the wardrobe door slammed shut. I heard the front door swing open and a man's thunderous greeting as I climbed out through a window into the back garden.

I took refuge in Jennifer's garden, trying to conceal my presence there. I hid in the trees during the day and only entered the shed late in the evening when all was quiet. There were two men hard at work on the next phase of the tennis courts, marking out a perimeter for a fence and laying grass. Whether slaves or contractors I could not tell from their appearance. But it was clear that Jennifer had no further use for me.

The shed was even more infested than before and I gave up trying to kill the beetles that tormented me. I sank into a state of numb complacency, indifferent to the bites and the stings. I had a recurring dream that I had become an insect myself, a worm-like larva with hopelessly short legs that was compelled to crawl to its own death under passing female feet. But what of such strange imaginings! I had four walls around me and a roof over my head. And when I wanted food I had only to scavenge in the bins like the foxes.

But word must have reached Jennifer that I was making secret use of the shed. Early one morning two burly servants shook me awake and frog-marched me off her property. Now I was homeless and hungry, just like poor Gregor.

Sixteen

*'You'll kiss my shoes because I tell you to
and because you need a job.'*

Maybe I'm just weak but I have a reserve of
compassion even for those who make me suffer. Why
else did I forgive my old rival and even come to
sympathise with him? Why else didn't I attack the
boy who opened Jasmine's front door to me? Instead
of being consumed by a jealous rage, I felt pity for us
both as he led me through to his Mistress. As for
Jasmine, I could feel nothing but desire when I saw
her. Her beauty atoned for all her sins.

She was reclining on a leather sofa and grinned
wickedly when I came into the room. I stood before
her with hands in pockets and the new slave took his
place, kneeling at her side. In addition to the G-string
and pouch, he wore a white shirt collar around his
neck complete with a black bowtie. He folded his
arms across his chest and looked at me with smug
satisfaction.

'This is Neil, your replacement,' she said. 'It's
nothing personal. I just get bored of men so quickly.
You have to admit, though, he is cute, isn't he?' He
was indeed a handsome youth, an Adonis fit for a
goddess. I watched her reach a hand down to his
buttocks and give them a possessive squeeze.

Jasmine granted me five minutes to pack my belongings into a holdall. She had Neil escort me through the hall to the kitchen, where he waited in silence while I went into the boys' room. Everything in here was as I'd left it. The bed had not been used and my clothes were still laid out over the desk and chair. I tried not to dwell on what this indicated about the privileges of the new drudge, that he perhaps slept on a mat at the foot of Jasmine's bed. I stuffed what I could into my bag, including the leather folder, and pocketed the money I had left from the sale of my car.

I'd expected to leave by the garden door but Neil shook his head and led me back through to the hall, where Jasmine was waiting. She was standing before one of the windows and the afternoon sunlight burst through her gauzy white dress, revealing the soft silhouette of her naked body.

Neil knelt down at the side of this blinding goddess and she stroked his cheek with her fingers. I sensed she wanted me to kneel too, or perhaps grovel one last time as my old rival had.

'Stay on your feet if you like but you'll always be a dog,' she scoffed.

'It's over,' I said, looking down at her heels with a sense of dread.

'No,' she said, 'it's just about to begin.'

Neil pressed his face against her thigh and closed his eyes, oblivious to everything but the warmth and softness of her flesh. Again it was pity I felt for him. In his slender, clutching fingers I recognised a weakness more profound than my own. One day soon Jasmine would grow tired of this fawning boy and abuse him just as she'd abused me and all the other men who'd come under her spell. Neil, I thought, as he began to bestow worshipful kisses on the white dress, working his lips down to the hem, you're only a head above me and both of us are falling.

I let myself out through the door and started along the driveway, determined not to look back. Jasmine called after me in a sweet voice.

'I spoke to Ms Lexington just a few days ago. Did you know she's sitting behind your old desk now?'

Kim, the bane of my days!

I turned around to see Jasmine standing in the doorway, a vision of gloating loveliness. Neil's head was down at her feet.

'You'll need a job, no doubt. Why don't you give her a call?'

Her laughter followed me all the way to the gate.

I reached the outskirts of town with a leaden feeling in my stomach and headed along the dock road in search of a cheap hotel. Freight vehicles rumbled past me, their power breaks hissing in complaint each time they were forced to slow down. The first hotel I came to was a run-down Victorian building at a busy junction. I went into the dimly lit lobby and my spirits dropped even lower at the sight of the flea-bitten furniture and the cigarette burns in the carpet. I fingered the roll of notes in my pocket, sorely tempted to blow it all on a taxi ride, a three-course meal and a night in the penthouse suite at the Park Hotel.

A clerk appeared behind the reception desk and his hacking cough returned me to my senses. I paid for a week's room and board and was given a key on an oblong of wood and directions to the top floor. I found my room at the end of a narrow windowless corridor with yellowing walls. I didn't bother to undress or even turn on the light. I put down my bag, lay on the thin mattress and closed my eyes.

The majority of the hotel's occupants were out-of-town contractors, dour men who carried their own toilet paper to the bathroom each morning and lathered their torsos with harshly scented soap. I did my best to avoid them and usually stayed in bed until they'd left for work. I simply could not face these leather-skinned grafters, especially first thing in the morning over eggs and bacon and strong tea. I was not ready for a working man's life yet, its open vulgarity, the scary, backslapping camaraderie. I needed time to readjust – and I often doubted I'd ever be able to rejoin my own kind.

But if you've a notion that I'd at least found shelter from pretty women then you're greatly mistaken. We were a community of plain men, it is true, and there was a monastic austerity about our existence; but we were not left in peace. Sirens summoned us from all sides and the other world's teasing beauty penetrated into our very midst. The room I'd been given looked out across the junction and when I pulled back the curtains on my first morning, I found myself staring into the cleavage of a proud giantess. All day long she flashed her Wonder Bra tits at the traffic passing below. Some days later, a tiny man on a ladder pasted a picture of her Pretty Polly legs on a neighbouring billboard. Her superbly arched feet were as long as a car.

The other lodgers made it worse for themselves and for me. They littered the place with tabloids and magazines and kept the TV on all night. I seldom went into the communal lounge in the evenings, as I hated to see my fellow men gazing lustfully at women they'd never possess. I limited my TV viewing to the afternoon when the room was usually empty and I was free to switch between Australian soaps, chat shows and old movies in search of my fix. When others were around I felt restricted. Worst of all, I realised I was just like them – without a hope of seizing what lay beyond the screen. I could not bear to sit in such company for very long; our communal deprivation was too shamefully apparent.

I walked the streets instead, preferring the company of orange lights and hurrying strangers. Or I'd find a lively pub somewhere and look at pretty girls from a table in the corner. On such occasions my long-standing wish to be an invisible pair of eyes seemed to have been granted – I was completely ignored all evening long. Even the frumpiest girls peered straight through me as they passed by on their way to the ladies' room. Quite drunk one night and teased to bursting point by a sexy student ass that had been pressed up against the edge of my table, I got my taxi to stop at a 24-hour garage while I bought a stack of pornographic magazines. I went through them all, page by page, as soon as I got up to my room, and laid my favourite images in an arc around the bed. I wanked until morning and resumed my solitary orgy after a rushed breakfast. But lying in a harem of paper ladies could not compare to being on the end of Jasmine's fuck-me heel.

I began to spend more money on magazines and beer with the result that after a month at the hotel I was down to my last few hundred pounds. But Jasmine's parting words, which I could hear as clearly now as when she'd spoken them, had left me negatively disposed towards seeking employment. Let me put it like this. I saw the world of work as a place dominated by practically minded Kims, people who were always thinking about the future and doing the right thing, cowards who were waiting to punish me for following my cock's desire. I felt compelled to defy them. I'd go out to buy an evening newspaper, with every intention of searching the classified section for a job, but instead I'd come back with a glossy magazine or end up in a student pub across town.

But finally I had no choice: it was work or starve. Bright and early, I went into the city centre, picked out a suit at a discount store and visited the barber's. Then I boarded a bus to my old office. I tried some breathing exercises on the way but they did little to pacify me and when I reported to reception I was in a bitter mood. I took a seat in the foyer and folded my arms across my chest. The familiar surroundings weighed down on me. I remembered the thousands of elevator rides up to the sixth floor to days that never seemed to end. And I remembered all the evenings I'd rushed out through the sliding glass doors full of hope, only to find an empty answering machine waiting at home.

Kim made me wait a long time before she called for me. If it was part of her strategy to provoke me, she'd succeeded. I reached her office, inwardly fuming, just as her assistant was leaving for lunch. She was a nondescript girl with thick glasses and I felt an immediate solidarity with her. It was a vicious slap in the face to hear her giggling as she closed the door behind her.

Kim was sitting behind my old desk – quite literally – which was now bare except for a monitor and keyboard. She indicated that I should take the chair opposite which was noticeably lower than her own. She'd changed relatively little since the good old days, though my expert eye could detect signs of Jasmine's influence. Her make-up was a touch bolder now, especially the lipstick, and her short hair was slicked back at the sides and seemed darker. But below the desk she remained the same old Kim. Her skirt reached down past her knees, her pretty calves were hidden in beige-coloured tights and her shoes were as good as flat. The sight of her castrated heels gave me courage. This was hardly the woman who'd flirted with boys in the park and sneered while I'd wiped the muck off her slutty sandals with my shirt.

'You wanted to see me?' she said with the calm authority of a company representative.

'I came about a job . . . Miss Lexington.'

'Ms Lexington,' she corrected.

'*Ms* Lexington.'

'The usual method of application is to send a CV. We consider candidates for interview if their profile matches the specifications of any positions that are available.'

As if I didn't know that! Bite your tongue, I told myself. I took a deep breath, focused on the severed heels and smiled sweetly. 'Yes, but there are exceptions to that procedure.'

She countered my smile with her own. 'So, you consider yourself exceptional? Tell me, Mr Crawley, what exceptional skills and talents do you possess? Are you a whiz with computers? Will you manage our developing cyber business? Or maybe you have outstanding . . . linguistic abilities?'

I ignored the insinuations in her last question. I stuck to my script and played the professional. 'I think I'd be an asset to the company. I have a great deal of relevant experience. I worked in this department for close to fifteen years.'

She glanced at the monitor. 'Yes, that's correct. I have your file right here.' I felt naked as she clicked the mouse and browsed through information that I was not privileged to see. Her eyes had a cruel gleam in them. 'If I may say so, there's not an awful lot here to recommend you. In fact, some of the appraisals of your performance read like thinly veiled warnings.'

She continued to read, shaking her head disapprovingly at what was displayed on the screen. I squirmed on my chair wishing I could see what she could see – the Matthew Crawley that others knew.

'I suppose I could find you something,' she said finally.

'You could?' I sat up straight, full of hope.

'How would you like to be my second assistant?'

I'd asked for it, I suppose. Whether I accepted her offer or walked out of the office cursing her she'd revel in her victory over me and my cock.

'You'll need to call me Ma'am and do whatever I order.'

I swallowed deeply. There'd be Kims sitting behind desks wherever I tried to find work.

'Well?'

'That won't be a problem ... Ma'am. When do I start?'

She burst out laughing. It was the very last reaction I'd expected.

'Did you really imagine I'd have someone like you in here as my assistant? That's too funny.' She clapped her hands in glee. 'I wish Donna had stayed to see this. You as my assistant! The very thought of it! I wouldn't even trust you to lick a stamp for me.' She sat back in her chair and pressed her fingertips together. 'No, I had something much more suitable in mind. A job that's right up your alley. I was considering recommending you to the agency that provides the office hygiene staff – that's cleaners to you.'

'I would be very grateful if you did, Ma'am.' My voice failed utterly to express the sarcasm I'd intended to convey. I stood up to leave.

'Now wait a moment,' she said with a sternness that made me freeze. 'You don't get a cleaning job that easily. If you want to work here in any capacity at all, you're going to have to ask me very, very nicely.' She flicked her tongue over her lips. 'I've become so used to seeing you grovelling on the floor that I just can't let you go until you've crawled under this desk and licked my shoes. I want to hear you beg me for a cleaning job.' She crossed one leg over the other and began to swing it back and forth, twisting her brown, workaday shoe around and around. I had to look away from the appalling spectacle.

'You're not in her league,' I said. 'I won't kiss your ugly shoes.'

'It has nothing to do with what you want. You'll kiss my shoes because I tell you to and because you need a job.'

I looked down under the desk again. Could I become a slave to this functional female footwear that made not a single concession to my desires? She flaunted the outstretched shoe even more meanly, showed me the flat, rounded toe and turned her foot sideways so I could see the stump of a heel in profile.

'Do I need to remind you that I'm responsible for writing your references? Unless you want to flip burgers until you drop, you'd better crawl under here right now and start cleaning my shoes. Come on, I'm running out of patience.'

I got down on my knees and crawled under the desk towards an ugly future. There, in a very ordinary office, I lowered my head and began to lick the suspended shoe of my social superior. Small pieces of gravel were embedded in the sole and the heel was worn down at one corner, but I forced myself to complete the horrible task to her satisfaction, which she indicated by tilting the top of the shoe down to my lips. This was no more pleasant to clean. The leather was hard and scuffed around the toe and the polish had the bitter taste of necessity. The muck from beneath her sandals would have been more palatable and once again I felt the bile rising in my stomach.

When I had washed every square inch of the suspended shoe I moved my tired tongue down to the shoe that was planted on the floor. Between long, passionless licks, I begged the owner to help me get a cleaning job, begged her to write me a favourable reference.

'No,' she said when both shoes were glistening with my spittle, 'I don't think so.'

Aghast, I watched her slide her feet away from my lips and rise from the chair. I spun around under the desk to see her heading towards the door, swinging a pretty handbag at her side. She walked with surprising elegance in those insulting shoes, transcending them, even while their bitter taste remained on my tongue. She let me know that when the man or occasion called for it, she could kick them off and step into her slutty sandals or any other teasing footwear she chose.

Kim was as good as her word. I had several promising interviews but even the most enthusiastic panels turned cold on me as soon as my references arrived. In an attempt to bypass Kim, I called up some old colleagues, her superiors, men I'd known for years, one I'd gone to school with. But one after the other they let me down. Company procedures needed to be followed, I was told. I approached them in the street after work in order to put my case in person. But, repeating the same excuses, each one walked quickly away clutching his briefcase and blushing. They all knew something dreadful about Matthew Crawley but they were not prepared to tell him what it was. I finally lost my temper and followed

240

my old schoolmate all the way to his car, demanding to know the nature of my crime.

'Level with me,' I pleaded. 'For old times' sake.'

He shook his arm free of my grip. 'Leave me alone. You're only making it worse for yourself.' I kicked the tail of his Audi as he drove away.

The next day I found a policeman patrolling the pavement outside the office.

In a bid to get to the bottom of it all, I contacted a loose acquaintance from accounts. The man had a reputation for being a depressing bore and never turned down the offer of a sympathetic pair of ears. I'd spent hours on the phone listening to him describing the progress of his wife's illness and interjecting the occasional word of sympathy. I reckoned he owed me.

We met at a pub and I bought the first round of drinks. But right away I had the feeling I was wasting my time. He seemed to have no idea that I'd resigned from the firm or that my life had changed immensely since our last phone conversation. I listened to him without interrupting, sipping my beer steadily and tasting nothing. Would I never get a break! The man's wife had gone into hospital that same afternoon and there she lay, even while he spoke, waiting for a surgeon to come and slice off her breasts. I could hardly press him about office gossip in such tragic circumstances.

I bought us each a double whisky and consoled him as best I could. He reached into his pocket and produced a photograph of the unfortunate woman. It had been taken on their wedding day, but the bride had big frightened eyes as if she'd sensed even on that happy occasion the horror life held in store for her. I went over to the bar and bought more drinks. I'd give him my ears for the night; it was the least I could do.

By closing time we were both quite drunk and he had tears in his eyes. I helped him onto his feet and out into a waiting taxi. I promised I'd call him the next day. Walking back to the hotel, I tried to imagine the life of a woman without breasts.

As I neared the dock road, I saw my giantess waiting up ahead. Her gorgeous face was on display now, gleaming beneath fluorescent lights. She was winking and blowing the world a sexy kiss with her Revlon lips. She had no cares. I stood beneath the billboard for a long time, ignoring the honks of passing cars, wishing it was my cock she wrapped her silky lips around each night.

Seventeen

A diet of images and work in the morning.

I woke up late the next morning with a bad hangover and lay in bed considering my options. I was dangerously low on funds and far too demoralised to go out and look for a job. There was only one thing a man in my condition could do: I'd have to throw myself on the mercy of a grudging welfare state. I went to the nearest job centre and after providing a few personal details came away with a bundle of forms. From then on it was an uphill struggle and I betted against ever getting back a penny of the thousands of pounds I'd put into the system. The questions on the forms made no allowances for one's privacy or the uniqueness of one's misfortune on this earth, and I twisted my hair in frustration as I turned each page. It was impossible to fit my employment as Jasmine's drudge into the neat little boxes they provided and there were some things I simply refused to tell the Department of Social Security.

It came as no surprise when I was called in to explain my evasive answers and the protests I'd scribbled down the side of the forms. My claim was sent to an adjudication officer and, while I awaited the decision of this God on high, I scraped together my pennies and went hunting for another place to live.

When you're poor and looking for a home, the city seems to be made up entirely of stale rooms with narrow beds. You notice the big houses of course, but you pass by these with merely an envious glance up the driveway on your way to meet the next landlord who, you pray, won't ask for more than a week's rent deposit. I moved from one hellhole to another in the months that followed. I admit it: I was a coward. I left the first place because the bathroom did not have hot water. I stayed only a week in the next, driven out by the reflection of my thirty-eight-year-old face in a speckled mirror on a wardrobe door. Then I fled from a dope dealer and his pack of terriers. But in between packing and unpacking my holdall and introducing myself to an endless succession of deadbeats whose habits and hang-ups I'd learn a little bit more about each day, I had an abundance of time on my hands. I was a member of the new leisured class. I rose at midday, had a pint of sweet tea and four slices of margarine-smeared toast for breakfast and, while decent folk were hard at work, I sat in front of the TV or went out for a stroll.

A group of Christians had set up a stall at the top of the high street and whenever I passed this way some young convert was sure to come running over. What failing did they detect in me?, I used to wonder. I eventually got so tired of making excuses and telling lies that I gave them my address. I was taken aback when I opened the door later that evening to find three of them standing on the doorstep in the drizzle. I'd never imagined my soul was such a prize. Without wiping their feet, they tramped up the stairs to my room and sat in a line on my unmade bed. I made tea for them all and took my place on the floor, listening mostly and answering when called upon. I waited patiently for an opportunity to steer the discussion about my salvation in a more interesting direction.

When the moment was right, I produced the verse my old rival had copied from the Bible and asked if they knew who the author was. They held the paper between them and absorbed themselves in the six lines. I watched their faces expectantly, hoping for that sparkle of recognition. But they shook their heads blankly and laid the paper down on the floor. Why did I worry about that kind of thing? they asked. Jesus was the answer to all my questions. Their collective condescension riled me and so did their easy faith in salvation. I chased them down the stairs and out into the rain.

'Infantile religion!' I yelled after them. 'Crucified fool!'

Whenever I was out walking, I kept a lookout for my old rival; but after that evening with the Christians, I began a deliberate search for him. I wondered why I'd delayed for so long or ever imagined that former colleagues or wide-eyed converts could help me. I had a destiny that was different, desires these cowards and greenhorns could never comprehend. But my supersensual guide was nowhere to be found. I became obsessed. I felt only he could provide the revelation I needed to move forwards. I sat down with derelicts and gave away money and cigarettes, hoping one of them might reveal something of his whereabouts. But if they knew anything – and I think a few of them did – they kept it to themselves and sent me around the city on one wild goose chase after another.

But my persistence paid off. My inquiries led me to a ticket collector at the main station and between streams of passengers he told me about a beggar whom he nicknamed 'Old Moses'. About six months before, Old Moses had wandered into the station, he said, dropped to his hands and knees and crawled about in the rush-hour crowd. He'd almost got himself trampled underfoot but didn't seem to care. People cleared a space around him and many stood and watched. The ticket collector shook his head as he recalled the scene. It had been a sickening yet compelling spectacle, a big man like that behaving like a dog, filthy and hairy and reeking of something terrible. It had taken three policemen to drag him away.

I had the supersensualist in my sights now. There was bound to be a police report and maybe something in the newspaper. I left the station satisfied with my work. It was only a matter of time before I caught up with him. And time was something I had in abundance.

Or so I thought. The next day was my fortnightly appointment at the job centre and, as luck would have it, I was called to the desk of one of the more zealous advisors. I passed my job search diary to him and he scrutinised each fictional activity I'd entered. I made my impatience apparent; a man's fate was waiting to be discovered and somewhere in his fate was a message for me.

'You're looking for managerial work, Mr Crawley?' he asked.

'Or admin,' I pointed out.

He searched his computer while I picked my fingernails clean; sitting in this place, I always felt somehow contaminated. Then he stunned me. He found a job that I was qualified to do and this time none of my usual excuses would get me off the hook. I listened in disbelief as he picked up the phone and arranged an interview for me. He handed me the details and grinned like a toad that had just swallowed a fly.

The following Monday I started work as an attendant in a multi-storey car park. The company provided me with a peaked cap, a navy-blue jacket and black trousers, and wearing this flunky's uniform I sat in a glass sentry box for nine hours each day, Monday through Saturday. I cannot say the work was difficult. Each day I watched about five hundred cars roll in and took money from the hands of resentful drivers when they rolled out. But it zapped my energy all the same – maybe it was all the exhaust fumes I was forced to inhale. Within a week my priorities had changed and I suspended the search for my old rival. I discovered once again that it was impossible to balance work with an obsession.

Planted on my stool, I had a clear view down a street of office blocks and I could not fail to notice the many fine asses that sailed by each day, usually in tight grey or navy-blue skirts. There were some real stunners among the secretaries and bank clerks and when they came for their cars at the end of the day, I shook my head and gave a sigh. They swayed right past my window, tossing their hair and clicking their heels. Save closing my eyes what could I do? I was trapped, a prisoner in a glasshouse. This really was no job for the struggling disciple of a grizzly patriarch who warns against looking at shapely women. Still, I earned enough money to escape the outrage of modern communal living. If there is one thing I'm sure of it's this: when you reach my age, enforced intimacy with strangers over a prolonged period will lead to insanity, suicide or murder.

I found a self-contained flat. It was nothing to compare with my bachelor pad of old but it gave me the space to take stock of my life. The first thing I did after I'd settled in was read the King James Bible from cover to cover but still that verse eluded me. After that, I lost the motivation to pick up the search for my old rival. Old Moses and his antics in the station diminished in meaning for me and I decided to take Ecclesiastes as my guide. I resolved to eat, drink and be just as merry as each day allowed. I would go to women too and if the pretty ones would not let me get close to them, I'd content myself with looking. I reverted to the man I'd once been. My aspirations fell and I accepted my limitations. Jasmine, if you can believe it, became less of a presence in my thoughts – it was time to forget her, or to try to at least.

Little by little I acquired the necessities to make the transition. I rented a big screen television and a video player with excellent slow motion and pause controls. I started my magazine subscriptions again, joined video clubs, got connected to cable, and looked into buying a fast computer and going online. I also put away a little cash each week, whatever I had over, saving for my pilgrimage to that holy city in the Nevada desert.

I got in touch with family and friends again too. It was only a matter of time before somebody using the car park recognised me and spread the word. I had to explain my absence and my changed circumstances, but the interrogation was not half as bad as I'd feared; I was far from being the only Crawley with an unlucky, messed-up life. I was a hot topic for about a week and then everybody's attention moved on to the next social casualty in the line.

It was a little different with my drinking buddies though, who, it turned out, knew a good deal about my time with Jasmine. They didn't push me to talk about it directly – that's not the way we did things – but my adventure was a lingering source of amusement and they never missed the chance to pull my leg. I remember coming back from the gents on one particular evening to see them all biting their bottom lip and trying hard not to laugh. There, lying on my stool, was a classy lingerie brochure, open at a photograph of Jasmine modelling a lacy black bodice and matching panties. I had to look twice. The angle of the shot did her nose a terrible injustice and the colour balance was all wrong, giving her face a red and vulnerable quality. But what am I saying! She was magnificent – that body! – more than any of us dopes could ever hope for. I calmly closed the brochure and put it on the bar.

'Right,' I said, 'the drinks are on me if any of you jokers can honestly say you wouldn't get down on your knees for the chance to fuck her.'

None of the assembled pricks would take up my challenge.

I was back with my own kind, visiting the city's many watering holes and trying to keep the wise counsel of good King Solomon. A new club had opened and I made that my regular Saturday night haunt. I took my position at the edge of the dance floor and, bottle in hand, watched firm teenage asses swaying in the ultraviolet light. White panties of varying cuts glowed angelically through tight skirts and ass-hugging pants. And when I woke up on the Sunday, to a throbbing head and a hot, insistent cock, I reached for the remote control.

Winter came and with it Christmas. I spent the day at my parents' house, cooped up with kith and kin, while outside dull snowflakes dropped heavily through the murk. Crushed around two pushed-together tables, we ate and drank and then, nicely stuffed, collapsed in front of the old TV that gave everything a blue cast. A parade of celebrities performed for us, singing, dancing and gushing enough sentiment for a whole nation. My two sisters shed tears over some of the outfits the women wore and made a vow to start a diet in the New Year. But my male relatives soon grew restless listening to the same songs and hearing the same jokes. They changed channel to the Bond movie, pulled open beers and eased back in their chairs.

I knew what was coming but there was nowhere to hide, no place to run. The whole country had shut down for a day so that fifty million of us could stay at home and watch Sean Connery cavort with Ursula Andress. The dreaded scene duly arrived and I squirmed in my seat as we all watched the blonde goddess climb out of the sea in her explosive bikini and walk across the golden beach. It was Venus rising from the foam all over again and, as in times past, the air was tense with awe and desire. My own cock too obeyed the primitive calling and grew and grew until there was hardly space to breathe in our small living room. What a merry band of sycophants and wankers we all were, the Crawley clan at Christmas, and what tearful lives we led. We'd survived the Egyptian deserts and ten thousand Russian winters – but for what? A diet of images and work in the morning.

* * *

It is summer again and now I see her, strolling towards me through the crowd, freshly tanned and wearing knee-length black pants. Her feet are strapped into tall black sandals and her toenails are painted the palest pink. Jennifer is at her side and each young woman shines in the other's effortless beauty.

She stops before me and grabs her friend's arm.

'Jen, look who it is.'

Jennifer's face clouds momentarily and she looks away, far away, further than I will ever see. Jasmine smiles at her reaction and I smile too, this time.

'I could use you for a few days,' she says.

I murmur that I have a job.

'It's your choice.' She takes her body away from me. 'I can always find someone else.'

She draws level with Jennifer, who has walked on ahead, and side by side they continue along the street. They are in no hurry and wander over to a jeweller's to look at the display in the window. I study them both as they stand with their perfect faces close to the glass, reflecting the brightness within. But my eyes come to rest on Jasmine, on the silky black pants she has squeezed herself into.

She walks on again and my eyes follow the agonising movement of her ass; her hips promise to burst out of the hugging fabric with each strutting step she takes. I focus on the sharp cleft between the rolling cheeks, and the soft friction I see there lights a fire inside of me. Consumed by desire, I follow, hesitantly at first but my pace quickens. Soon I am trotting and then running breathlessly down the street. I must not lose her.

She stops before another window and, as I get closer, my gaze drops from her devouring ass to her pink-tipped toes. Her feet are raised high above the cracked and battered pavement, each one shaped into a disdainful arch by the sandals. Turning her long heels, she continues on her way without regard for the world below and I am dragged along behind the diamond sparkle of each black step. I hear a loud, clear whistle. It cuts through the clamour of the traffic, the blur of voices and the last whisper of dull reason. I am being summoned to heel and my soul sings.

nexus

The leading publisher of fetish and adult fiction

TELL US WHAT YOU THINK!

Readers' ideas and opinions matter to us so please take a few minutes to fill in the questionnaire below.

1. Sex: Are you male ☐   female ☐   a couple ☐?

2. Age: Under 21 ☐   21–30 ☐   31–40 ☐   41–50 ☐   51–60 ☐   over 60 ☐

3. Where do you buy your Nexus books from?
☐ A chain book shop. If so, which one(s)?

_____

☐ An independent book shop. If so, which one(s)?

_____

☐ A used book shop/charity shop
☐ Online book store. If so, which one(s)?

_____

4. How did you find out about Nexus books?
☐ Browsing in a book shop
☐ A review in a magazine
☐ Online
☐ Recommendation
☐ Other _____

5. In terms of settings, which do you prefer? (Tick as many as you like.)
☐ Down to earth and as realistic as possible
☐ Historical settings. If so, which period do you prefer?

_____

☐ Fantasy settings – barbarian worlds
☐ Completely escapist/surreal fantasy
☐ Institutional or secret academy

☐ Futuristic/sci fi
☐ Escapist but still believable
☐ Any settings you dislike?

_____

☐ Where would you like to see an adult novel set?

_____

6. In terms of storylines, would you prefer:
☐ Simple stories that concentrate on adult interests?
☐ More plot and character-driven stories with less explicit adult activity?
☐ We value your ideas, so give us your opinion of this book:

_____

_____

_____

7. In terms of your adult interests, what do you like to read about? (Tick as many as you like.)
☐ Traditional corporal punishment (CP)
☐ Modern corporal punishment
☐ Spanking
☐ Restraint/bondage
☐ Rope bondage
☐ Latex/rubber
☐ Leather
☐ Female domination and male submission
☐ Female domination and female submission
☐ Male domination and female submission
☐ Willing captivity
☐ Uniforms
☐ Lingerie/underwear/hosiery/footwear (boots and high heels)
☐ Sex rituals
☐ Vanilla sex
☐ Swinging
☐ Cross-dressing/TV
☐ Enforced feminisation

☐ Others – tell us what you don't see enough of in adult fiction:

_____

_____

_____

8. Would you prefer books with a more specialised approach to your interests, i.e. a novel specifically about uniforms? If so, which subject(s) would you like to read a Nexus novel about?

_____

_____

_____

9. Would you like to read true stories in Nexus books? For instance, the true story of a submissive woman, or a male slave? Tell us which true revelations you would most like to read about:

_____

_____

_____

10. What do you like best about Nexus books?

_____

_____

11. What do you like least about Nexus books?

_____

_____

12. Which are your favourite titles?

_____

_____

13. Who are your favourite authors?

_____

_____

14. Which covers do you prefer? Those featuring:
(Tick as many as you like.)

- ☐ Fetish outfits
- ☐ More nudity
- ☐ Two models
- ☐ Unusual models or settings
- ☐ Classic erotic photography
- ☐ More contemporary images and poses
- ☐ A blank/non-erotic cover
- ☐ What would your ideal cover look like?

_____

15. **Describe your ideal Nexus novel in the space provided:**

_____

_____

_____

_____

16. **Which celebrity would feature in one of your Nexus-style fantasies? We'll post the best suggestions on our website – anonymously!**

_____

THANKS FOR YOUR TIME

Now simply write the title of this book in the space below and cut out the questionnaire pages. Post to: Nexus, Marketing Dept., Thames Wharf Studios, Rainville Rd, London W6 9HA

Book title: _____

NEXUS NEW BOOKS

To be published in June 2007

BEHIND THE CURTAIN
Primula Bond

Sheila Moss moves into suburban Spartan Street to lead a quiet, respectable life with a handful of lodgers for company.

But she soon discovers that her glossy neighbours, bored with their perfect lifestyles and their absent husbands, are on the prowl, hunting for excitement wherever they can find it, and the more varied and kinky the better. It's not long before they set their sights on number 44 and arrive on Sheila's doorstep, demanding that she come out to play.

Sheila is soon caught up in their intimate world of so-called coffee mornings and 'truth or dare' parties where anything goes so long as it's totally debauched. Anyone crossing the threshold must submit to their erotic games. And it's not long before they reckon they've unleashed the devil in Miss Moss.

But behind her curtains, behind her prim façade, Sheila hides her own dirty secrets. Secrets that those perfect neighbours are determined to find out.

£6.99   ISBN 978 0 352 34111 2

THE ISLAND OF DR SADE
Wendy Swanscombe

Fleeing the gathering storm-clouds of war in 1939, a party of British débutantes are shipwrecked on an uncharted tropical island. It seems a completely deserted paradise ... until, one by one, they begin to disappear.

So who was the Marquis de Sade? And what deviant secret is his distinguished descendant, the Nobel laureate Dr Louis de Sade, concealing far from the eyes of the world? Does he plan to use his beautiful and not wholly unexpected young guests as accessories? In her ninth Nexus book, Wendy Swanscombe gets right to the bottom of all these darkly delicious mysteries.

£6.99   ISBN 978 0 352 3411209

NEXUS CONFESSIONS: VOLUME THREE
Various

Swinging, dogging, group sex, cross-dressing, spanking, female domination, corporal punishment, and extreme fetishes . . . *Nexus Confessions* explores the length and breadth of erotic obsession, real experience and sexual fantasy. An encyclopaedic collection of the bizarre, the extreme, the utterly inappropriate, the daring and the shocking experiences of ordinary men and women driven by their extraordinary desires. Collected by the world's leading publisher of fetish fiction, this is the third in a series of six volumes of true stories and shameful confessions, never-before-told or published.

£6.99   ISBN 978 0 352 3411306

If you would like more information about Nexus titles, please visit our website at www.nexus-books.co.uk, or send a large stamped addressed envelope to:
Nexus, Thames Wharf Studios,
Rainville Road, London W6 9HA

NEXUS BOOKLIST

Information is correct at time of printing. To avoid disappointment, check availability before ordering. Go to www.nexus-books.co.uk.

All books are priced at £6.99 unless another price is given.

NEXUS

- ☐ ABANDONED ALICE — Adriana Arden — ISBN 978 0 352 33969 0
- ☐ ALICE IN CHAINS — Adriana Arden — ISBN 978 0 352 33908 9
- ☐ AQUA DOMINATION — William Doughty — ISBN 978 0 352 34020 7
- ☐ THE ART OF CORRECTION — Tara Black — ISBN 978 0 352 33895 2
- ☐ THE ART OF SURRENDER — Madeline Bastinado — ISBN 978 0 352 34013 9
- ☐ BEASTLY BEHAVIOUR — Aishling Morgan — ISBN 978 0 352 34095 5
- ☐ BELINDA BARES UP — Yolanda Celbridge — ISBN 978 0 352 33926 3
- ☐ BENCH-MARKS — Tara Black — ISBN 978 0 352 33797 9
- ☐ BIDDING TO SIN — Rosita Varón — ISBN 978 0 352 34063 4
- ☐ BINDING PROMISES — G.C. Scott — ISBN 978 0 352 34014 6
- ☐ BLUSHING AT BOTH ENDS — Philip Kemp — ISBN 978 0 352 34107 5
- ☐ THE BOOK OF PUNISHMENT — Cat Scarlett — ISBN 978 0 352 33975 1
- ☐ BRUSH STROKES — Penny Birch — ISBN 978 0 352 34072 6
- ☐ CALLED TO THE WILD — Angel Blake — ISBN 978 0 352 34067 2
- ☐ CAPTIVES OF CHEYNER CLOSE — Adriana Arden — ISBN 978 0 352 34028 3
- ☐ CARNAL POSSESSION — Yvonne Strickland — ISBN 978 0 352 34062 7
- ☐ CITY MAID — Amelia Evangeline — ISBN 978 0 352 34096 2
- ☐ COLLEGE GIRLS — Cat Scarlett — ISBN 978 0 352 33942 3
- ☐ COMPANY OF SLAVES — Christina Shelly — ISBN 978 0 352 33887 7

☐ IN FOR A PENNY	Penny Birch	ISBN 978 0 352 34083 2
☐ THE INSTITUTE	Maria Del Rey	ISBN 978 0 352 33352 0
☐ NEW EROTICA 5	Various	ISBN 978 0 352 33956 0
☐ THE NEXUS LETTERS	Various	ISBN 978 0 352 33955 3
☐ PLAYTHING	Penny Birch	ISBN 978 0 352 33967 6
☐ PLEASING THEM	William Doughty	ISBN 978 0 352 34015 3
☐ RITES OF OBEDIENCE	Lindsay Gordon	ISBN 978 0 352 34005 4
☐ SERVING TIME	Sarah Veitch	ISBN 978 0 352 33509 8
☐ THE SUBMISSION GALLERY	Lindsay Gordon	ISBN 978 0 352 34026 9
☐ TIE AND TEASE	Penny Birch	ISBN 978 0 352 33987 4
☐ TIGHT WHITE COTTON	Penny Birch	ISBN 978 0 352 33970 6

NEXUS CONFESSIONS

☐ NEXUS CONFESSIONS: VOLUME ONE	Ed. Lindsay Gordon	ISBN 978 0 352 34093 1
☐ NEXUS CONFESSIONS: VOLUME TWO	Ed. Lindsay Gordon	ISBN 978 0 352 34103 7

NEXUS ENTHUSIAST

☐ BUSTY	Tom King	ISBN 978 0 352 34032 0
☐ DERRIÈRE	Julius Culdrose	ISBN 978 0 352 34024 5
☐ ENTHRALLED	Lance Porter	ISBN 978 0 352 34108 2
☐ LEG LOVER	L.G. Denier	ISBN 978 0 352 34016 0
☐ OVER THE KNEE	Fiona Locke	ISBN 978 0 352 34079 5
☐ RUBBER GIRL	William Doughty	ISBN 978 0 352 34087 0
☐ THE SECRET SELF	Christina Shelly	ISBN 978 0 352 34069 6
☐ UNDER MY MASTER'S WINGS	Lauren Wissot	ISBN 978 0 352 34042 9
☐ WIFE SWAP	Amber Leigh	ISBN 978 0 352 34097 9

NEXUS NON FICTION

☐ LESBIAN SEX SECRETS FOR MEN	Jamie Goddard and Kurt Brungard	ISBN 978 0 352 33724 5

------- ✂ -----------------------------------

Please send me the books I have ticked above.

Name ....

Address ....

....

....

.... Post code ....

Send to: **Virgin Books Cash Sales, Thames Wharf Studios, Rainville Road, London W6 9HA**

US customers: for prices and details of how to order books for delivery by mail, call 888-330-8477.

Please enclose a cheque or postal order, made payable to **Nexus Books Ltd**, to the value of the books you have ordered plus postage and packing costs as follows:
   UK and BFPO – £1.00 for the first book, 50p for each subsequent book.
   Overseas (including Republic of Ireland) – £2.00 for the first book, £1.00 for each subsequent book.

If you would prefer to pay by VISA, ACCESS/MASTERCARD, AMEX, DINERS CLUB or SWITCH, please write your card number and expiry date here:

....

Please allow up to 28 days for delivery.

Signature ....

Our privacy policy

We will not disclose information you supply us to any other parties. We will not disclose any information which identifies you personally to any person without your express consent.

From time to time we may send out information about Nexus books and special offers. Please tick here if you do *not* wish to receive Nexus information.   ☐

------- ✂ -----------------------------------